THE AN
VERSUS THE GOOD BOY

ZACHARY FINN

PRESS

VULPINE

PRESS

Published by Vulpine Press in the United Kingdom in 2021

Cover by Claire Wood

ISBN: 978-1-83919-093-3

www.vulpine-press.com

To Desmond. Here's an adventure you deserved.

PART I

CHAPTER 1

I guess it all started at the shelter, when those sad eyes peered up at me from behind the thin wiring of the kennel. He had those knowing eyes that, for whatever reason, pitbulls have perfected despite their troubled breeding legacy, which has seen humans inflict all sorts of cruel treatment towards them. And well, I'm sure you're familiar with how they're treated today. Despite it all, they've mastered that look that rips your heart out of your chest, that makes you feel like the biggest jerk in the world for not fixing all of their problems that second. It's a soulful gaze, I suppose.

I swear, all animals can make it, but pitbulls have it down pat. Especially Desmond. His eyes seemed so vibrant compared to the concrete beneath him that had a zealously buffed shine about it. Almost as if somebody was trying to scrub something away.

That's my first memory of Desmond. In fact, it might also be the first memory of him at all, from anyone still living anyway, so I prefer to think of it as his rebirth. Or, perhaps more accurately, a reentry into the world of the living from the gray area between life and death. Up from the shadows where nobody wanted to venture and nobody had, as until I met him Desmond had sat in a forced purgatory for a sin that he didn't commit...but I'll get to that. And look, I'm sorry for waxing poetic right at the start of things; it's hard not to when you're talking about your dog, right?

Desmond was a handsome dog and although it's stupid to admit as I write this, that made the fact he'd been cast aside all the worse.

Desmond was a mix of light brown and tan fur that ran down half his body, while the other half was white with grey and blue speckles. To top it all off he had a blocky head that could put a T-rex to shame. How could anyone not want this guy? You could've pictured him happily running around a farm or hiking some dangerous mountain while his tail wagged excitedly throughout the harrowing adventure. But no, there he was locked up in a three by six-foot cage that he hadn't left for the past week.

During that first encounter Desmond had done all the right things. He had walked up to the kennel when I approached to greet me, which, as I learned in training, was a good sign that he was friendly and wanted some attention. Then when I looked him over for any surgery scars or reasons not to bring him out, he'd sat there plopped on the ground, just staring up at me with those knowing eyes.

No injuries, no barking, and no posturing or behavior that gave me any concern for that matter, either. He just sat there like a good boy, waiting and watching me…almost like he was surprised I had noticed him. I looked him over once more to make sure I wasn't missing anything, *anything* that might explain why he had been passed over by the other volunteers and left alone without getting walked. From all I could tell, all he wanted was some love.

Maybe he intimidated people?

His fur was short and revealed a heavily muscled body that may have been a concern for some, but there were bigger dogs that came in and got walked all the time. Typically, there were volunteers forming *lines* to walk dogs like Des. Still, I settled with that being the explanation since it was the only thing that could *possibly* explain why he hadn't been walked yet.

As I got ready to open the kennel gate, Des had just sat there, still staring up with those grey eyes, helpless despite his athletic and powerful frame. And those eyes were enough to make me want to hunt down whoever had put him in the shelter and make them regret it. Desmond seemed like the perfect dog.

I quickly glanced over his paperwork to see if there was anything of note, and nothing stood out. The only things I learned about him were from a few generic notes, hastily scribbled in a dying blue pen on the little information card, which was clipped to his kennel. I had to tilt my head to read the crooked notecard, but it read "American Staffordshire/heeler mix" and put him at 75lbs and (about) two years old. All of which made sense and passed the eye test to yours truly.

What didn't make sense, as I mentioned earlier, was the fact that everyone had basically ignored him since I'd arrived at the shelter that afternoon. Come to find out, for that *whole* week Desmond had sat ignored by the world, stuck in the kennel by his lonesome as the "walked" column belonging to A9 (his specific section of the cage) remained unchecked. The longer I stood there hunting for an explanation, the less my intimidation hypothesis held any water. He could have been a statue with how calm he was waiting for me to get him outside, which was typically a moment when most dogs were going berserk in excitement.

It wasn't just the other volunteers who seemed oblivious to him, either. I mean, normally a dog like Desmond would get snatched up quickly for adoption. He was young, had no clear health issues, and looked adventurous. However, in the brief time I had been in the shelter that day I had watched the whole gambit of potential adopters walk past his kennel without so much as a sideways glance. No *oohing* or *awwing* at the sight of him. Nothing.

He was a ghost that only I could see. It seems likely, however, especially as I reflect on it enough to write it down, everybody who ignored him had some intuition of self-preservation that I apparently lack, which is how I found my way into this story. I should probably introduce myself.

My name is Jonathan Riley, but everyone calls me Jon. I started volunteering at the shelter as a way to feel better about myself. It sounds lame and self-serving, I know, but I had just retired from kick-boxing at the ripe old age of twenty-two and I was starting my first full-time job at a museum; if you know anything about starting a new job, I'm sure you know that issues seem to rain down from above before you even have your footing. The whole time, you're doubting your competency as you make slip up, after slip up, after...

So basically, I was feeling like a failure for leaving the sport I loved, and to top that all off, feeling like an idiot on a daily basis while at work. I needed to find some way to convince myself I wasn't the biggest screw-up in the world. It was my dad who recommended volunteering at the Richter Street Animal Shelter, something he'd been doing for a few years at that point.

And volunteering at a dog shelter seemed like a good way to do something positive. I loved animals, always have. Plus, I figured it might help remove that little voice in the back of my mind. The one that whispers constantly about being just a blip in the universe: a nobody doing nothing that matters.

I never realized just how wrong I was going to prove that little voice. The shelter I volunteered at was in a, how do I say it, *unsavory* part of the city. I kind of liked that too if I'm being honest, and I might as well be straight-shooting since this story really depends on you trusting me throughout. There was something about walking through a sketchy part of town that most people never see that made me feel alive. Being accompanied by a giant shelter dog didn't hurt either.

The shelter sits central to everything here in scenic Buffalo, NY. Bars, restaurants, clubs, it's all within walking distance of those valuable establishments, and then just outside the reach of the nice areas. The shelter even has a nice little park to walk the dogs around, where

4

the volunteers can bring them to get some fresh air. I wouldn't suggest any family picnics there, but it's a good spot for dog walking. And boy, do the dogs love it after another day cramped in their enclosures, with a host of noisy neighbors barking at their doors.

The park was not exactly a clean or friendly family destination by any means, and the day I met Desmond was no exception. It was surrounded by a city that seemed on the verge of engulfing the park, and the pathetic attempt to add some nature to the otherwise industrialized cluster around it seemed in vain. There were some picnic tables scattered throughout, a giant hill, and a few trees, all of which the walkway meandered through—pretty standard stuff. Still, despite the simplicity of it all, there was something so serene about the little area, and I found myself daydreaming about it during those long hours at work.

As I'm sure you can imagine, the shelter stays pretty full. It's mostly pits, though there's a good mix of all breeds. Sometimes it's people moving, or sometimes it's just people who realize having a pet requires actual work who drop their dogs off. They'll make a brief scene about being heartbroken at the counter before they disappear guilt-free, leaving their former pet shell-shocked. On top of that, animal control is always bringing in strays (that's how Desmond was brought in, they found him wandering the streets...but I'm getting ahead of myself). It's always full—usually too full—and it always sucks to see good dogs without a home.

So as a volunteer walker, my job was nice and simple: just get the dogs out for a bit. Walk 'em, play with 'em, the whole nine yards. It's the perfect level of excitement and relaxation for me. It's hard to describe without waxing poetic as I've already done, but there's always a bit of a rush working with a new dog. I mean, you have to corral the dog in the kennel to leash it, and if it goes rogue, well...you know.

But you get the dog on the leash and realize you were concerned about nothing, and that the dog's a good boy or girl who wouldn't hurt a fly. Then you get them out on a walk around the park and they're thankful the whole time: tails wagging, tongues out, living in the moment. It makes you feel pretty important while they run around this little park most people would sneer at, having the time of their life, and being thankful for that small reprieve of getting let out to explore the world with someone who cares about their well-being. Even if it's only fifteen minutes you spend with them, you're the dog's whole world for that little bit, and if that doesn't make you feel a little better about yourself, I don't know what will.

The day I met Desmond was pretty normal. I had just gotten out of work and had made my way from the artsy district of the city, where the museum I work at is, to the shelter. It was early summer, and the weather was pretty warm, which meant short walks and making sure the dogs had plenty of water in their kennels. I signed in like normal at the front desk and began working through the rows.

The way it works is that the walker would sign the dog out on the clipboard at the front of the shelter, making sure to include the time they were taking the dog out on the walk. That way, the actual shelter workers always knew where the dogs were, and the volunteers could make sure the dogs who needed to get out did. Simple, but efficient. If there was a blank space underneath a kennel number for the day it meant the dog hadn't been out yet, so you got 'em out and let them stretch their legs a bit.

However, just because a dog was in the shelter, it didn't give us the green light to get them out strolling the mean streets of Buffalo. They had to get the go-ahead first. Sometimes a dog couldn't be walked if they were new, or untrained, or scared, or something, but normally once they were brought in, there would only be a day or two before a vet-tech would clear them for walking. It took a very rare circumstance for a dog not to get walked daily, and usually they would get out multiple times a day at that. The staff there was excellent, and all the walkers truly cared about the dogs. It was a nice place to be and I felt good helping out there.

On that particular day, I picked up where the last volunteer had left off and walked two dogs pretty quickly. They were both bigger pit-mixes and the warm weather takes a toll on them, so the walks were pretty succinct. Just enough time to let them see something outside their kennel, do their business, and basically tire them out. Both walks were uneventful, aside from the fact it was my last with them; the next time I was in neither dog was still around since they were both adopted (score for the good guys).

I was going to call it a day after those two, and how different my life would be if I had. I'm not like those superstar volunteers who walk *every* dog (that's my dad, but I'll get more into that later). My style is to get two or three dogs out to enjoy themselves, which helps silence the demons of weird, internal self-loathing then go home to read and relax.

Which I was about to do, but I knew there had been that long column void of handwriting on that front clipboard: A9. That was strange, since it meant either the kennel was empty, or the dog couldn't be walked at all. And I *knew* I had seen a dog in there when I walked past it from one of the earlier walks. I *also* knew I had seen other volunteers walk past it without so much as a downward glance along with some people looking to adopt. So, I went to talk to one of the shelter employees to try and figure out what was going on and whether I could get the mystery dog out.

"Hey Shelly, is there a dog in A9?" I asked, speaking as quickly as possible.

The workers at the shelter were always busy, and normally stressed, so as a rule of thumb I try not to waste their time. Also, again, I'm not there for human interaction.

"Uhm…I didn't think so…but let me look," Shelly said, scrambling behind the desk.

Her curly brown hair flew wildly about as she searched for her clipboard, which made her look frazzled and overwhelmed. No denying it, Shelly was a cutie, though the dark bags underneath her eyes made her look like she'd just been in a particularly brutal fist fight. It's a tough line of work watching people surrender their dogs, I'd imagine.

"Hmm…looks like there is a dog in there. I haven't heard anything about him though…That's weird." Shelly scrunched her face in momentary scrutiny, then went back to whatever she was doing without giving it another thought. The Desmond effect, I'd soon come to know it as.

"Thanks Shell!" I said as cheerily as I could. I grabbed a leash and made my way back to the kennels. I figured if the dog there hadn't been out all week, the least I could do was help them see the world a bit before I went home to my copy of *The Mountains of Madness*.

When I first stepped into the kennels, the usual commotion stirred up almost immediately. Dogs excitedly yipping, the sound of aluminum water bowls being knocked about excitedly, and the *tip-tap* of paws on kennels all filled the cavernous room with their deafening echoes. However, as I walked back towards A9, it grew quieter until I was about three feet away, and then the shelter went silent. You could have heard a pin drop, and, like in a corny western movie, I could practically hear the piano *rip* then slip to silence in the ol' saloon as the gunslinger burst through the swinging gates. It was as if all the dogs knew what I was getting myself into, and they were giving the young, stupid well-doer a moment of respect. I've always found that animals have much better intuition than humans.

As I stood in front of the kennel looking down at A9 who, according to the little sheet clipped on the top bar, was named Desmond, and who sat there so well behaved, there was nothing to indicate that my life was about to completely change. No indicator about how I was about to be thrust into a supernatural freak show…but, I suppose life doesn't normally give you a heads-up on such things.

CHAPTER 2

After I'd gotten Desmond out of his kennel and on the leash, I quickly walked him past the other dogs and out to the main hallway. From there, we took a few winding corridors past the veterinarians' and animal control's offices towards the exit. Sacks of dog food and crates of brightly colored toys ran along the hallway, and above were pinned posters and pictures of dogs that had been adopted over the years.

"You'll be up there soon, buddy," I informed Desmond, who had picked up his trot excitedly.

Finally, we took a sharp right, and there before us was the door leading outside. As we made our way outside the shelter, Desmond and I were forced to dodge a partly smashed bottle of some cheap liquor that made the cement around it sparkle in the sunlight, and something that looked like a partly chewed cheeseburger that was regurgitated on the sidewalk. Cars sped by, torn up pieces of old "missing pet signs" swirled about the air daintily, and the smell of burning rubber drifted from somewhere down the street.

As we made our way through a landscape that would have fit right into a *Mad Max* film, my first impression of Desmond was that he was a good walker and a well-trained pup. I mean, back in the shelter he had let me put the leash on him without any fight, something which is *normally* a huge pain. On top of all that, he had walked past all the other dogs in their kennels without so much as a sideways glance, which is *always* a pain, as all the dogs want to say hi to each other (some more aggressively than others). As impressive as he was leaving the shelter, he was even better once we got outside.

Desmond also didn't pull on the slip leash I used, distracted. Instead, he stayed focused on whatever I was doing closely by my side. Running into a dog that could walk well at a shelter was a rarity; you find that the same jerks who up and cut a dog loose normally aren't the type of involved owners who train their dogs before doing so. So typically, part of the walking process as a volunteer also involves a bit of training, specifically not to pull. During my time at the shelter I've had a few dogs I was worried might be trying to off themselves because they pulled so hard on the slip leash, which is basically a soft, humane noose that tightens against their force. It takes a lot of treats and patience, but normally you can get them walking better after a few minutes.

None of that was necessary with Desmond though, he walked perfectly from the start. Occasionally he would stop and smell something along the sidewalk that caught his fancy like any other dog might. But even then, I noticed that after the brief moment of inspection, Desmond's eyes would dart up frantically, as if he was scared he'd lost me amongst the tangled heap of buildings that lined the walkway to the park. It was the first time I had ever felt like a dog was focused on protecting me or was strictly worried about my well-being. I mean, I'm sure most of the shelter dogs I've walked in the past would have given any mugger the business if they attacked me, but Desmond seemed to be actively making sure I was safe.

Almost like he felt it was his duty.

"You're a protective little guy, aren't you?" I'd said after seeing him repeat the process for the third time. Desmond glanced up from a crumpled candy wrapper that had been carried over by the wind. He stayed looking up towards me as if he understood what I'd said, then returned to the crumpled snickers wrapper for a final inspection.

Above us, a telephone wire draped in ivy let me know we were getting near to the park, whose nature sometimes bled out into its surrounding. It was funny seeing a vine dangling in the midst of a cityscape, but where there's a will, I suppose there's a way. Des noticed me looking at the telephone wire and followed my gaze upwards. He peered up at the stringy green plants that had been brought to life by a soft breeze, watching curiously as they drifted above our heads. I looked down at him and decided to make official introductions.

Desmond's fur was soft to touch, and as I began to pet him, he looked up at me with the same interest he had just inspected the overgrown plant with. It's tough to pinpoint an exact moment when I decided that whatever happened I was going to be there for him forever, but I'm pretty sure that was it. With each stroke of the head, his muscular shoulder pressed his weight further into mine, and soon, he dropped his head onto my bicep and peered up affectionately towards me. As I pet underneath his chin, he softly shook his head as if saying thank you.

There's something about a tough-looking dog with a soppy personality that I'm an absolute sucker for. Desmond was that in spades. The fact that he seemed so keen on my safety I think, in a way, made me feel the same way about him. I didn't know it yet, but this would be the beginning of our bond, that would make us such a good team in the upcoming months.

As Des pressed himself against me, I momentarily understood why humans first took in those wolves who gathered around early fires: both entities just trying to survive against a surrounding darkness that contained all sorts of things that went bump in the night.

We sat there for a moment, me petting Desmond and him resting his head and body on me. Everything seemed picturesque, until a slight fluctuation in the wind sent his body rigid. Desmond continued to drop his weight into me, but something had changed, and he began to shift back and forth. His attention drifted past me, and he began glancing around with laser precision as if he was looking for an attacker as his body went tense. Throughout the whole thing, he stayed composed though. No yipping, or barking...just intensity; like a composed fighter before their shot at the belt.

But as we crouched in that alleyway, a soft scowl began to take over his face. The grimace pinned the corners of Desmond's lips up and exposed the tips of his white fangs. As he snarled, I saw him cast a quick sideways glance towards me, who he was still hovering close towards. It was like Des was trying to not appear aggressive in front of me, still wanting to be a good boy, while also trying to warn something not to mess with us. He seemed aware of the delicate line he was treading.

Meanwhile, I looked around trying to locate what was bothering him. I figured it was someone drifting a little too close for comfort who had managed to escape my limited senses, or someone who was hiding in the bushes talking to themselves (people will do that occasionally), which sometimes excites the dogs. That, or another dog walking further down that Des had caught the scent of. While the walkway leading to the park was far from mundane with the collection of litter strewn about it, I couldn't locate a dog, a drifter, or anything for that matter that would explain what had set Desmond on edge.

There was nothing.

So, I stayed sitting, hoping he would calm down and we could continue our stroll. The two of us were stuck in the alley, which, similar to the wires above, was overgrown with vines and leaves that penetrated any crack in the sidewalk they could. The wind seemed to pluck at these tall shoots as they fluttered in the pull of the breeze. As I sat there with Desmond shielding me from the unseen attacker, I noticed a chill in the air, despite the fact it had just been unbearably warm not minutes before. The wind that was responsible for the swaying weeds now whipped more violently around us. I stupidly looked around to see if we were by a vent or something that I would have blamed for the temperature change.

Still nothing.

Despite it being a beautiful summer afternoon, the air around us had gone from a chill, to an impossibly bitter cold, and there was nothing that I could locate to explain it. Any of it. Still, I looked around not knowing what I thought I was going to see. Maybe a talking snowman telling me about friendship, like one of those kids' cartoons…maybe not. All I saw was a destitute walkway filled with discarded trash and some unhealthy-looking vegetation, clinging to the living world.

I was just about to start moving, to pull Desmond away from whatever it was that I couldn't see when a sharp whistle cut through the silence, setting Desmond's growl a few octanes lower.

That was when I saw it. The dark figure.

At the time, I didn't think much of it. I let my brain rationalize it as soon as it registered seeing something. I told myself the sun had reflected strangely off some debris or that all I was seeing was a shadow cast from the top of a nearby building, or something like that. I should've known it was something worse though. Maybe I did, and I just wouldn't allow myself to process it. Hindsight's 20/20 after all. The shadow moved quickly along the chalky bricks and rusted grey tin walls that made up the warehouses around us. For a brief moment, it seemed like the whole walkway went dark, as if night had come early or I had been punched from behind and was coming back to the land of the conscious. The wind had continued to grow in intensity, choosing that exact moment to begin its loud howling. It was then that the shadow grew into its giant form, skating across the walls, ignorant of my gaze. And then…it disappeared from sight.

Looking back, the whole thing was creepy, but it was all over so quickly, and everything went back to normal, so I just had to tell myself I was seeing something. I convinced myself that I'd imagined it or that, if it were real, then I had just seen some freak anomaly of light and dark.

"C'mon Des," I said standing up when I felt him relax a bit, and not realizing I had just met the very thing that would torment both of our lives in the upcoming months.

"Let's go see the park, buddy!"

The walk was supposed to be a short one, but that went out the window quickly. It went from fifteen minutes, to a half an hour, until finally, after an hour of scampering about the park, we found ourselves on top of the hill which overlooked the city.

It was too pristine a hill to belong in the particular park it was situated in. The hill looks like something taken from a cartoon, it was so green and well-manicured. It was also oddly spherical, like someone cut a giant grass covered ball in half and plopped it down. Truthfully, it looked like something from a yuppy golf course, but it wasn't. Instead, it was in a rundown park, and I was thankful for that. This was a nice place to bring the dogs and relax outside for a bit. Plus, because it was so steep and always in the sun, very few people cut across it from the sidewalk, so there wasn't a ton of garbage littering the area around it.

After tiring ourselves out exploring that little blip of green amongst the grey, Desmond and I sat up at the top of the hill and gazed across the perfect silhouette of the city before us. The baseball field, tall buildings of industry, and other ancient looking structures all stuck into the air like the ragged bottom half of a jack-o'-lantern's smile, illuminated by the disappearing sun. In the little park in front of us, other volunteers strolled by with dogs who they walked on the serpentine sidewalk that cut through the park. A homeless man slept peacefully, resting on the top of a picnic table he had pulled into the shade. The red glow of the setting summer sun gave everything a soft, warm appearance.

That moment, everything was perfect in the world. There was no school debt, or worrying about rent, or wondering whether I screwed up in quitting kickboxing. All that just disappeared. It was just Desmond and me, watching as the world spun around us. We might've been two blips in existence, but we were two content blips. Des rested against my leg, before picking his head up and looking out at the city in awe. For a dog that had spent the last week alone and ignored in a metal crate, walking around the park must have been like discovering a new world. Desmond peered over the city like a noble gargoyle, but his gaze broke as he looked back at me for a second before he returned his watch to the city in front of us. You could almost hear him sigh in appreciation…maybe that was the moment he decided he'd do anything to save me. Who knows?

"C'mon buddy, I think it's time we get you back…they probably think I got mugged or something," I said after a few more minutes of enjoying the world.

Looking back at it now, if I could go back in time and talk to myself, I would give myself a piece of my mind. *Stupid…shut up and enjoy this. There's no rush. Why are you trying to end this any sooner than it has to? Just be happy with this.*

But no time-traveling Jon showed up to tell me to enjoy the moment for as long as I could, so we began making our way back to the shelter. Maybe it was some subconscious instinct that was amped up after the encounter with the shadow, or maybe I wanted the walk to be a bit longer, but for whatever reason, I decided to take us the long way back to Richter Street Animal Shelter.

The back way to the shelter looped around some rundown houses, and similarly old industrial buildings. These ancient buildings had been left to the mercy of both the elements and squatters for the past fifty years as jobs fled the largely blue-collar city, which left such places to rot in the city's proverbial gut. The peeling fronts of old factories flew past us as we strolled, but I slowed down for a moment. See, there was one particular door leading into one of these abandoned buildings that had always drawn my attention. Once, in a sad attempt at being artsy, I had even taken a picture of the entrance hoping to impress somebody, somewhere. Of course, the photo sucked and didn't do the faded door justice, but there was something so out of place about it that just always demanded a moment of my reverence when I walked by. The door looked like it belonged on a farm or something, not in the middle of a city.

From some later research carried about before writing this, I found out that the building used to be either an industrial butchering center, or a place where animals were stored in order to provide fresh meat for city-dwellers. Either way, it's where a lot of things died, and it went deep down. That second part is key. See, this particular door led down underground where the recently frozen slaughtered animals would be stored. I know this, because in my online search I found a blog post from some local urban explorers who had broken into it. They had posted a few pictures of the underground freezers, which they plastered on various social media channels as well as their blog, for whatever reason (I mean, it was a freezer in the dark…c'mon).

The plant had been closed down for at least forty years when trucking made it wildly impractical for such a place to survive. The door still stood though. Its huge, wooden bulk was split down the middle so that the two doors can swing open. Again, like a barn door. The wood of the door has become soft and waterlogged, and the white paint was chipped or had been scuffed without mercy. So much so that the greying wood underneath blended in with the flaking paint.

It looked like what a normal doorway would look like if you blurred your eyes or looked at it in someone else's glasses. And it led underground...that's where the big-bad preferred to be. It probably liked hiding out in a place that had seen so much death too.

But I'm jumping the gun.

As we walked past, Desmond switched the side he was walking on. Like I mentioned earlier, Des is a great walker, and leading up to that moment he had positioned himself between myself and the road. However, once we were in sight of the door I loved so much for whatever weird reason, he crossed over quickly and wedged himself between me and the wall the door was on. It was sudden, but not enough to really draw any of my attention as it happened.

That was until we were about five feet away from said door, and Des went full-on hunting mode. Ears slicked back, body positioned to explode forward and attack. His body was a coiled ball of muscles and bad intentions. He was even more primed than earlier. He was ready to tear into something.

Normally when a dog gets like this, we're supposed to call another volunteer ASAP. It's a safety precaution, since a lot of dogs have triggers no one knows about when they first get dropped off at the shelter. Some dogs distrust guys, some women, some children and normally it's warranted due to a traumatic past experience with whichever one messed up their lives before. While the specific volunteer never personally hurt the dog, someone like them probably did and sometimes calming a dog down is easier with another person by your side. So, the rule is a reasonable one, but unfortunately, this story is not one about playing it safe, or even smart, so please if you plan on volunteering do *not* follow my forthcoming example.

So, of course, I didn't call anyone for backup. Instead, Des and I slowly walked forward toward the door. Truth be told, I was a little interested to see what was going on. I *love* horror movies, and if that wasn't the start of one, I didn't know what was.

With each step forward, Des was growing more agitated and on edge. Chest down low, teeth bared, the whole nine yards. Meanwhile, I'm getting ready to fend off either the dog I had thought was my new best friend, or a serial killer that's hiding behind the door who was just *waiting* to add a handsome, young museum worker to his skin collection...

When, all of the sudden, Des went back to normal. The second we passed that door leading underground *boom* no scary dog. I swear, he even looked up towards me as if to say, "Sorry you had to see that." It was such a rapid transition I didn't know what to make of it and opted to file it away with the rest of the memories I attempt to forget.

The rest of the walk back was uneventful, but I think walking past that door was the first time I realized something wicked was coming, and that I'd be too dumb to step out the way. Even if it was only some unvoiced premonition that *really* knew how deep in it, I really was.

CHAPTER 3

"No. You signed the rent agreement. Remember? That was the rules then, and it sure as hell ain't changed now!"

Chuck's voice slurred softly from the fat wad of chew he had packed into his lip, which gave him a comical lisp that reminded me of Elmer Fudd. He stared at me like I had asked to kill his wife or something, while I stared back wishing his puffed-out lip was a result of a right cross from yours truly.

Normally, I tried my hardest to avoid Chuck outside of shoving checks into his absentee fists the first of every month. Sure, I liked the place he rented me enough; but make no mistake, he was a piece of trash slumlord through-and-through. If I didn't know how a screwdriver worked, or god forbid own a lawnmower, I'd be royally screwed. Since I had both a minimum understanding of home care and access to lawn care supplies, I was able to keep the house I rented looking halfway decent without needing to come in contact with Chuck often. Which, in turn, allowed Chuck to focus on his true loves: evicting families and telling Tiny Tim that this would be his last Christmas. Certainly, a win-win for all parties.

He hated animals too, or at least banned them from his properties, so forget that guy, amirite? I know, I know...renters' insurance goes up if you allow animals and they can potentially make a mess of a place. Trust me though, with the state my place was in when I first moved there, a pack of Siberian wolves on uppers couldn't have done any worse damage to the place than what the previous tenants managed.

Even before I brought up getting a dog, I had known how the conversation would go with Chuck. Which is why I made sure I had an ace up my sleeve. The nice thing about greedy people is that if you speak their language, they're the easiest to manipulate because they *just* want more. Sure as the sun sets.

"I know Chuck, but you know I'm not going to mess up your property. I mean, look what I've done with this place," I said gesturing around. I'd been there two years now, and the house had gone from being a potential health violation to an actual home.

We were standing on the neutral ground of the front porch of the house that he owned, but that I had made livable. He slung his hands to his hips like a teenager about to complain. I could practically hear the slow grinding of the rusty gears in his think-box as he thought about a way to blame me for some made-up problem in the house. He knew I had at least equal footing in this dispute, and when your living is based on kicking the downtrodden, equal footing is a dangerous playing field. I decided to cut him off before he could spew any made-up lie that would just piss me off.

"Look, Chuck, I know you got the property on Filbert. The one you were so excited about. I also know that place has a pool…"

Research friends: it'll getcha what you want. He had yammored on and on excitedly about the next house he had planned on buying to rent during one of his visits to take my money. Once I had seen the FOR SALE sign go down from the property's front yard, I had checked the place out to see if I could upgrade. Too big for little ol' me, but it had a pool…and I had spent summers cleaning pools all through college.

"So!?" he said indignantly, as he slowly slobbered into the energy drink can he was using as a spitter.

"So, that's a lot of work to take care of a pool. Plus, with county regulations and safety codes, your new place could become a real financial black hole if you don't have someone who knows their stuff working on it. I used to see people drop four figures on a visit at the pool store. That was just on chemicals."

"I could do it! Can't be too hard," he retorted immediately

I actually feel a little bad about how hard I laughed. I'm talking back-bending over, heaving laughter. He almost looked hurt as I doubled over cracking up at the thought of him doing *something*, while he stared at me like a kid who had just been told Santa was really his alcoholic stepfather. Sometimes I forget people aren't aware that they suck, so Chuck probably thought he was a great landlord. Christ, life would be so easy if I could be completely oblivious like him.

"You're too busy I'm sure." I managed to get out when I finally stopped laughing. "But look, I made $50.00 a visit back when I was doing this all summer when I was younger. You pay for the chemicals, which I know how to get dirt cheap, and I'll clean the pool for you. Then *you* let me get a dog." His eyebrow arched up. Despite his feigned disinterest I could tell he was interested in the offer, and I made a mental note to play poker with Chuck should the opportunity ever arise.

"You'll be making out like a bandit. I'm telling you, I've seen people dump tens of thousands into a pool that they forgot for a measly week…you trust your future tenants that much? If they ignore it for a week or two, you're looking at a swamp you'll be trying to rent in the future."

He looked down and shook his head: no, he didn't want that. I swear, sometimes it's like dealing with a child. His bald head sparkled in the sunlight that cast through the porch as he thought. I could almost hear the inner turmoil going on in his head. I suppose he thought my happiness with having a dog would somehow inconvenience him.

But with everything I'd done for him, plus keeping up the pool on his new property (which meant he could charge more every month) I knew I had him. He was a prick, a stupid prick at that, but he really liked money and this deal made him a fair bit.

"I s'pose," he finally said. "But'cha gotta sign a sheet that says the dog's your problem."

Of course, I agreed. Five minutes later, after we jotted it down on two crumpled loose-leaf sheets of paper so we could each have a copy, he was gone. I think it was the longest interaction Chuck and I had since I agreed to rent the place from him.

***

"Shelly, where's A9?" I asked, trying not to sound frantic.

I had arrived at the shelter early the next day following the conversation with Chuck, and I was ready to adopt Desmond. I had practically floated through work. For once, everything seemed to be going right.

Only problem was that when I had gone back to get him, his crate was empty which spelled trouble for your protagonist, dear reader. He was either adopted or...

I had sprinted from the kennels to find Shelly, who was now (thanks to me) at least aware there was a dog in that pen.

"After we... well, after we noticed there was a dog in there, we realized we had to make room. A whole litter of dogs in rough shape were brought in. Doc thinks they might be bait dogs, and well, we needed to make room. I think the doc just grabbed—"

I didn't let her finish. I normally don't like making waves, but if the vet had grabbed Desmond there were two ways the following minutes could've gone down. Either I was barging into that vet's office, heroically saving Desmond from death and parading out with my new dog or, I was getting dragged out of the shelter kicking and screaming about how they're all murderers.

As I ran to the vet's office, I weaved through the crowded hall of the shelter, which was filled with vet technicians busily moving around and potential adopters eyeing the available dogs. If somebody could have hit pause at that moment, and somehow stopped both time and me mid-stride to ask: why does this dog mean so much to you? Why have you already gone to such lengths to adopt him after one walk? I wouldn't have been able to formulate an answer. I mean, I had worked with plenty of other dogs I really liked at the shelter. Dogs who might have gotten adopted, or put down, who I could've adopted as well. Truth be told, I didn't know why I was doing what I was, all I knew was that I needed to. Des needed a home, needed me. And not to be cliché, but I think that went both ways.

I burst into the vet's office without so much as a knock.

"Where's Desmond...A9?" I demanded, looking around frantically.

The vet, Jim, I'm pretty sure his name is, stared up at me like I had just kicked his kid. Which I might've considered had he put Desmond down, assuming he had a kid.

"He's in the back. We got a new—" he stuttered. He was wearing light blue coveralls, and his bloodshot eyes scanned the room as he tried to make sense of why I was in his office demanding things. I was surprised he answered. I mean, he would have been well within his rights to tell me to screw off, but I think he could tell I meant business.

Before I go on, I want to point out that the vet is a great guy, so is everyone who works at the shelter—they're all better humans than I am. They have abnormally stressful jobs, and they are forced to stare into the worst parts of human nature on a daily basis. If at any time

through this part of the story I seem disparaging of them or their efforts, just realize I was stressed and wanted to save a dog I connected
with, while they were trying to save a whole batch of dogs.

"Is he ok? You didn't?" I asked, both hands gripping his paper
strewn desk.

I didn't know what "in the back" meant, but it didn't sound good.
The vet leaned back and rolled his chair a few feet away from his desk.
I think he was worried I was going to flip it like the Hulk if I didn't
hear what I wanted to.

"Yes, he's fine right now. But we're going to have to—"

"I'll adopt him. Today. Right now. I got permission from my landlord."

The vet stared up at me, confused. We'd never really talked before.
Yet here I was, in his domain no less, being pushy. I expected an earful
back (it certainly would have been deserved) but he only smiled, with
a tired gleam in his eye that let me know there were parts of his job he
really, truly hated. He seemed relieved.

"I'm glad," he said. "I think the poor boy hasn't had a fair shake of
things. Let me call a vet tech to bring him out with you, and you can
do the interview and all that."

From somewhere in the back of his office, I could hear Des shifting
around. I can't be sure, but I like to think he knew what happened.

***

"Are you sure this is the one you want? I mean, we still got Bonnie.
And everyone absolutely loves her! You've walked her, I'm su—"

Shelly continued on for some time, talking about all the walkers'
current shelter favorite dog, Bonnie. She was a great dog, but she
wasn't Desmond. I let Shelly drone on without interrupting, though I
had no intention of taking her advice. I liked Shelly, she was nice

enough, but this was one of those times I really wished she would have sped up her abnormally long interview process.

When Shelly was done talking, she sat there staring at me like she expected me to have changed my mind. There was an awkward moment of silence, until I realized she was waiting for me to say something.

"Uhm…no thanks. Desmond is the one," I finally managed to get out.

I was actually a little taken aback that Shelly had tried to get me to rescue another dog, which would have basically been a death sentence for my man Desmond. I decided to gather a little intel on the situation since I was rushing headfirst into adopting a relatively unknown dog, but planning is for lames, amirite?

"Shelly, why don't you want me to adopt him? And why was he getting put down? Did someone see something aggressive or something?" Afterall, I had only walked Desmond once. And while he was great with me, that doesn't mean it's the same with every interaction.

Sometimes (like I said earlier), a dog will have had a *real* bad interaction with a man, woman, child, or you name it, and the same dog that was an angel with a female handler would give the guys hell, or vice-versa. I needed to know what I was getting into. As I looked down at Desmond who was resting calmly on the ground next to me, I realized that being aggressive probably wasn't the reason he was on the chopping block.

"No! We're glad you're adopting him!" Shelly practically shouted, as if she had just woken up from some sort of hypnosis. "I mean, why wouldn't we be? It's just, we know nothing about him. He was picked up off the streets by animal control—no issues there, but he's a bit of a mystery."

"Well, yeah," I said with a bit more sarcasm than intended. "Of course, he's going to be a mystery, he hadn't been walked the whole week. How's anyone going to know anything about a dog stuck in a kennel? Did the volunteers just skip over him? I mean nobody could be troubled to get him out on a walk that whole time?"

Shelly's eyes widened with horror. They normally run a very tight ship at the shelter. How a dog slipped through the cracks like that was a bigger mystery than anything about Desmond, who was now sitting up. His head was going back and forth between whomever was speaking like we were playing ping-pong.

"I…I have no idea. I think everyone just…*forgot* about him." As she said it, Shelly looked down at Desmond with a mix of pity and embarrassment. "I mean, I swear I walk back there daily. But I just can't remember him for the life of me."

Shelly looked like she was near to tears, so I decided not to pester her any further, and went back to filling out the adoption form she had provided

Fifteen minutes later, Desmond was my dog.

CHAPTER 4

"Welcome home, buddy!" I said, beaming as I led Desmond into his new house. "It's not much, I'll admit, but I'm still damn proud of it."

I'm close enough to everything in Buffalo that matters, and best of all, I have the whole place to myself since it's an old house that was purposefully built small for working families. For some reason, while all other similarly sized houses in the area were torn down and replaced with duplexes, mine stood the test of time. It's called a craftsman bungalow, technically speaking, though it's missing the front porch most have. As such, it's about as plain a house as one could imagine: gable roof, long vertical windows that sit beside the door. I read somewhere that you could order houses like these from a catalogue back in the early 20th century then build it yourself. Supposedly they were pretty popular back in the day.

The house has a little front and backyard, and a creepy unfinished basement I rarely used. If you've ever read *Pickman's Model* by Lovecraft, I'm pretty sure mine was the cellar he was picturing while he wrote. The front and backyard were nice for Des though.

"C'mon buddy!" I said excitedly as I led him in. Desmond bounded up the steps and sprinted into the place, while his tail wagged the whole time. I had expected him to be more timid moving into a new home but, boy, was I wrong. Desmond had acquainted himself with the house before I had even managed to lug in his dog food, newly purchased toys, and all the other things needed to give the good boy a decent home. On my last trip back from the car, I was greeted by two grey eyes and a black nose pressed up against the screen door, staring up at me.

Everything was right in the world.

Desmond stayed glued to my side as I carried everything to the walk-in pantry. As I did so, he occasionally glanced up at me with the carefree look of a dog who was doing his job of keeping an eye on me. I loaded all the new dog stuff onto a newly bare shelf that had previously held a few boxes of pasta and cans of tomato sauce, while Desmond stood in the doorway watching. His long brown tail slowly wisped back and forth, and his head tilted slightly to the side in curiosity.

We spent the rest of the day playing tug-of-war and watching travel documentaries while Desmond got acclimated to everything. It was a pretty low-key day to start things off, and to my surprise Desmond settled right in without missing a beat. He was clearly used to living in a home, despite the fact he had been found wandering the streets. He was nuzzled into the couch with what I could've sworn was a grin across his face when I finally made my way upstairs, tired from work and the trials at the shelter. As I crashed into my bed, ready for a night of uninterrupted sleep in which *surely* nothing weird would happen, my mind seemed to shut off immediately. I think I was out before my head hit the pillow.

***

Desmond's growl echoed through my bedroom like a gunshot being fired right next to my ear. I jumped up, guided only by the neon light of my alarm clock which read 3:17 a.m., and rushed to where I was pretty sure the light switch was. The world began to make sense as I slowly came to.

I have a dog now. Desmond. It's Desmond's first night here…he must have heard something outside, or a mouse in the cellar…

I noticed the air was abnormally cold in my bedroom while I made my way over to the light switch. Usually in the summer heat this would've been a blessing, since the electrical bill is a real bitch when I use air conditioning, but there was something…sinister about the chill. Even in my half-asleep state, I recalled the two instances on the first walk with Desmond. And in my gut, I knew something was wrong. The threat of danger was like a bucket of ice water being poured over me. My mind was soon firing on all cylinders as déjà vu tried to take over, and memories tried to flood my conscience. I was too focused on figuring out what was happening at that *exact* moment to let the past sink in, however.

Looking back, had I stopped to analyze the feeling in my gut, I might have been more prepared for what I was about to see when I turned on the light. I'd only ever felt something comparable to the energy in my room that night once before. It was during my first kick-boxing fight and it was the moment when I first got into the ring. I felt like I was floating above the crowd, and the energy of the surrounding mass of humanity surged at me like a wave of pure electricity.

That cold, bitter energy was suffocating in my small bedroom. All the while, Desmond was raising bloody hell, growling like a grizzly bear on PCP and pacing back and forth. The patter of his nails on the hardwood floor let me know he was circling all around. I was glad he was only growling though, the last thing I needed was one of my neighbors complaining to Chuck about a barking dog. Still, in the immediate space, the sound of Desmond's growl might as well have been a bass drum the way it filled the room.

I finally managed to find the light switch after accidentally kicking over a stack of books that rested on the floor next to my bed and stumbling like a drunk through the dark. As the light flickered on and my eyes adjusted to the scene in front of me, I tried to convince myself that I was still asleep and just having the most terrifying nightmare of my young life.

Unfortunately, though, I was *very* awake, and what I was seeing was as real as could be. The corner of my spartanly decorated bedroom was encompassed by a dark shadow which seemed to pulsate in contempt. It shouldn't have been there. I mean, there was nothing in my room (in the world for that matter) that could have cast a shadow like that. As I stared in horror at the growing blot of darkness, Desmond stared in defiance from directly underneath it, growling and positioned to pounce. His shoulder muscles flexed, and his head moved slightly from left to right like he was slipping punches and looking for a weak spot.

I must have stood there paralyzed for a whole minute trying to make sense of everything before I snapped to and made my way over to him. I had no clue what I was supposed to do, but it seemed like the right move to make. We were only about three feet from the shadow, and there was no doubt where the cold air I felt earlier was coming from. It seemed to spew forth from the shadow in icy waves. From the new vantage point I could now make out a slight movement, which wriggled on the outside edges of the dark void like there were bugs crawling around its outline.

At first, it only looked like a few ripples in murky water; but in a sudden, violent explosion, a dark arm shot out from the edge of the black pit. It was immediately yanked back in by some unseen force. As soon as the arm had disappeared from view, a full shadow of a body seemed to do the same thing. But it too was pulled back at the last moment before escaping. I stood there watching in a sick, confused daze. Whatever was happening, I didn't want to miss a second of it.

The writhing rim of the shadow jerked forward suddenly, which added another foot to the thing's radius. Then another shadow spewed out. This one came even closer to breaking free and stayed suspended on my ceiling.

Another followed it…and another.

The shadow beings kept flashing across my ceiling, making my room look like ground-zero of the world's creepiest rave. To make things worse, each shadow got closer and closer to getting loose. I looked up at my ceiling and noticed they all seemed to be turning their heads in my direction. I was about to move until the air in front of me began to change; it filled slowly with a dark mist emitting from the pit. As soon as I noticed it Desmond leaped towards it, and the thing disappeared in a puff of blackness. Without missing a beat, Des landed and placed himself between me and the void, growling loudly.

The whole time these shadow creatures were trying to get out of the main pit, my ears had begun to ring with an obnoxious noise that sounded like static on a megaphone. It was the same feeling as when you first take off on an airplane before your ears pop, where everything feels more sensitive, and it wasn't just white noise for long. Soon, there were whispers too, too hushed to make out. Even though they were quiet, the intensity of it became overpowering. It took everything in me not to just get the hell out of there and pretend it was just a nightmare. I bent down, covering my ears and looking away. It was all I could do.

But as I looked down there was Desmond, and I saw he had no back down in him, which helped steel my resolve. I fought to stand back up. When I finally managed to get to my feet, I was about to start screaming out the three Latin terms I know in an attempt to exorcise whatever was in my room (*de jure, de facto,* and *terra incognita,* if you must know how learned and cultured I am) when I noticed the shadow had shrunk slightly. At that moment, it seemed less like an empty void, and more like a blurry, cloaked human. Without a moment's hesitation it darted across my room and out the door, leaving me and Desmond alone.

"What the hell?!" I screamed when the room was empty. I'd finally managed to find my voice and was able to hear myself clearly without that overpowering ringing. I looked down at Desmond like I expected him to sit me down and tell me the origins of the primordial evil that had just decided to make its residence in a very small home in Buffalo, NY.

No such luck.

Desmond jumped up on my bed, walked around a few paces, and then plopped down without a care in the world. He was done doing his duty and seemed quite content with himself. I stood in my room with what I'm sure was the world's most bewildered and confused look plastered across my stupid face, while Desmond fell asleep.

***

The next day I left the museum an hour early, after telling the director I had an appointment. A pretty basic lie but, at that moment, I didn't really care; my main focus was getting some sort of protection, anything, which might help me sleep.

I don't really know why I bought a gun. Hell, if I'd had one the night before it might have only made a bigger mess of things. But I figured I'd rather have it and not need it, as the cliché goes. After what I had seen the night before, I just wanted something that I could defend myself with. Even though I had absolutely no clue if a gun would do anything to the shadow. I won't bore you with the nitty gritty, but after a very brief background check, I got to choose my boomstick. I grabbed a shotgun because, I mean, if they're good enough for Ash from *Evil Dead*, they're good enough for me. As I made my way to the counter, a horrible thought crossed my mind.

Desmond's been alone...what if that thing came back.

The thought hadn't occurred to me at work. Truth be told, it was so busy, and I was so tired, I don't think a functional thought crossed my mind since I had left my house that morning. I was running on autopilot, while I'm sure my subconscious attempted to figure things out or forget them completely. As my mind shuffled about to make sense of the new realities I had been exposed to, the cognizant part of me seemed to check out while my body just went. However, my mind had begun to work in the gun store for whatever reason. Maybe it was being around so many weapons that forced me back into the present moment. Whatever the reason, I hurried out once the shotgun was bagged.

As I rushed back home, I made some rather self-deprecating comments to myself about how stupid I was for not taking the day off. Sure, I'd only been at the new job for three months now, but if there was a better reason to call off, I couldn't think of it. I tried to remember the day and couldn't even remember if I had swung home for lunch. It was like I had been sleepwalking for the past ten hours.

I remembered one thing though, Desmond looked at ease when I left that morning. The foggy memory of him sleeping on the couch began to form, and I remembered that I convinced myself to leave because Desmond clearly had everything under control. Much more than I would (or could) have. He had been fine in the morning, I *knew* that.

I hoped nothing had changed...

CHAPTER 5

Before I had even managed to get the key in the lock, I could tell my worries were unfounded. Everything was ok. Desmond was ok.

Through the glass panel of my front door I could make out his giant beige-and-white head looking up at me. I could also see the flurry of his tail as it whipped around frantically. It wagged with such force, I was a bit worried he might take flight before I could unlock everything and make my way in. When I finally opened the door, I managed to squeeze my way in leading with the carefully packaged shotgun standing upright to make sure Desmond couldn't get out, then shut the door behind me as quick as I could. Desmond jumped up to greet me. His giant paws landed delicately on my chest before he pushed off and began tapping his feet excitedly on the living room floor.

I peered nervously around the living room, looking for anything suspicious. I was happy to find everything as it had been when I left this morning. The books on the ledge under the tinted window, the posters of old horrors movies, beer brewing companies, and places I had traveled, the old grey couches I inherited from my aunt; it was my living room, as it always was. Nothing sinister, just my house and Des who was happy I was home.

Yet, despite the fact that everything appeared fine, I couldn't relax. I distrusted everything there; every nook and cranny could have been a hiding place. I felt a horrific mix of the terror of the threat, the shame of feeling weak, and a twinge of melancholy that I wouldn't wish on my worst (human) enemy. It was like I was a stranger in my own home.

Unlike Desmond, I was not able to shake off the previous night's encounter and fall asleep like everything was alright in my little corner of the world. No, I had spent the rest of the night clutching a baseball bat and flinching every time a car drove by when their headlights filled up my room with long, stretched shadows.

I was terrified.

I stayed that way until the sun had made its way through my bedroom window that morning. I found myself staring at the growing shadows cast by its light with mistrust, ready to swing on anything that moved in a way I didn't like. When my alarm clock went off, I had rolled over, turned it off, and then went about my day barely able to function. The rest of the day passed in a blur. What I did, how I did it, or any other details about what my day looked like between waking up to returning home was lost. That was, and I suppose is it, little more than a foggy memory that I can't recall.

I'm sure the lack of sleep didn't help my state of mind either. I was in just as much confusion as I was scared. I mean, what do you do in a situation like that?

I couldn't call anyone for help without sounding like I was losing my mind. Plus, there was no comparable situation I had lived through that I could use for a point of reference to direct my next move. I felt like I was alone on a raft in the middle of the ocean with swells on the horizon, but at the same time, even with that danger so clearly looming ahead, I knew I had to carry on with my day-to-day life as if everything was fine. If I did anything too drastic, I would end up in a mental institution, or pumped so full of pills I wouldn't know my own name. I knew I was going to be forced to play the long game.

After a day of essentially sleepwalking through existence, I felt myself perk up a little after finding Desmond safe and sound. Just in case

I did a quick lap around the house to make sure there were no shadow people lurking in corners unchecked, then settled down on the couch. I was quickly joined by Desmond. He leaped up on the faded grey loveseat and managed to wedge himself between my shoulder and the armrest.

It was then I remembered I wasn't alone on that raft heading into danger, and that I wasn't alone in carrying on as if everything was alright. I had someone with me to face whatever beast lurked beneath those waves. A friend who, somehow, had managed to fall asleep in what must have been a wildly uncomfortable square foot of space between my bony frame and the couch.

I looked over at Desmond who had woken back up without my knowing after the short doze, and who was now staring intently at me in the way only dogs can without it being creepy. He looked like he wanted to say something, or at the very least, do something. So, I decided we should get out of the house for a few. After all, a walk would do both of us some good.

"Wanna go for a walk, boy?" I asked.

I was answered by an explosive leap from the couch. It rattled the house when Des landed. Now, make no doubt about it, Desmond was quite graceful, but that didn't help buffer the noise the old place made when there was any hint of movement within.

After he made contact, Desmond lowered his chest to the ground, and took off in giant leaps. Those jumps soon turned into wild puppy (I know he's not a puppy, but that's what I'm calling 'em) sprints. He zoomed back and forth so comically; I couldn't help but collapse to the couch he had just bounded from in a fit of laughter.

So yes, to answer the earlier question, he very much wanted to go on a walk. I leashed him up, and out we went on the breezy summer day.

The park, which was much nicer than the one we explored on our first walk, was right by the house. We made our way in that direction like two adventurers searching for cities of gold. Despite living in what I'm pretty sure could be classified as a doll house since it was so damn small, we were close enough to all the colleges that everything artsy and nice was within walking distance. A quick stroll could take us to any number of art galleries, small cafes, or even the public market. There was no lack of things to see or do. A fact that I was certainly appreciative of, and I'm sure Desmond was too.

It was dusk and the soft glow of the summer sun engulfed everything. A red glowing ring was cast along the horizon, which seemed especially warm and comforting, like staring into the embers of a dying fire.

The smell of freshly cut grass and cigarette smoke brought me back to earlier summers spent at my grandparents', and my mind slowly began to slip into the comforting backdrop of nostalgia where shadow people weren't, and I was just a normal guy out walking a normal dog.

As my mind strayed, Desmond stayed by my side bouncing with excitement, his eyes lit up in pure, unabashed joy. I looked down at him and wondered if he ever thought about the good ol' days. He had to have had some. I mean he was trained, he knew what "walk" meant, and he had a great disposition, all of which led me to believe that at some point in his life, things couldn't have been *all* bad. The shadow couldn't have always haunted him, and he must have had a loving family who let him be happy.

But maybe he forgot those happy days, before the shadows, and the shelter, and being ignored. How else could Des go on as cheerfully as he did on that walk, if he knew what had been ripped away from him unfairly? Sometimes, I think knowing how good life could be, especially while going through the bad, is what jades humans, not the situation itself. It's the fact you had a taste of the green grass on the other side that makes it so easy to be bitter when you're back on the other side.

Maybe dogs don't have that, because they forget, or maybe they're too focused on the present to let the past drag them down. Who knows?

Whatever the reason that allowed him to cope with the past, on that walk, Desmond was as happy as could be. His gold fur seemed to turn copper-red in the setting sun's rays, and his eyes darted around looking at all the new sights like a tourist on the most spectacular vacation.

As the park appeared in the distance, I felt Desmond begin to pull excitedly for the first time since I started walking him. He knew what the park was, and I mentally kicked myself for not bringing a frisbee or a tennis ball to toss around with him. He didn't seem concerned though, as he hustled towards the patch of green which lay ahead.

We walked around a giant loop that brought us past a water fountain, and a giant metal amorphous entanglement of beams. It looked like two octopi discovering their love for each other, but was really some forced attempt at contemporary art. I stopped for a moment, trying to make sense of what we were looking at. As I tried to figure out what the artist was going for, I noticed the shadows from the trash art begin to stretch out towards where we stood. It ripped me back to the night before, when we were staring into the black pit with the evil whispers, and the lurking bodies that seemed to spew from it. I quickly resumed our walk to get as far away from that thing as possible.

It was not a far-reaching conclusion to assume that whatever was happening at my house was bad. Real bad. It did not take a leap in logic, either, to know whatever I had seen the night before was most certainly linked to my new partner in crime.

I looked down at Desmond, who was happily walking at my side without a care in the world, and I suddenly felt a deep remorse. Toxic guilt, like everything wrong in his life was my somehow fault.

Sometimes you feel bad about something you didn't do or couldn't have prevented, for that matter. There are those times when you read about something horrible: about some genocide, or pointless death in the news. Things so evil and cruel that it makes you shake your head in disbelief, and feel that sick, burn of guilt in your gut. But that's nothing compared to watching someone struggle through a horrible situation in front of you. To watch them put on a brave face as they slowly decay while you are nothing but a stupid, helpless witness to the cruelty of the universe. Unable to do anything but be an audience to misery.

I couldn't, I wouldn't, let that be my role in whatever we were now entangled in. I was never good at being a spectator anyway.

Sometimes there are situations that, for whatever reason, you find yourself forced into; situations that you're a part of but there's someone who deserves to be involved even less; and you owe it to them to keep fighting, even if it seems hopeless.

That was going to be my role in this story.

Somehow, I feared I might be both the damsel in distress, and the brave (albeit stupid) sidekick, but I was okay with that, as long as I wasn't just sitting back being useless.

As I watched Desmond happily explore what was a completely new world, I realized what I'm sure I always knew in my gut. Whatever was going on might be attached to Desmond, but it wasn't his fault. Maybe it was the universe having a laugh, or maybe it was just bad luck; whatever it was, Desmond deserved to be dealing with it even less than I did. I wasn't going to abandon him.

So heads up reader, for the rest of the book whenever I do something brave, or reckless, or whatever, you need to know it's not me being any one of those things, it's because sometimes you have to kick-back against the chaos we're all engulfed in.

And because me and Desmond were a team.

CHAPTER 6

We walked for another hour through the moonscaped park, just a man-child and his dog, before finally heading towards home. A home that might've been swarmed with evil entities, or might not…who knew? The hazy glow of the moon on the streets we haunted reminded me of old noir films. Something about the fuzzy light the moon casts down, which filled the walkways, reminded me of those old black-white films.

The house was dark when we arrived back from our walk. Normally, I wouldn't have given this a second thought. I'd plunge right into the living room—dark though it might be—and root around until I found the lamp. No big deal. But that night was different, because I knew there might've been something waiting for us, cloaked in darkness.

Nevertheless, Desmond and I made our way up the front steps towards whatever awaited us, since there was really no other choice. I knew my front door was now a potential portal to a world of hurt, but we couldn't exactly stand outside all night. At some point I was going to have to face the fear of what might wait inside, and I figured it might as well be then.

I stopped for a moment in front of the door and willed myself to fumble through my pockets until I had my keys, all the while trying to clear my mind. Desmond sat down patiently next to me on the stoop as I took my time fishing out the keys. Once I finally had them in hand, I took a deep breath and inserted them into the lock continuing what typically was a mundane chain of events, but that I was convinced would be the last thing I did on this earth.

With the door swung open, we plunged into the darkness of my living room guided only by the eerie glow of the streetlights behind us. Since Chuck was cheap, he had never installed a light switch in the living room, or any form of lighting for that matter. Instead, he depended on the tenant bringing their own free-standing lamp to lighten the area. To add to it all, there were no outlets by the front door so I had been limited to where I could put a lamp.

After what I had seen the night before, however, this former annoyance was now much more problematic. The last time I had turned a light on I was greeted by an unpleasant, shadowy surprise. So, there was added stress to this particular game of "find the light."

I walked into the dark abyss with my left hand glued to my cheek, primed to fire off a jab if anything popped out, though I had very little hope a punch would do anything. As I made my way towards where I knew the lamp to be, I dropped Desmond's leash so I could use both hands just in case. I expected him to stay by my side as I clumsily navigated the room, but instead he sprinted off into the house the second the leash hit the floor. Apparently, he wanted to do a preliminary sweep and I was moving too slow.

I could hear the soft *pitter patter* of Desmond moving around somewhere in the kitchen, then it went silent. Immediately assuming the worst, I dove towards where I *thought* the lamp was and missed by a solid foot. Instead of light filling up the room, I felt the arm rest slam into my hip as I collapsed onto the couch. I pathetically rolled over after falling and finally managed to flick the light on.

Looking back, it's too bad the shadow wasn't there in the living room to see that display of raw athleticism. If I'd been so lucky, I imagine it might have opted to move on to destroy someone else's life after deeming me too pathetic to waste time on. No such luck though.

With the room no longer pitch black, I was finally able to confirm that there was nothing in there with us. The room was completely void of anything unexpected, but the silence had now broken in the next room and I could hear Desmond sprinting around excitedly in the kitchen. There was another noise coming from the kitchen: a soft metallic scraping, which sent my heart into my throat. It sounded like a weapon being dragged menacingly across the floor.

Throwing caution to the wind I made my way to see what trouble Desmond was in. I burst into the kitchen and stood in the doorway, only to find Des toying with his empty food bowl. The metal bowl swirled about the kitchen floor in a sparkling blur, spurred on as Desmond flipped it with his paw anytime it looked like it was about to stop rolling.

A little embarrassed, I went into the pantry to grant his request. I poured his food from the Tupperware container into the shiny silver bowl after it had finally settled still on the floor. As Des began chowing down, I made my way back to the living room where I collapsed onto my couch, yet again, in defeat. Desmond followed shortly after. He hopped up onto the couch and plopped his giant head onto my shoulder as if to say: *Hey friend. Sorry you're so on edge!*

I knew I was unsettled. What made it worse was that even as I told myself to calm down and relax, I could feel a tightness in my chest that let me know I was doing the exact opposite. I was getting more worked up and more nervous. I sat up on the couch and buried my face into my hands. I could feel Desmond inch closer in an effort to console me.

What did you used to do before fights?

The thought made sense—thinking about how I used to handle stressful times of uncertainty, that is—and I knew the answer right away.

You wouldn't think about it. You'd relax and push it as far back here in your mind as you could. You can react, and at the moment, that's about all you can do.

Even weeks before a fight I would get so nervous I would have trouble sleeping. It took time, and several training camps, but eventually I learned how to purposefully distract myself before the looming competition. I decided to take my own advice and apply the learned skill in this particularly demanding instance. I reached over Des and grabbed the remote from its perch on the coffee table.

It was already late for me at 9:00 p.m., a time when I would normally be curling up in my bed and passing out. However, I knew that I wouldn't be able to fall asleep no matter what mental gymnastics I tried; the thought of going into the dark immediately sent an adrenaline rush pumping through me. If I was going to try to act normal, I knew I'd need some background noise to fill my attention, especially since sleep was out of the question.

I opted to fill that background with a documentary: a perfectly mellow and mundane choice of watching pleasure. As I flipped through the documentary options that were streaming, one particular film about the history of the Himalayas caught my eye. I've always been a sucker for adventure books and films, and I'll admit that visiting the Everest base camp is on my bucket list.

"What do you think, bud?"

Desmond barely moved at the sound of my voice. At this point, he was curled up so tightly he looked more like a cinnamon roll than a dog. The soft sound of his snoring let me know he didn't care much what I decided to watch on that particular evening.

Soon, I was listening to some British narrator's soothing description of the first human settlement in the treacherous area. My oversized, grey box of a TV was far from being hi-resolution, but despite this, the beautiful shots of the almost otherworldly landscape made me forget about my problems for a few minutes. The stunning mountains, while beautiful from my couch, were no doubt fraught with peril for those early people. A point the voiceover made over, and over, and….

About an hour into the film, and despite all odds, I had begun to doze off a bit. The documentary had started to fade to black, as did my conscious as I felt myself *really* relax for the first time that day. I was *so* close to sleep, but an expected word caught my attention. It snapped me back to the realm of the living with the same suddenness that somebody slapping me might have done.

"…Vampire."

I don't know why (probably because I was already on edge about anything involving the supernatural) but hearing that word sent shivers through my already tense body. I leaned closer to the TV as its light bathed my living room in a soft glow. Before I got too engrossed, I looked next to me to make sure Desmond was still safe. He was twitching in his sleep, but otherwise appeared hunky-dory. Knowing he was alright I turned my attention back to the documentary.

"In Nepal's Mustang region, the burials of its earliest settlers are unique, carved high into the cliff walls so synonymous with the mountainous area. It's in these tombs, which require a treacherous ascent to access, that we discover signs of 'staking' where stakes are driven into the deceased who are thought to be haunted by a sinister being. Researchers at first were baffled…"

I felt like a little kid watching Saturday morning cartoons as I continued to lean further forward while sitting cross-legged on the couch. The only thing that was missing was a giant bowl of some sugar laced cereal. I was worried if my attention flickered for the briefest moment, an important nugget of knowledge might escape my grasp.

"The closest translation for these beings in English is 'vampire,' though Tibetan and Nepalese folklore differs greatly from the European mythology, describing them as dark beings whose presence was accompanied by bouts of bad luck and death. These burials being unearthed in the cliffside, where individuals are found with a stake driven through their center, anthropologists now believe, were either thought to be a carrier of the spirit or the victim."

As the narrator switched to describing the ties these settlers had to other early Buddhist cultures, I snatched up the remote and rewound the film to where I had first begun to fall asleep.

"—these burial sites coat the northern part of Nepal, all the way to its border with Tibet. As archeologists brave the difficult landscape, they have made a startling discovery. None of these settlements are exactly the same. Some are simply tombs dug from above the cliff to bury the dead, while further north, there are examples of complex tunnels and labyrinths in caves that appear to be a part of a network resembling a city…"

The film continued on, eventually picking up at the point that had demanded my utmost attention…but something that distinguished British voice had said sent butterflies on a rampage in my gut.

Dark beings, whose presence is accompanied by bouts of bad luck and death.

I shut the television off and made a beeline for my laptop that was tucked away in my backpack. I heard Des grunt behind me from the couch, apparently annoyed at being stirred from his sleep.

"Sorry, bud, I've got work to do."

47

I spent the rest of the night reading Tibetan and Nepalese mythology, learning about the mountain gods and the hungry ghost. It was fascinating, so much so that I forgot for a moment that I was likely being haunted by some shadowy creature, and actually found myself enjoying the hunt for information. There was something about looking at the words on a brightly illuminated computer screen that made everything seem so distant and not real.

As I dove into the underbelly of eastern culture, studying like a monk in a monastery with nothing better to do (certainly not sleep!), I found myself beginning to formulate a hypothesis about what was going on in my little house. As I bounced from website to website, I continued to look up to make sure my living room was clear of any bats or pale, caped creeps. By this point, my working hypothesis was that I had seen a "dark being." As the documentary had mentioned, the early settlers of the Himalayan mountain range—who no doubt had to be some of the toughest people to ever walk the earth—believed that evil spirits could attach themselves to certain families, or villages, or whatever. When you think about it, it's more similar to modern beliefs in ghosts or possessions than vampires.

Due to the alpine terrain, these settlements were independent enclaves forced to survive on their own for extended periods of time. In stark contrast, they could also be busy hubs of trade when passes opened, which basically connected India and China by being located in the only walkable area. The geographic situation created very interesting communities that would have to survive long isolated stretches for undisclosed amounts of time, but that would still be introduced to other cultures and ideas intermittently, where these new ideas could grow into something unique to that village.

In Tibet, "Sky Burials" left the bodies to the elements to decompose and be scavenged by animals (mostly birds, thus the "sky burial" name, because the body would end up flying in the belly of some giant scavenger). It's a Buddhist practice meant to remove the traces of a previous life so that the person can move on to the next phase of existence.

Which is why the tombs in the cliffside were so interesting. The early communities who used these graves predate the Buddhist practice of sky burials, or supposedly even Buddhism taking root in the area, but there are signs they were doing something similar to the modern-day practice of stripping the flesh off the bodies or reburying them once they naturally lost flesh. Then, a stake would be driven through their core until it pierced their spine.

I couldn't find any more in-depth information about what types of bad luck would lead to a body having a stake driven through it, outside a few theories from anthropologists who guessed it was the normal stuff: disease, a rash of unexplained deaths, increased infant mortality, etc. All of which were par with the course of early settlements in any region.

Everything I looked at was written through a historic or scientific interpretation and glossed over anything supernatural, which was to be expected, I suppose. But those authors didn't see the shadow. They didn't feel the gut-wrenching realization that there were things out there beyond comprehension, learning this as their bedroom turned into a very real nightmare. That ancient evils might sometimes take interest in those living very average, very mundane existences. Or, had Desmond not been there to save me, I might be suffering some eternal cosmic fate. They didn't get all that, but I did. As I thought about the night before, the sleep deprived wheels in my head started turning slowly.

What if it wasn't natural occurrences that led to the unusual burial practices?

What if there was something attaching itself to people in those early settlements, and making bad things happen?

And what if, assuming such a thing might be real, it decided to attach itself to a lovable dog? A dog, who at least on some level, knew something wicked was afoot and could at least temporarily fight back?

I thought back to the night with the shadow and the way Desmond was able to back the thing down after the standoff. Like I said before, dogs seem to have better premonitions about certain things. What if that was one of them? Maybe Desmond was both the reason that thing was in my house, and also the reason why I'm still alive and kickin'? At this point I also remembered the weird happenings that first time I walked my good boy, and everything slowly began to make sense.

I looked at him, all curled up without a care in the world on the couch next to me. The walk had apparently wiped him out and I swear he was grinning as he slept.

He looked so serene.

Probably because he didn't have to do any research or hadn't tried to figure out what was going on. Des was just doing what he does, same as all dogs. Hell, all animals. No overthinking, no worrying about whether something bad might happen. Just reacting.

I decided that, at least for the night, I would follow suit. I needed sleep. A lot of sleep. So, I followed Desmond's example and curled up on the couch next to him. Despite what I'd just learned, it was easy falling asleep knowing he was there.

CHAPTER 7

"The Old Stone House" is what we in the industry call a cabinet of curiosities. That means it's a hodge-podge assortment of what the original owner, a nineteenth century tavern owner named Edward Smith, thought was interesting and collected throughout his life. Smith had inherited enough money to travel the world, which was certainly not common for a tavern owner of his time, so we have some cool artifacts lying around. And since such a place is a rarity, we stay busy enough to justify having me as a full-time employee.

It helps that ethical tourism and archeology were not around during Smith's time and nineteenth-century travelers snagged whatever they could get their grubby hands on. We have chunks of every ancient monument you could imagine being defiled by a nineteenth-century tourist. There are pieces of linen from mummies, dried out leopard skins, books from around the world…basically, you name it, we got it. All the things that make work a little less like actual work, especially when you see them stuffed away in some back corner waiting to be brought out to the light.

The house itself is not a mansion by any means. The first floor would have been home to the tavern and above that are six rooms: three of these rooms would have been for paying guests, and the other three would have been for the Smith family. Then, above the second story, there's a large attic that mostly serves as storage. Since it was turned into a museum the house had gone through several changes, but the basic bones of the old place were still there.

As I made my way into work the day after watching that documentary, I was a man on a mission. Not only had I been able to sleep uninterrupted for six hours the night before, but I also felt renewed with the possibility of a quick victory over the shadow, which I had deemed mine and Desmond's mortal enemy. Needless to say, after my morning pot of coffee I was raring to go.

"Morning Jon!" Rick said cheerily as I walked into the break room.

Rick was the museum's curator, and a good one at that. He had turned the Old Stone House from a jumbled collection of oddities into an actual museum that interpreted Smith's peculiar place in history. Trust me, I'd seen the original photos of the place from before his time and it looked like a hoarder's wet dream. No order and no emphasis based on accurate historical interpretation. Just a shamble of *things.*

Now, everything was catalogued, organized, and presented in a manner that was befitting of the collection. Rick had been working at the museum for twenty years at that point and knew more about the collection than any other human on Earth. Which is exactly why I needed to talk to him.

"Rick, just the man I was looking to see!"

The break room, which was a small room that contained one folding coffee table, a coffee pot, and a sink, sat in the back of the first floor where the original kitchen for the tavern would have been. My office shared a wall with the break room.

It wasn't a glamorous set up by any means, but it did its job and at least there *was* a break room.

Rick sat at the table; a half-eaten glazed donut rested in front of him. The other half seemed to be either mashed into his grey beard or crumbled on the T-shirt that was much too big for his wiry frame. Rick didn't dress up much since he worked behind the scenes, and the fact that he was the phantom of the museum was probably for the best;

Rick could be a bit rough around the edges, which, coupled with a love for his own voice, could get him in some trouble. I liked him still.

"Why's that?" he asked curiously.

Rick knew I was working on some new merchandise for the gift shop and I knew he had some ideas he wanted to pass along. That's my job, by the way: I work on merchandise design, tours, and research facts to add to the tours.

"Question about the collection," I began. "I was watching a documentary about Nepal and Tibet, and I was wondering if Smith ever got out to that area or if we had anything from those places? I know he went east to India twice during the 1838 and '49 trips; do you think he might've ever gone further east?"

Rick stroked his beard.

"Yeah," he said slowly, hand still on his beard, "he went there for a bit. Wanted to see Everest during his Victorian adventure stage, or right before it, I suppose. I think he brought back a few trinkets. We can look at the catalogue later if you'd like." He paused like he was done, then added: "Oh, and I can show you something I was thinking about for a new T-shirt!"

I was waiting for that, and he shoehorned it in rather clumsily, but if he could find anything that might be of interest to me and Desmond's predicament, I'd put a picture of him on a T-shirt for all I cared.

I hung around the break room for another minute or two, making forced small talk, then after filling up my coffee mug with the jet fuel Rick had brewed, I made my way to my office.

Since I was ahead of my work for the week, I spent the next hour continuing my research on the shadows that plagued the Mustang area of Nepal. I don't know how long I spent flipping from website to website, but the screen had just begun to turn to a translucent blur when Rick saved me.

"Hey, I found some Nepalese stuff in the attic storage room if you wanna come see?"

His head peered from the side of the door with the rest of his body completely obstructed. I could tell he was excited by the tone of his voice, which was a tenor I had never heard from him before. His face was a rosy red and a trickle of sweat dripped down his forehead, which meant he had bypassed looking through the catalogue, and instead had just gone up to investigate the attic. The fact he had to put in some (literal) legwork to find whatever he wanted to show me meant that it interested him as well.

We made our way up the steep stairs leading to the stories above while Rick began telling me about the find in breathless rasps.

"It was in a box tucked away in the back. I hadn't seen it. It's not catalogued either, but I was certain we had *something* from Nepal. Must've been put there by the old curator and I just never saw it when I was organizing."

He stopped at the top of the first flight of stairs, regained his breath, and pushed on. Each step was labored, and he was favoring one side of his gangly body as he lurched up each step.

"There's a whole bunch of artifacts in there…some Buddhist stuff that must have been traded from India…a dagger…I think there's a bone fragment and some burial ritual stuff too. Too bad we can't put it as an exhibit."

He was sounding pretty bad towards the end there, so I didn't pry into the reason why we couldn't use it in the museum.

After another set of the grueling stairs, that were built at a nearly 90-degree incline to take as little space as possible, we arrived in the attic. Before we even opened the latched door the heat from the space suffocated the stairway. It was like standing in a dry sauna. There was even the smell of dried, heat-baked cedar that gave me flashbacks to cutting weight for fights.

"Jon…" Rick was huffing and puffing like he wanted to blow the door down. I was too busy inspecting the door to realize how bad of shape he *actually* was in. He continued talking from behind me in short, choppy sentences.

"I think we gotta part ways here…I pulled it out…you can't miss it. Feel free to investigate as much as you…as much as you want. I don't think we can use it in displays—little too rough. No real story…but maybe a researcher would be interested. We can reach out…I don't know if I can stay up h…here."

He started to wheeze; it sounded as dry as the air coming from the attic's hatch. I was worried that Rick might lose that donut from earlier, and the prospect of cleaning vomit up here in the sweltering, cramped stairwell was enough to make me consider booting him down the stairs to speed up his descent.

Rather than kicking Rick down several flights of stairs, I nodded to let him know I understood. Rick's face was sickly pale, and his grey T-shirt was changing shades by the second with patches of sweat that grew larger and larger, clinging to his skinny body. This was his second time up to the attic that day. I made a mental note to buy him a beer as a thank you the next time we found ourselves at a bar.

As Rick hobbled slowly down the steps, his weightless body barely making a noise on the steps, I lifted the latch and entered the attic.

It was like stepping into a clay oven. The heat hung so thickly in the air, I swear I saw it ripple like a mirage. I pressed forward as the smell of dry must and old books flooded my nostrils, which would have been comforting in a weird way, had I not been walking into the hottest level of hell.

As promised, the box was pulled out on the wood slat floor and impossible to miss. I walked towards it gingerly and each step creaked eerily as the weathered wood beam flooring shifted underneath my weight. I tried to spread out my weight as much as humanly possible.

The loud creaks I heard with each slight movement was enough to fill me with the irrational fear of falling through to the museum below; even though I knew the attic floor had managed to support Rick before me who only weighed slightly less than me. Still, there was no harm in being careful.

The box was already open revealing its contents, which might have been garbage by the way it had been crammed in there haphazardly with no regard. A few notes were stuck to items throughout, but as it was, there was no way to verify anything in there. Like Rick mentioned, Smith's trip to Nepal must have been fairly uneventful if he didn't mention it in any of our records. Without a written trail it would be hard to justify dedicating some of the already limited gallery space to these artifacts.

I hovered above the box as sweat poured down my face. I quickly leaned back to make sure none of the sweat dripped down onto the trinkets. As I moved back, I felt my shirt cling to my chest and droplets of sweat beaded to my forearms simultaneously.

Still, I was there for a reason, and I began to lay out the menagerie of items on the attic floor as neatly as I could. There was an old rug hanging on another box next to me, which I gently laid out on the floor to view whatever I found in the box.

I began unpacking the crate. There were a few copper Buddhas as well as some pieces of various clothes, and coins. It was all very mundane, that was, until the dagger Rick had described emerged from the rubble. Rick knew his stuff, but why he described this as a dagger was beyond me—though I'll give him the benefit of the doubt and say that the heat stunted his judgement.

The "dagger" was a long gold pole, about eight inches in length and ornately designed. It was tough to tell *exactly* what the figures were that had been carefully folded and carved into the weapon, but they appeared to be either dragons or birds of some sort. Even with my limited knowledge I knew I was holding a stake, which was exactly the type of thing I had hoped to find.

It didn't hurt to see that stuck to the handle was a note that read "Cliff Burial," which affirmed what I already knew. The writing had been done in marker and the faded yellow paper was old; it was clearly not written by Smith, or the son who had inherited the tavern after his father passed.

I guessed the curator before Rick was responsible for the cryptic and unspecific note. There was no additional data or information about how Smith had acquired it…nothing of substance to go on. I sat down on the stovetop of a floor feeling frustrated. Still, it was better than making the trip to the attic and leaving empty-handed.

By that point, the heat was really getting to me. As my head began to grow light, I quickly put everything back into the box the way it had been for the last thirty years. I made one change though. I put the stake on top of everything else for easy access when I wanted to investigate it again. My head was swimming by the time everything was put away and I knew if I stayed up there any longer, the next visitor to the attic would discover the dried-out Mummy of a twenty-four-year-old museum worker.

I practically crawled my way back down to the operating floors of the museum; the rush of the air-conditioned downstairs felt like a rebirth. If I could bottle and sell that rush of refreshment, I'd be a millionaire.

Desmond greeted me at the door again, but I could tell by the concerned look in his eyes that something was up. But more telling than the concern in his eyes, I suppose, was the fact that he was covered in a chalky white powder. He looked like he had just returned from the wildest bender this side of Vegas.

I stood outside for a second and braced myself for the worst. Though at this point in my little adventure, my limited imagination couldn't even come up with a situation to prepare myself for. I just assumed it would suck. Hard.

I burst through the door with my hands up and ready to give whatever was there the old one-two. Meanwhile, Desmond began to bark simultaneously, as I made my hero's entrance. I was relieved to see the living room was alright. For a fleeting moment, I allowed myself to hope that I had only imagined Desmond's call for help. I mean, the powder could have just been some loose drywall that had sprinkled him, or him getting into some normal dog mischief. It all made perfect sense for a moment in the living room. However, as soon as I made my way into the kitchen, any relief I had misguidedly felt went up in flames.

The kitchen looked like a hurricane had made its way through my humble abode. Among many other things strewn across the floor, I found the culprit for Desmond's current dusty state: a broken jar that was shattered on the painted wood flooring. It was one of my ceramic containers that had watercolor robins painted on, a move-in gift from my grandmother, which I used to hold cooking supplies. This one in particular had spilled its powdery contents all over the floor when it was knocked over, and the layer of flour on the floor painted a vivid play-by-play of the earlier events that I missed while I was at work.

I stood in the entranceway of the kitchen and surveyed the scene. Closest to me—and providing enough evidence to make this the world's easiest whodunit—were prints. Paw prints.

Now, in any other situation that'd be that: mystery solved. Just a dog left to his own devices making a mess. Desmond even looked up at me with a guilty look on his giant T. rex head, but I knew better. I looked back at the war zone that was my kitchen, and as I expected to see, noticed that it wasn't only paw prints in the floury dusting. There were several other prints all around the room that were most certainly not canine in origin.

And by room, let me be clear, I don't mean just the floor of the kitchen. The walls, counters, even the ceiling, were covered by flour dusted footprints. It seemed like there had been a great migration of *something* that had occurred in my kitchen, and the prints were *almost* human.

Almost.

There were so many, and they were blurred together so frantically that there was no chance at figuring out the exact anatomy of whatever had left the print.

Desmond's paw prints didn't stray far from the initial spot near the entrance of the kitchen where I had first seen them. The other prints went everywhere in the room, except for the three-foot radius surrounding the area where I stood, peering in, and where Desmond had stood during the attack. There was one line of paw prints that made its way to the center of the kitchen though, which explained how Desmond had gotten coated in flour.

The shadow's prints seemed to be most heavily focused above the basement door and the areas surrounding it. Looking at it you would be hard pressed to believe that the particular area in the kitchen was actually painted a putrid yellow and not white; that's how smeared in flour it was. The flour completely coated the area, and the only spots where a hint of yellow managed to peek through were the areas so highly trafficked that the flour had been completely kicked off.

I thought back to the last encounter with the shadows. I remembered how they had culminated in one dark amorphous mass before shooting out for their individual attacks and figured that the giant flour spot must have been the nexus of the attack, while the footprints all around must have been their mad dashes towards Desmond. As I sat in the entrance way of the kitchen dumbfounded, I tried to piece together any new information this newest attack might have told me.

They left prints…which meant…

They're real…there's something sort of physical about them…and they're scared of Desmond. They were trying to scare him off.

He had stood his ground though, and apparently turned them back. I reached down and pet his giant head. He seemed to smile; his giant jaw unhinged as his tongue rolled out in an excited pant. Des seemed proud of his work and I couldn't blame him, from the looks of things, he had turned back an army. An army that I now knew had retreated to the pit of a basement that sat beneath my house. A basement that could even possibly be described as little more than a cave.

"Let's clean this mess up, buddy," I said, grabbing a broom to begin the painstaking process of cleaning up my kitchen. As I swept, my eyes never drifted from that cellar door.

Believe that.

CHAPTER 8

Force must be met with force, and they started it after all, so I was done being on the defensive. Besides, the way I saw it, they looked to set-up an ambush while I was gone so the gloves were already off. It was my turn to attack.

The gun was heavy in my hands, and walking down those crooked, shambled steps made me feel as if I was making my way into a crypt where a vampire might store their coffin. This was only my second time down into the cellar since I moved in. The first time I had been down there was right after I had signed the lease to the place and paid my security deposit. It was not an endearing first encounter, since I had stepped on what may have been an old needle. After I had sprinted upstairs to clean the cut, it took everything I had in me to not immediately dial Chuck to tell him to rip up the lease agreement. Needless to say, the subsequent doctors visit, shot, and bill left me with an unfavorable view of the space.

Yeah, that's the type of basement I had.

So why I decided to make my way down there again was anybody's guess. The steps creaked and groaned with each shift as if they were alive and suffering underneath my weight. Adding to the creepiness, I was led only by a single dangling light bulb at the bottom of the steps. The bulb flickered about excitedly as I plunged toward it. Each flashing explosion of light seemed to reveal a new cobweb, all of which dangled in heavy clumps from the ceiling. The long strands of web would catch the light in a silver sparkle with every hiccup of the bulb as a sparkle of light would trickle down the strand before disappearing at the end of the net.

There was a musty, earthy smell in the air, like the scent of stagnant pond in oppressive summer heat. The rust brown watermarks on the crumbling concrete walls explained why it smelled like that. I felt like I was stepping down into a deep, carved out cave.

Just like a cliff tomb.

Before I could give the idea any more thought, a soft sound filled the stairwell. Behind me, I could hear Desmond whimpering and softly scratching at the basement door.

I knew it was not because he was scared, of course, but because I had quickly closed the door behind me when I began my little adventure to the basement. I had blocked him out of my excursion because I wanted to see what I could do to this thing myself. It seemed stupid even then and looking back it certainly was.

But the basement was no place for a dog.

Besides, I had a bit of a hypothesis going, which I was apparently confident enough in to bet my life on that particular night. There were two parts to my idea (which I formed sleep-deprived after watching one documentary, mind you). One, that these shadow things like the underground or cave-like dwellings; and two, that a stake could hurt them.

Part one was pretty evident. I mean, with the whole concept of cave burials, the flour above the cellar, and the first walk with Desmond when he freaked out at that door leading underground. I had very little doubt that I could be wrong about this. I mean, the European versions of vampires prefer dark places, so why wouldn't these shadow ones? Maybe that's where the odd translation comes from.

As for the second part, which I'll admit was a bit more of a leap of faith then I'd like to take, if all those ancient bodies buried in Tibet and Nepal had stakes driven through them (and again, European vampires' aversion to the same instruments) maybe there was some truth to it. Besides, I can't think of anything in this world that *likes* having a stake driven through it, so why would the shadow?

Of course, I had the gun with me just in case, but that wasn't all. Tucked into my jeans and running down my leg out-of-sight, there was a metal tent stake I'd snagged from the camping supplies in the garage. I figured since the camping tool had stake in the name, it would suffice. I wasn't overly optimistic though, and I figured a measly tent stake wasn't going to kill the thing completely. But maybe I could scare it enough to remind it that there were better places for it to hide than my house.

The stale air in the basement seemed to quiver as I hopped down from the wooden stairs to the broken cement floor. I turned the corner ready to scrap. I was facing the back of the basement, and the only thing I could see was a collection of broken wooden furniture scattered throughout. The whole room was a cluttered mess, and I strained my eyes to try and make out more details. I felt like I was peering down a twenty-foot alleyway of darkness, an alleyway that you were almost guaranteed to get mugged walking down.

The house was old, and for some reason the ceiling was so low that even I, all five foot eight of me, had to crouch down a bit to make my way towards the back of the basement. Various metal pipes and columns jutted down from the ceiling, which made it even more difficult to traverse.

The old furniture I had seen scattered about had presumably belonged to earlier tenants. There was a battered set of dining-room stools, a rocking chair, and what looked like a small table that had been hit by a truck. Chuck being too lazy to properly dispose of these items had opted to just throw them down in the basement, I suppose. It gave the basement the same decor that an abandoned and haunted asylum might have in a lazy cliché-ridden horror movie. I wouldn't have been surprised if the wooden rocking chair that was missing an armrest somehow began to rock by itself.

My eyes began to adjust to the darkness and started to make out more of the landscape in front of me. As I travelled through the piles and broken furniture, I encountered a dark blob that nearly paralyzed me, I was so scared. That was, until I realized I was looking at the heater. The mangled shape of the central heating tank, with its various protruding metal pipes that led somewhere into the house above, appeared sinister for some reason. In the dark, the twisted metal looked like the silhouette of Cthulhu.

It also blocked the view behind it. This posed a major problem, since there was only a two-foot walkway past the heater. It was a narrow space that I would have to make my way though, with no hint as to what lay in front.

I walked towards it slowly, trying my best not to make any sound. There was only so much I could do though since each step forward was marked by the sound of crunching corroded concrete. When I finally arrived at the heater, I wasted no time and instantly began to squeeze through the small passage running past it. I was careful not to touch anything too much, seeing as I had no clue when I had gotten my last tetanus shot. As I worked my way through the tight space I could still hear Desmond's whimper from up above and desperately wished he was by my side.

I knew it was the right choice not to bring him down to the basement though; there was too much that could go wrong and in such a small space, two might have been more of a hindrance than a help. Still, at that moment I felt as lonely as I ever had, as the rotted walls of the walkway seemed to press down on me like the panels of a garbage compressor.

I made my way through the small walkway as fast as I could, which was difficult with a shotgun in one hand and a stake digging into my leg. The rancid smell of mold and wet earth flooded my nostrils, and I felt my forearm bump against something slimy. I recoiled and tried not to think about what it could've been as I walked deeper into the all-encompassing darkness.

When I emerged from the walkway, I felt a swift change in the air, and almost immediately, I knew I had hit the world's worst jackpot. I wasn't alone anymore.

The air had changed from a putrid but natural smell, to a putrid, evil stench that hung stagnant into the air, and was accompanied only by a sinister coldness that chilled to the bone. If possible, the darkness even seemed to grow a little inkier as well, which made it seem as if I was in the bottom of a well. The chamber beyond the heater was small, I could tell that from the few specks of light that managed to shine through from behind, but in that moment, the room felt like it stretched on for eternity in complete darkness.

The shotgun felt useless in my hands and seemed to grow heavier by the second. Before that moment, the thought of having a gun and being hopeless seemed impossible. I mean, I figured if you had a gun, you had a fighting chance, right? That was before I was in that dark cramped space, and before I realized there were some spots humans weren't supposed to venture into. That instinct of self-preservation I keep mentioning, that one that I think the people who ignored Desmond had, finally reared its ugly head, and hit me like a ton of bricks.

Run you idiot. This isn't an action movie where you're the hero. This is a horror movie where you're the unnamed character, and you're in for a world of hurt you stupid—

The darkness seemed to seep all about me. The light at the other end of the cellar might as well have been in another galaxy. I felt like the last doomed survivor of a spaceship drifting through a black hole, the one who knew the darkness would soon swallow him whole. I stood still, hoping I had gone undetected, but knowing that was about as likely as me surviving the next twenty minutes. That was when it dawned on me.

Cell phone.

Of course, I had brought it *and* it had a flashlight. No longer caring if the shadow knew I was there, I rested the shotgun on one arm and reached into my pocket to pull out the only chance I had, maybe not of surviving, but at least a chance of seeing what I assumed would be my killer.

I fumbled about for a moment, before finally opening the lock screen and finding the flashlight app. The whole time the room seemed to grow colder, and more still despite my bumbling efforts. As soon as the light was on, however, the room brightened up as if a police floodlight had been aimed in the small space. The white light bounced off the grey, crumbling bricks. It made it look like I was in the middle of a black-and-white film where I was just some poor, sad stiff, sitting in a 1920's movie theatre watching the show of my life.

As my eyes adjusted to the other extremity, I saw exactly what I feared I would. In front of me was the dark outline of a human that crawled slowly along the wall, reaching and pulling with its hands and feet in a synchronized motion. I tried to follow its movements, but the wicked hum of voices began pounding in my ears; harsh whispers that seeped above the drone and into my being enveloped me.

"You'll be dead in the hour…"

"The beast can't save you this time…"

"Devour you. Devour you…"

Each voice seemed more sinister than the last. With a clatter that was overpowered by the voices, the gun fell to the floor as I reached up to shield my ears to stop their wretched threats from getting through. It didn't matter though. I was in their domain, and there was nothing that could stop those horrific voices from making their way through as I clutched powerlessly at my ears.

Laughter.

The whispers seemed to die away as a deep, guttural chuckle rattled around the small room. The laugh was so loud I swear I saw small bits of crumbling rock fall down from a decayed portion of the wall. Even with all the noise happening around me, directly above where I stood, I could still make out the sound of scratches on the floor above me.

Desmond's trying to get through.

But the sounds of Desmond's frantic attempt to get to me were overshadowed as the laugh echoed deafeningly in the chamber. I frantically looked around to find its source, waving my phone around in a jerky motion that only made everything more disorienting. Aside from the shadow, the only anomaly in the area I could make out was a deep cavern, about three feet in diameter, that was carved into the same crumbling surface I had seen the rocks tumble from earlier.

The climbing shadow had stopped moving as the light filled the gap. It stood there on the wall as if it were watching me. I barely paid attention though, since I was still recovering from the horrid voices, and that sick laughter.

That was when it attacked me.

A dark blur surrounded me, knocking me down next to the fallen shotgun. It momentarily crossed my mind to reach for the weapon…but then I realized how pointless it would be.

What would you be shooting at? It's practically a mist.

I kicked out at the shadow as violently as I could, but the dark figure seemed to dissipate into the air. I then tried to stand up, only to be knocked back down. There was nothing I could do to it in its domain, I was too slow. I could feel the icy grip of a hand pawing at my throat and squirmed back as far as I could until I was sitting prone against the base of a wall, feeling particularly defenseless. Still, I kept kicking because that was better than lying there and dying without a fight. Even one as pathetic as that.

My head was spinning in confusion. While the whispers and laugh might have been gone, a horrible sound like magnified static had replaced them.

This is how it ends…

That was when I felt it, a sharp twinge in my leg and I recoiled back from kicking at shadows. It was the stake digging into my skin. I shoved my hands in my pants, a gesture I'm sure the shadow misinterpreted as an attempt at me dying a happy man and grabbed at the unsharpened aluminum end of the stake. The green plastic handle might as well have been the hilt of Excalibur with the surge of confidence it gave me.

As I pulled the tent stake out and began jabbing at the air like a blind Zorro, I felt the icy cold hand that had recently gotten a hold of my leg let go. And in a matter of seconds, I saw the shadow appear back on the wall. The noise in my head had died down too, and I began to re-orientate myself in the spinning cellar. The stake had temporarily worked, and for whatever reason, the attacking shadow had been weary enough of the lame excuse for a weapon to back off.

That was all I needed.

I wasted no time getting out of there. Still brandishing my stake, I snatched up the fallen shotgun and sprinted back through the small walkway next to the heater and hurried toward the flickering light bulb at the base of the stairs. Only once I got there, did I chance a glance back.

There was only darkness. Just as it had been when I first came down.

A quick look was enough for me, and I hurried up the stairs towards safety and Desmond.

CHAPTER 9

The kitchen might as well have been an oasis in the middle of a desert, judging by how I dove into it. As soon as I slammed the basement door closed behind me, I took in the fresh, non-musty air like it was water and I had just managed to get to it in time. As my eyes acclimated to the bright light that was amplified by the yellow-painted room, I muttered a thank you to whatever gods may be that I was still alive.

Desmond scurried about me excitedly as I placed the shotgun and stake on the table. Both items settled to a still after rattling around the glass top for a brief second. They looked startlingly out of place on my dinner table resting in a spot where there should have been a bowl of fruit or some flowers.

As for Desmond, he was clearly relieved to see I was still alive. As he scampered about my feet he occasionally bumped into my leg as if he was checking to make sure I was real and not an illusion. His feet pit-patted against the ground at the pace of a machine gun and at times it looked like his back legs worked faster than the rest of him, as he would begin to curl up before fixing his posture. Despite the obvious excitement, he seemed still cautious. I saw Des sniff the air with distrust at least twice during his little celebration dance. He could tell that I had been close to the thing, and the fur on his hind legs rippled instinctively as the excited sprints slowly turned to a purposeful stride.

I pulled out one of the two chairs that sat at the kitchen table and sat down. I hate to admit it, but the loud *screech* of the chairs being dragged across the floor sent my heart fluttering in fear. After I looked around the kitchen to make sure it really *was* my chair that made the noise, I buried my head into my forearm for a minute and allowed myself to wallow in self-pity.

All I wanted was to help a dog. Why would this happen to me?

I sat up suddenly as if some invisible force had slapped me and brought me back to my senses. That voice, that driveling, searching-for-pity voice I had allowed to take over for a moment was enough to make me vomit.

You live for this. This is a messed-up situation that only you can survive. You're built for this. This is just another fight.

I stood up after the internal pep talk, walked to my fridge and grabbed a beer. It seemed like a momentary return to normalcy, as if getting a beer and acting like everything was okay would actually fix things.

The click of the can opening sounded like it was miles away, and I took a long pull of the cheap beer that tasted like water with a hint of aluminum. The single sip wasn't enough though, and soon the bottom of the can was face to face with the ceiling.

As I chugged, I noticed out of the corner of my eye that Desmond was at the basement door. He reached his paw up and scraped at the door, apparently wanting to go down and raise some hell. I'm not going to lie, after letting the self-doubt seep through for a moment, I was tempted to join him in a blaze of glory. If for nothing else to convince myself I wasn't a coward. I imagined just sprinting down there with that stupid metal pole and seeing how much damage we could do.

Even with my personal pride in a sorry state, I knew it was a bad idea to confront the shadow thing again. Unfortunately, so likely was the alternative route I chose to take that night in an effort to soothe by nerves. I don't remember exactly what happened, but I do know the half of a bottle of JD I had on top of my fridge disappeared that night.

The next morning my head felt like it did after a brutal fight or sparring session. I could practically feel my brain trying to expand within my skull as the dull pain of the hangover filled the front of my forehead. I blinked my eyes rapidly in an effort to see the world and make out what time it was. The cool air of my bedroom seemed to soothe the pain for the moment.

My alarm clock read 4:32 a.m., nearly an hour and a half before I normally wake up, but I knew I wasn't going back to sleep. Instead, I decided to go to the gym. Even in my hungover state I knew that getting a sweat was my only chance at making the forthcoming day anything but miserable. I sat up and looked down at Desmond, who was still asleep at the foot of my bed. I was certain he had stayed up all night protecting me while I got ripped, so I tried to move without waking him. Despite my best efforts, however, I was accompanied by my personal four-legged bodyguard the whole stumbling escapade to the front door. He had snapped to attention the second I'd gotten up to change into gym clothes.

Ten rounds on the heavy bag and a cold bottle of water did me well, and after sweating out all of the booze from the night before, I made my way back home feeling the best I had in some time.

I walked into the house and even before the door was open, I knew something was wrong. Desmond hadn't met me at the door after hearing me pull into the driveway, and the living room had the strange yet familiar smell of a pond in the summer heat. I knew what it was instantly.

The smell of the basement.

I sprinted towards the kitchen, the whole time my mind raced with a slideshow of progressively worse possibilities.

You got drunk then left. You didn't even think about what the thing might do after you challenged it. You dumb, selfish—

The kitchen was as I had left it (best as I could remember) other than the fact that the basement door was swung wide open. The stake was still on the kitchen table, and I snatched it up as I flew down the creaky basement steps. I didn't even take the time to turn the light on—not that would have mattered.

I was pretty sure this was the moment it would happen: the final confrontation. I didn't know what that would entail, but I tried my best to hunker down and be prepared for anything.

As I turned sharply around the bottom of the stairs, Desmond sprinted towards me from the abyss of blackness that was my basement. His giant frame seemed to appear out of nowhere, as if he was being spewed out of a black hole. I was so distracted in my joy that he was alright that as I swiveled around the staircase, I caught my side on the rusted metal of the stairwell's ancient handrail.

"Crap!"

The pain felt like a lightning bolt jolting up my left side and I paused for a moment. Between the pain, the excitement at seeing Desmond was alright, and the fear of what trailed behind him, my mind seemed to short-circuit for a second. The brief pause and reboot were just long enough so that when the dust settled, I saw Desmond's copper-red and white body only a few feet from me still on his way to the stairwell. He was gracefully floating through the dingy and cluttered cellar floor. Behind him, I could hear sinister whispers cut through the silence, like a horrible echo floating up from a well.

I might have imagined it, but along with the whispers I swear there was a screech that came from the same spot where I'd been the night before. Not wasting any time to see what the shadow would do, I turned and climbed up the steps. Desmond, of course, followed closely behind.

When I stepped into the kitchen, I turned around and saw Desmond had paused a few steps down. He looked at me with distrust, and I realized he was trying to guess my next move. He was worried I was going to lure him up, only to sprint back down like I had the night before. Behind him was the sound of pure chaos; he just wanted to make sure he was between me and whatever was going on down there. After what felt like an eternity, Desmond seemed satisfied that I wasn't going to do anything rash and skipped up the last three steps without a care in the world.

It wasn't until the basement door was slammed and locked (which didn't matter, I'm sure, but it made me feel better) that I stopped to inspect my side. It didn't tear through the shirt thank god, but there would definitely be a pretty brutal bruise there the next morning I figured.

"Dammit that hurt..." I started to complain, but I was never able to finish my whining because that was when I noticed the black and maroon liquid smeared across Des's face. It reminded me of those animal shows where they zoom in on the lion's face as it rips into some poor zebra or gazelle's guts as the animal's blood smears across the lion's powerful jaws.

It hadn't struck me until that moment of seeing him with a blood-covered muzzle, but Des was the same copper gold as a lion. As I stood there with my own jaw hanging open in dumb amazement, *he* stood there in my kitchen proud of what he had done. In that moment Desmond's eyes were lit up with excitement, his tail *thwapping* happily on the kitchen floor. He had exacted his revenge.

"What did you get, bud?" I said squatting down as I tried to get a better look at the thick dark liquid smeared on his face.

It wasn't quite blood in the same way the footprints weren't *quite* footprints. Whatever stained Desmond's face was much too dark to be blood, but it did have the same, thick consistency as the stuff. I was scared to touch it—I mean, it could've had ghost diseases or possessed me for all I knew—so I got a wet dishrag from the sink and cleaned Desmond's face before planning on tossing the towel in the garbage. As I cleaned him, he tossed and turned his head in slight annoyance.

It was as I washed Desmond that I tried to piece together the chain of events I had stumbled upon. Now obviously I wasn't there until the tail end, so this is all conjecture, but I'm sure I have a pretty good guess as to what happened while I was at the gym.

After I left, Desmond heard the basement door creak open. The shadow thing, having come to the realization that I now knew it hated stakes, decides it's done playing around and is going to send one of its goons to ambush me when I walk in. It would be the perfect plan; I mean, I wouldn't have expected it at all. Plus, if the assassin got to the living room quickly enough the shadow could slip past the sleeping Desmond.

Only it didn't make it.

Maybe Desmond caught it when it was moving into the living room, or maybe he just sprinted down into the basement to attack them at their home base. Whichever it was, I'm sure Des was irritated at having to stay out of the scrap the night before and was likely out for blood.

As I finished cleaning him up, I knew he'd only hurt the shadow, maybe just annoyed it even. Still, once he was no longer covered in shadow blood, I went into the cabinet and emptied out a bag of chicken jerky treats.

"Good boy," I said, scratching behind his ear.

I mean, after all, a job well-done deserves a reward.

After that start I figured my day would almost certainly go downhill. I mean, what could top *that* for a wakeup?

I got to work extra early since I planned on taking a long lunch to check up on Desmond. Although I knew he was more than capable of taking care of himself, I figured it would let me rest a little easier for the remainder of the day if I knew he was safe.

I thought I was going to beat everybody in, but Rick was already in the break room along with Samantha. Samantha was the executive director of the museum and also my boss. When I first walked in, they stared at me confused, clearly surprised I was in so early. It was similarly weird that they'd both be in so early as well, so I knew something big was going on. Since I was the new person, I was usually the last person to know what was going on.

"Hey everyone!" I said trying to sound as cheery as possible.

Although the lingering hangover was still there, my morning had already improved. I knew it looked good for me that they both saw me arrive so early. Plus, I was interested in whatever had brought them in at that hour.

"Hey Jon," Samantha said as she drifted towards her normal seat with a steaming cup of coffee. Samantha was about thirty with curly black hair, and as she sat her hair seemed to bounce wildly as she adjusted herself in the folding chair at the end of the breakroom table.

She was homegrown through-and-through and had lived in Buffalo all her life. She had taken over as the executive director at the museum about two years ago, and since then, the museum's visitor count had skyrocketed. She had also been responsible for getting the museum on the map for the local tourism industry. Originally it was just her and Rick, but with the museum becoming more popular the board had decided to create a third position to handle tours and various odds and ends. That's how I came into the picture.

"Rick, do you want to tell him?" Samantha asked, as she peered over her thick-framed glasses and took a sip from her coffee. She was dressed up, wearing a navy-blue pantsuit. Even Rick was wearing a dress shirt…which meant whoever was visiting was important.

"Of course!" Rick said happily. He's a talker, especially when it involves something with the Old Stone Museum, so having the floor made his eyes light up. He had a yellow legal pad in front of him that was already so packed with scribbled notes that the sheet appeared to be more blue than yellow.

"That Nepalis stuff you found the other day. Well, I contacted the state school's Asian History department on a whim and they're sending someone over to look at it. I didn't get a name, but it's supposed to be some important researcher involved in burials or something like that. Sky burials? I think that was their focus. I'm hoping it's the head of the department…I think he was just published in *National Geographic*. Could be big news for—"

"Today," Samantha said, cutting in. "Which is why we got here early. I'm glad you did too. Rick's going to take the lead on this one but if you're interested in the topic, you're more than welcome to join as well."

"I'd love too!" I said, probably with a little more enthusiasm than either Rick or Samantha were used to seeing that early in the day. This was too good an opportunity to pass up. I mean, sure, I had managed to do some research on my own but having access to an expert to ask questions could be a game-changer. I knew I'd have to ask the questions in a non-suspicious way, but I also knew anything could help. Any small tidbit of information could be a literal lifesaver for yours truly.

"Sounds good. Just see if you can find an extra volunteer to cover the floor since you'll be busy," Samantha said as she stood up and made her way to her office.

Two phone calls and I was able to find a volunteer to cover and lead tours, so Rick and I were sitting in his office bidding time, waiting for the researcher to arrive.

"This could be huge," Rick said with a giant grin smeared across his face. He had rolled up his sleeves, and the sweat was already beginning to pool on his forehead in glimmering droplets. Since the museum isn't air conditioned even the early morning could get unbearably hot. And boy, was it already unbearable on that morning. I was already dreading the thought of going back up to that furnace of an attic.

As if reading my mind, Rick said, "We'll bring the researcher up as soon as they get here, then have them pick out anything they think might be important. We can have them use the basement to look at it. It should be at least bearable down there."

The basement was the coolest part of the museum and where we typically had any important meetings, so it made sense that anything involving prolonged research would end up happening down there.

As Rick spoke it looked like he was having flashbacks to his last time in the attic, and if he was already sweating down here on the first floor, I doubted he could make another ascent to the top of the house.

From outside Rick's office we could hear some light scrambling and muffled conversation at the front volunteer desk. As we slowly stood up ready to make our appearance, I realized I was more nervous for the pending arrival than I had anticipated...I mean, who knew what big shot could be coming to see the trinkets we had found.

What if they had questions for me?

And what if I bumbled the answers?

77

I tried to calm myself down as Beth, the volunteer I was able to finagle into coming in on short notice, poked her head into the doorway.

"Uh, there's someone here to see you, Rick."

As soon as she was there in the doorway, Beth was gone like an apparition and Rick and I were rushing to the front desk, which sat in the gift shop.

When we arrived, I think we were both momentarily taken back by our visitor. Rick and I had both assumed we were going to be meeting some old decrepit academic, who (we also assumed) would spend the next few hours talking down to us like we were some grad students desperate for an A. It had been unspoken, but Rick and I both had our Masters, so we knew the type.

However, standing in the gift shop was the exact opposite of the weathered ivory tower castaway we expected. I'll try not to drone on about how attractive she was, but she was a redhead (which I'll admit I'm a sucker for) and even from across the room her emerald-green eyes seemed to sparkle in a way I'd never seen before. I mean, she was absolutely breathtaking. I tried my best not to stand there with my jaw dropped like some middle-school kid.

"Hello!" Rick finally managed to stumble out. He was older and married for god knows how long and I'm going to venture a guess he was surprised our visitor was so young, rather than being enamored.

"Mr. Jenson," she said as she extended her hand out to him.

"It's nice to meet you, and thank you for contacting our office. We don't hear from many local museums who might have artifacts pertaining to Nepal, so I'll admit it was a pleasant surprise."

As she spoke, she gazed around the gift shop looking quizzically at the various trinkets we sold. The gift shop was small and probably not what she was used to, or expected for that matter, and I half expected her to turn around and walk out. But then she smiled, and any doubt I might have had about pretensions seemed to vanish.

"I'm excited to be here on a personal note, too," she continued, "I've been meaning to visit since arriving in Buffalo, but…well, I'm sure you know how busy everything gets." She caught my eye, seeming to notice just how awkwardly I was standing there, listening to her talk. She smiled, as if she had just remembered she was supposed to introduce herself.

"I'm Christina Kingsley." She reached out to shake both our hands. "Dr. Bradwick couldn't make it today, but I'm one of the doctoral candidates with the history department. I'm actually the only other person at our university focusing on Nepal and early Himalayan societal development for their thesis."

Christina said it like I was supposed to know who Dr. Bradwick was, and while I certainly didn't, I nodded like I was impressed to hear the name drop. After a moment of connecting the dots, I finally pieced two and two together and realized Dr. Bradwick must've been the *National Geographic* guy mentioned by Rick in the breakroom.

While I was lost in trying to make sense of everything, Rick had the common courtesy to explain why the baby-faced newbie with glazed over eyes was standing in the gift shop with the two of them. Gesturing towards me, he said:

"This is Jon, our newest employee; we only have a staff of three here, so he does a bit of everything. It was his interest in the subject that led us to find the artifacts I emailed you about."

"Perfect. I was glad to hear you'd found something."

I'm pretty sure Christina realized I hadn't peeled my eyes off her yet. Not wanting to appear like a love-struck puppy tagging along, I decided to drop some academic jargon to try and impress her.

"It was just luck. I'd been researching early social development across various cultures and was particularly drawn to the possibility of

79

the Indian influence on Nepalese and Tibetan culture's Himalayan outposts. I think there are some artifacts from a 'sky burial' that we found, which is certainly an anthropological oddity. We have a lot here thanks to Smith's travels, and apparent hoarding habit."

Translation: "I watched a show about weird graves and might have a ghost problem, so I'm invested in this. Also, I'll throw in a mention of anthropology to sound well-versed across a discipline or two, which I'm most certainly not. Smooth, huh?

"Well I'm excited to see what you guys have unearthed," Christina said. "I've recently sent an article on sky burials for publication, which…we'll see how that goes. But any artifacts, especially ones that have been tucked away for a bit, could help reveal something that could help us with our research. Where is the display?"

As she asked, Christina looked past the front desk towards the doorway that led to the rest of the museum.

"About that…" Rick said, shifting uncomfortably.

"Attic. I mean, we have them in our attic. They've been in storage and we haven't brought them out yet," I chimed in, smooth and collected I'm sure.

"Well let's go see them." Christina smirked, she had clearly picked up on my awkwardness and was either into it, or thought it was hilarious. Either way, I didn't hate the attention.

Rick glanced over at me, his wrinkled blue dress shirt was already soaked underneath the armpits with sweat and the way it stuck to the sweaty skin made him look like a scarecrow. I figured I could be of some use by not making our guest climb into the inferno of the attic.

"If you two want to wait downstairs where it's a bit more comfortable, I can run up and get the box," I offered. Rick glanced over as a look of relief washed over his face.

"Sounds good. While you get that, I'll show Ms. Christine around our little museum here."

The box was a nightmare to get downstairs from the attic. After fifteen sweat and curse filled minutes of lugging the awkward haul down those steep stairs, I heaved it onto the folding table in the basement. The cool air could have been the fountain of eternal youth with how refreshing it felt. It was so cool and comfortable down there that it took everything I had to not just sit down and pass out on one of the folding chairs littered throughout the room.

As I waited for Rick and Christina to join me, I looked down at the box and realized that our visitor was going to have her work cut out for her. Down here in the light of day, especially when I wasn't concerned with dying from dehydration, it was even more evident that the collection had not been stored correctly. I closed the box back up quickly in an attempt to prolong the inevitable.

"Oh wow…" Christina said as her and Rick entered the room. Having heard them walk down the rickety basement steps, I was no longer a visibly exhausted shell of a man and was now standing poised when they strolled in.

"And how did Mr. Smith come by all this?" Christina asked as she slowly peeled open the crate. I could tell she was a bit disappointed by the state of the find, so I decided to help out Rick and make sure she knew it wasn't his fault these things were in their current state.

"It's a little rough, I know, but I think this stuff has been up there since before this was a museum. So, it's about as primary of a source as you could have; really, this is a snapshot of nineteenth century international tourism. It may have been stored directly by Smith himself, or perhaps, more likely, his son."

I didn't want to throw any earlier curator under the bus in my explanation, so I figured saying the box had been up there untouched (even though I had seen a note on it the first time I opened it) was the way to go. It then dawned on me that I hadn't answered her question yet.

"Mr. Smith really was a world traveler, and well...I'm sure you know most nineteenth century explorers weren't too concerned about whether a very *hands-on* approach to souvenir collecting was ethical. A lot of these things were gifts; some were probably sold to the gullible traveler as something they weren't, and maybe some he got himself. There's no real way to be sure, since the paper trail doesn't mention either Nepal or Tibet."

Christina nodded, and if Rick appreciated the gesture of making sure she knew it wasn't his curating skills that led to the artifacts looking like this, he didn't show it. I didn't care, he was a difficult book to read anyways; maybe he *truly* didn't care what people thought since he knew he had done all he could for the place.

"So, what do you think?" I asked as she scanned the contents methodically with those livewire eyes. She was also tough to read and I hoped there was something of worth in there.

"It's very interesting...definitely some artifacts from the cliff tombs, but this...this was, well I guess still is, important," she said in awe. Apparently whatever Christina had seen there was enough to win her over, despite the state of the storage I had been fussing over.

Christina reached into the box tenderly and pulled out the item I had stored on top during my earlier trip to the attic. In her white-gloved hands the golden stake swirled about, sparkling under the lights above.

She carefully turned it every which way. She looked at it like a doctor might hold up a newborn baby to make sure it had all ten fingers and toes. Down here, I could see that the engraved handle contained a depiction of several hawks that wrapped their wings around the weapon as if they were diving in for a kill. By their direction, it was clear their target was whatever found itself at the end of the stake.

"You know why they had these?" Christina asked, though clearly, she meant it rhetorically since I'm sure she doubted that we had any clue what it was. No way I wasn't going to let my newfound knowledge *not* impress her though.

"The shadow vampires…" I murmured. Her shocked expression gave me the confidence to continue on. "Well, maleficent spirits they thought had attached to a family or village."

Even Rick seemed surprised that I knew what the item was. This was a very niche topic, and certainly not something usually covered in your average American History graduate program.

"Very good, Jon!" Christina said, impressed. She continued:

"They would use these posthumously if they thought a death was caused by a cursed spirit. The stake would go through either the heart or the very center of the deceased individual, and supposedly the evil spirit would die as well."

What if Desmond's cursed? Would he have to die for this to end?

As I stood in the cool basement and watched Christina inspect item after item like the prettiest mine inspector you'd ever seen, the horrid thought made my stomach drop.

No. You'll figure something out. That's not an option. Desmond is your dog and he's going to survive this. So are you…

"Well, I'm sure glad I came here," Christina said. "I'm not going to lie, I expected at most a few random trinkets which is what we usually get called for, not all of this. You have a real treasure here."

Christina's red hair hung down gently over the left side of her face and her eyes shone with excitement as she spoke. A huge smile was plastered across her face, while the notebook she'd brought with her was filled to the brink with jotted notes that were taken after looking closely at each artifact.

The three of us had spent the last three hours in the basement and we were now saying our goodbyes in the empty gift shop. Christina seemed less formal by this point and was leaning relaxed against the counter.

"Seriously, I expected junk given to some American tourist for an outrageous price with some tall tales attached, not the remnants of an early Himalayan burial. I wonder how they even got to them. I mean, they're so high up!"

Rick, who had been quiet for most of the visit finally spoke up.

"Smith was pretty brave himself, to the point of being foolhardy sometimes. I wouldn't be surprised if he climbed up so see one with a guide. He also had a strange fascination with local legends. He went through a stage where he was obsessed with seances as well…interesting man. Or maybe he just bought them from a local peddler." He shrugged and smirked. "Who knows? Glad we could be of help though."

Christina nodded appreciatively.

"Well, I'm going to take my notes back and see how it fits in with my research. I'll be back later this week if that's ok?" she asked, and of course, Rick agreed that it was fine. We exchanged business cards and promised to stay in contact if any new information came up. With that, she was out the door.

After she left, Rick spoke up.

"Damn, I thought it was Dr. Bradwick coming; he had that article published in *National Geographic*. Oh well. Maybe we could still get him to come in later." He shrugged again and lumbered into the break room for an early lunch.

I stood in the gift shop after Rick left and passed Christina's business card back from hand to hand. I had learned a lot in the past two hours, and, with Christina as a contact, I began to feel confident that whatever was attached to Desmond was in for a hurting.

***

I normally don't dream. Sleep for me, unless it was right before a fight, tended to be a visit to the darkness, shattered violently with the sound of my shrill alarm clock. The week of a fight though, that was different.

I'd always had the most vivid dreams leading up to my kickboxing matches; sometimes they were about the fight, sometimes they were about abstract things I couldn't remember. Other times they were simply about girls. For whatever reason, my sleeping mind tends to wander during times of stress and when I should be having the most disturbed sleep, I end up having the most restful.

The night after Desmond attacked one of those things and Christina's visit to the museum, I think most people would have trouble falling asleep—there was certainly enough going on to ponder over all night. As it was, that night I stumbled into the house after work, my whole body felt numb with a deep exhaustion that seeped all the way down to my bones. I barely managed to get Desmond out for a quick walk before I crashed into bed. I mean, I was so tired that the brief thought of shadow things retaliating wasn't even enough to keep me awake.

I was out.

The next thing I knew, I was blinking my eyes rapidly to make out that the alarm clock read 2:12 a.m. I hazily remembered I had fallen asleep around 8:00 p.m. after walking Desmond, and that I had been overwhelmingly tired, but my mind was still too focused on the dream I had just had to be sure of anything real.

The few dreams I've had, even the ones I would have leading into fights, tended to dissipate into thin air once I woke up. This dream, however, I can *still* remember just as clearly as I did when I first woke up that morning.

Lying in bed, drenched in a cold sweat, I thought that maybe it was from talking about the subject in such depth with Christina, or perhaps it was just my brain trying to make sense of everything. It even crossed my mind that it might possibly be the shadow trying to scare me. All I knew was that whatever it was, it was powerful. As I thought about the dream, I felt Desmond's warm body pressed against my feet at the bottom of the bed.

The beginning of the dream seemed to fade in from darkness. It was like I was stepping out of the blackness into something: into the dreamscape. I had simply gone from sleeping to *there,* wherever *there* was. And from that moment of first realization, there was nothing but chaos. Shades of darkness seemed to snake about all around me in coiled anger. The ripples didn't seem like anything immediately threatening though, just deep shades of black emptiness squirming around. I stood completely alone, and watched the sky around me writhe and creep with no clear order or purpose.

Staring at the orchestra of disorder, I began to see colors slowly drip into the surrounding world. Just a few drops at first; splotches that seemed to splatter against an invisible dome, which then slowly trickled down.

The blankness was quickly filled in with those dreary shades of color that crept and expanded against the dark ridges. Soft colors.

Earth tones.

A dirty beige from some unseen paint palette dripped across the area immediately in front of me. It was followed by an explosion of soft blues, dull whites, and pale greens. The colors filled in around me, and soon I was standing in an unmistakable landscape that had been painted out of nowhere. Tall mountains stretched around the horizon all about me, and towering dirt-colored cliffs seemed to engulf all of space and time.

Not all the darkness had been vanquished though. Black pinpoints of complete darkness littered the fronts of these cliffs. Those darks specks were the only thing that mattered though. I knew they revealed that the cliffs were a mere facade for the void of emptiness that existed beneath their surfaces. I might as well have been walking about an abandoned movie set…there was no substance to the structures that had appeared. They were a mask for what lurked behind. Even in the dream fog that I was in, it was clear that the only thing *truly* there was the darkness beneath the flimsy exterior.

From one of the tunnels came a cry, a familiar howl from deep within.

Desmond.

His howl came from somewhere *in* the cliffs, in one of those snaking pits of blackness, and I rushed to get there. No matter how hard I tried to sprint, I couldn't move, as if I was stuck in quicksand, but I refused to stop. I powered through the invisible weights that tried to drag me down, that made each lunge forward seem like complete exhaustion of the limited strength I had.

It felt like I spent an eternity slowly moving forward, but soon, I was standing in the entrance of a cavern. I have no recollection of how I scaled the wall, but somehow, I had managed to. The tunnel was grooved in fragmented breaks and chips of fallen rock, and the walls were an unnatural red hue that made me feel like I was standing in the esophagus of some giant creature. I might as well have been.

Then, for a blinking moment, I was in my basement staring into the darkness and no longer staring into the pit.

Then in a flash, I was back in the cavern as a wicked wind bellowed from somewhere deep within the long passageway. It carried with it a smell I didn't recognize but knew was evil on instinct.

Pure evil being hurled up from the rotten gut of the cliff.

I hiked forward into the foul gust. Desmond's bark continued to echo up the long cavern from somewhere deep within, from wherever the stench had come from, and willed me forward still. He sounded scared.

The walls of the cavern began to blur, and I knew that if I stopped to inspect them, I'd see an army of shadows fighting to escape. It didn't matter. I was moving faster now, and Desmond was growing closer. His barks had switched from frightened, to angry. The shadows screeched down the passageway with the echoes bombarding me from all directions.

How could you let this happen to me? Desmond seemed to ask in those fast-paced yips. Even asleep, I could feel my stomach drop in guilt.

"I'll save you!" I tried to scream out, but my voice was stuck in my throat. It didn't matter, I told myself he would be ok, and that Desmond could forgive me. I just had to keep descending into the darkness, no matter what. I just had to get to him.

A sudden drop of orange appeared in the empty black in front of me. Then another.

As my eyes adjusted, I could tell that I was seeing two burning torches in the distance. I knew I was almost to *whatever* it was that I was heading towards. Quick bursts of air fluttered past me as I felt the shadows moving by me now, as if I didn't matter.

Another few steps, and I emerged into a giant cavern that somehow, I hadn't seen—even though it must have been only a few feet in front of me. The room was washed in the orange hue of the two flickering torches light. A giant throne sat in the middle.

Desmond was chained to it. His howls were back to sounding frightened. I had moved towards him to cut him loose, when I felt a presence engulf me that froze me in my tracks.

"You're both dead. There's nothing you can do…"

It was a whisper, but it felt deafening in the cavern as it bounced around the granite walls in a soft growl.

"Did you really think your little escapade in the basement hurt me at all?"

I tried to move, but my body felt like it was made of lead, and I was sinking into the depths. It was like I was stuck in the murky bottom of the ocean, the soft mud swallowing me whole. I was falling into a pit of darkness.

"You'll never kill me."

I awoke. My sheets were drenched in ice-cold sweat, and my heart was pounding. I had looked over at Desmond in a panic, desperate to make sure he was still there.

He was asleep at the foot of my bed keeping my feet warm.

As I retraced the dream over and over, I felt my heart flutter in fear; fear at what might happen to him.

My bedroom window was open that night, and as I tried to make sense of everything, a warm summer breeze drifted through the room gently causing Desmond to stir slightly. He looked so serene. I hoped he never had dreams like the one I had.

I didn't sleep the rest of the night. My mind wandered and tried to formulate a plan to save us. Nothing came; no stroke of genius for me that night. Just the memories of the shadow and its throne in the cliffs.

CHAPTER 10

"You look tired. Is the new dog keeping you up?" Shelly asked.

She was sitting behind the front desk at the shelter, which was un-
usually slow. Normally, the shelter would be bustling with drop offs,
volunteers, and trainees all running around at that time of day but for
whatever reason, it was slow enough that Shelly was trying to start a
conversation. I hadn't realized it until that day, when there weren't a
million other things going on to distract me from making a fairly obvious observation, but the shelter could easily be confused for a hospital: the overly polished tile floors, the bright colored signage with tips
and reminders, and the harsh smell of cleaning chemicals all could
have belonged to the foyer of any emergency room.

"No, no, it's not that at all. He's a good boy. Just some…rough
nights. I've had a tough time sleeping these past few nights. That's all."
I still hadn't completely forgiven her for trying to get me to adopt
another dog instead of Desmond, though I tried to be as polite as I
could. I *knew* it wasn't really her fault, but still.

Shelly nodded in sympathy for a moment, then something dawned
on her that made her eyebrows shoot up in sudden realization. As she
spoke, her whole face seemed to stretch out in excitement, "Both Ri-
leys in at once! Your dad's here too, I'm sure you saw it in the sign-
in."

I hadn't. The whole shelter could've been on fire and I doubt I
would have noticed, that's how tired I was, but I was happy to hear
that he was there. Talking to somebody, even if I couldn't tell them

everything that happened, would no doubt be a good thing for my unraveling mental state.

I quickly grabbed a dog from the kennels, remembering at the last minute to make sure they had a blue slip on their crate: the blue tag meant they were not reactive with other dogs and could go in the play yard, which is where I was heading. The pup I grabbed was a short little bulldog whose stubby tail wagged furiously as I put the leash on him. He calmly strolled past all the barking dogs in their kennels with his head held up at a slight angle.

With the stocky bulldog waddling happily about, I bustled to the park to intercept my dad and whatever dog he had out. The bulldog stayed glued to my side, softly snorting the whole way.

My dad looks a lot like…well, actually, I guess *I* look a lot like a shorter version of him. We've both got an athletic build and the same facial structure. In fact, we look so similar that at my first kickboxing fight one of the other fighter's trainers had confused my dad for my brother.

I've been told I act like him too. He was one of my main sparring partners during my kickboxing career, and it was him who suggested that I work at the shelter, so I guess that accusation wasn't unfounded with so many shared hobbies.

I found him walking a giant pit bull in the park. The dog had a thick, chocolate-colored coat of fur and bounced around excitedly as we approached. I could hear the bulldog to my left snort more rapidly, and I looked down to see his stubby tail flail about in bliss. He coiled his body to begin bouncing about, which made him look less like a dog and more like a bundle of beige wrinkles.

"Surprised to see you here! I figured you'd be at home with the new pup," I heard my dad say over the sounds of the two dogs who were happily greeting each other. They were so close to each other that their snouts were practically touching, while both their tails were still whipping around in a blur of happiness. I loosened my grip on the slip-lead and the two dogs began sniffing each other in a whirlwind of paw-taps and unabashed joy.

It was in that moment as I watched the two dogs meet that I realized I had completely forgotten to tell my parents I had adopted a dog. This huge change in my life, one that was now driving the majority of the decisions I made, and I'd failed to mention it to my parents. I tried to figure out how my dad had found out, since I had forgotten to tell him, all the while the bulldog pranced about the giant pit bull who had playfully lowered his level to be eye-to-eye with the little guy.

He must have found out from Shelly. I think she said she had spoken to him earlier, didn't she?

Before too much guilt managed to set in about leaving my parents out of this big news, I remembered that he and my mother had just gotten back from a vacation. Plus, with everything going on, some things were bound to slip my mind.

"I got out of work a little early and I figured I should swing in here before I go and see Des. It's been a few days and I was starting to miss it. Des is probably sleeping right now, anyways," I said, finally answering his question. "When are you and Mom going to come over and see him?" I continued quickly, as the pit bull and bulldog resumed circling each other curiously, taking small leaps at each other and clearly wanting to play.

"Tomorrow works actually, if you're free. Want to bring them"— he gestured to the dogs—"to the play yard so we can catch up?"

The play yard was a fenced-in dog park owned by the shelter where dogs could run around together supervised by the volunteers. Since it was easy to monitor, it was a great place to begin socializing dogs with each other before (hopefully) they would be adopted. The fenced-in yard sat just behind the hill Desmond and I had hung out on during our first walk. It really was an impressive little complex the shelter had managed to carve out in the middle of the city like that.

The four of us made our way through the park towards the gates. Both dogs excitedly pulled at their leashes, forcing my dad and me to jog. Once the gate was closed behind us and the two dogs were unleashed, we watched them sprint away in the play yard. They were both so thrilled to be there they took off running with no clear end in sight. The bulldog's short bounds looked comical next to the pit's giant strides; they were both having the time of their lives.

And that's what mattered.

Eventually, the two of them found a giant plastic ball to push around in a game of keep-away. Their little game looked so fun I would be lying if I said I wasn't tempted to join in, but before I could, my dad started speaking.

"Shelly couldn't tell me anything about the dog you got. Hell, she had to look up his name." We leaned on the fence and watched the two dogs take turns chasing each other with the red ball always in the middle. Despite his small stature, the bulldog's sharp cuts as he ran managed to keep him a step ahead of his bigger counterpart. Both of them had huge, goofy grins glued to their faces the whole time.

"No one could. I mean, listen to this: he hadn't been walked for the *entire* week. He was cleared to, just no one walked him."

My dad looked at me in disbelief. "You're kidding me?"

"Not at all. He wasn't barking and no kennel fighting either. Everyone just completely ignored him and he's such a good boy, who deserves a good home. I have to clean a pool for my landlord now, but I managed to get the okay to have him. Good thing too, because he was in the room of no return when I picked him up. The vet was about to put him down."

"I was going to ask you how you managed to swing that with your rental. Well, good, I'm glad you were able to get him." He smiled.

Both dogs soon grew tired from playing keep-away and had moved on to exploring the various other plastic and rubber toys that littered the fenced in enclosure.

"Vacation went good?"

He nodded, and for the first time since I'd seen him that day, I noticed he looked tired. Almost as tired as I felt. His hair was less kept than normal, and he had dark bags under his eyes.

"It did. The beach was great, but I think I ate something bad towards the end there—there was so much seafood. I started having the weirdest dreams for the last night or two we were there. It was weird; I felt fine during the day, but the second I'd fall asleep…I don't know. Must've been the seafood."

"What kind of dreams?"

I felt a chill in the wind even though the sun was beating down on us. It did not escape me (even at that initial moment) that Christina had mentioned whole villages would suffer from the dark spirits of Nepalese folklore, not just one, handsome dog owner.

"I kept feeling like someone walked into the room or was standing next to me. I couldn't make out what they looked like, but they—"

"Were like a dark shadow?" I ventured an unfortunately informed guess.

"Exactly! I think I was driving your mother nuts. I had…what's it called, sleep paralysis?

I nodded, even though I had a sinking suspicion that the dreams weren't any form of sleep paralysis that a normal doctor would be familiar with.

"Anyways other than that, the vacation was awesome. I'm glad to be back here though. You miss these goofs after a day or two away."

We sat there watching the dogs for a little while longer, making small talk about the vacation, beers we'd drunk recently, and workouts to try. Since the next day was Saturday and I had it off, we planned for my parents to visit and meet Desmond.

Eventually, we wrangled up the exhausted dogs who were ready to make their way to their air-conditioned kennels. As we walked back to the shelter, I found myself desperately hoping that Christina responded to emails on the weekends. I had some important questions that needed answers.

I walked a few more dogs to clear my mind, and despite all odds, it somehow seemed to work. With each walk, I found myself slightly more grounded in the moment than I had before. By the last walk everything almost felt normal again.

Before I left, I walked down the winding rows of kennels and gave each dog a treat. Some dogs took the treats immediately and gobbled them up, while others left the small milk-bones for a later time, but either way, it would have been impossible to not feel a tad better about yourself after seeing all their grateful eyes peering up at you.

Still, I hadn't completely forgotten about the bitter reality I was now a part of. When I was done for the day and about to leave for home, I took a moment to reach out to Christina. Sitting in my car outside the shelter, I rapidly began mashing buttons as I typed up the email on my phone.

Hello Ms. Kingsley,

It was a pleasure meeting you the other day, and I hope you enjoyed your time at the museum! I've been conducting my own research on a few of the items we inspected during your visit, and had some questions regarding the mythology attributed to the burial practices you mentioned; specifically, the role of the maleficent spirits in how the early communities understood death, or unfortunate events.

I guess what I'm primarily interested in, is what type of accidents, or events, would lead to these

95

"stake" burials. Was it disease, crime, etc? Also, were there any other signs, outside of an unexplained accident, that would lead them to believe they were being attacked by these spirits? Would people claim to see them, or feel their presence, dream, etc.

If you could direct me to any sources you recommend on the subject, that would be hugely appreciated. I apologize for emailing you on the weekend, and hope we have a chance to work together on this in the future.

Best,

Jon Riley

As I drove home, the usual sense of satisfaction that came from volunteering never emerged. Instead, in its place was a growing sense of dread. I tried to stuff it down, ignore the feeling and hoped it would disappear, but no matter how loud I turned the radio, or how focused I was on the road ahead, there it was.

As I stopped at a red light two blocks from my house, I reminded myself that I was almost home, and that waiting for me was a giant bundle of fur and excitement who no doubt would be happy to see me. While it didn't remove the feeling of apprehension completely, it stopped me from overthinking and dwelling on it. The second the light turned green my foot hit the gas, and I sped past those last two blocks in record time.

***

"Hey buddy!"

Just as I had hoped, Desmond burrowed into me as I entered the doorway. His giant head nuzzled into my knee as if I had been gone for eons, instead of hours. It was the best feeling in the world, walking into *my* place and being greeted by *my* dog. I doubt I can describe it adequately, but I guess it made me feel as if I was important. That I mattered to *something*. I was still trying to ignore the feeling that had started on the drive home, and as predicted, Desmond was doing his part in helping with that.

Desmond sniffed me, smelling the dogs from the shelter, and after he was done examining me, he plopped down underneath the row of hooks his leash was hanging from. With intuition that rivaled Sherlock Holmes, I deduced Des wanted to go on a walk. And even though I had been at the shelter walking dogs for the last hour, I figured another one couldn't hurt. Besides, Desmond seemed determined to get out.

I leashed him up and locked the door behind me. As soon as he was outside, Des beelined for the car, catching me off-guard. I was surprised to see him head in that direction. Normally the immediate neighborhood was our normal stomping grounds, but it seemed like Des had his heart set on going somewhere that night. He wanted to see something different than the usual stroll.

"Where do you want to go, boy? Okay fine, let's go for a ride."

I opened the door, and Des leaped into the passenger seat so elegantly that an Olympic diver would have been jealous. He sat down as soon as he landed, then stared at me as I closed the door carefully behind him. As I walked around the front of the car his eyes followed me with a look of pure joy.

As I got into my seat and began tinkering with the windows, I felt Desmond rest his giant head on my arm. When I looked over to see him, I saw that his body had relaxed in the small space. He had coiled up in the seat so comfortably that he appeared to melt into the plush. It dawned on me that Des seemed to have the ability to make anywhere his home, even if just for a moment; it was a skill that I'm still jealous of, I'll admit.

We started driving, and honestly, I had no idea where we were headed. It was still light out, but the vibrant splashes of color that trickled into the horizon let me know it wouldn't be for much longer. My mind went to autopilot, and before I knew it, I was pulling back in the (now) abandoned shelter's parking lot. The lights were off in the building and no visible activity stirred within.

Everyone was gone, everyone except the dogs with no homes, that is. There was something melancholy about seeing a building that looked so empty at first glance, but that I knew held so much life and potential within its somber chambers.

I imagine it's the same feeling a lifelong business owner feels as they close the door of their store for the last time, or returning to a childhood home, only to find it has fallen into disrepair and neglect. You knew what was there, or rather, what was *supposed* to be there according to the memories, but instead, that place of nostalgia stared back like a stranger who never knew who you were.

Memories whispered from the shelter that night, but there was no one there, save me and Des, to listen or pay them any mind.

Desmond sat up in the seat when he realized where we were, no longer relaxed, and appeared to be listening to the same whispers I'd imagined I was hearing. Knowing him, he probably could hear something though, and we sat in the car for a moment taking it all in. The sun disappeared behind the shelter in an explosion of reds and oranges, casting the building as this dark, lonely place in the world.

I can't explain it, but something about sitting there and staring at a place of so much sorrow, but also so much hope, made me want to cry. I was tempted to just start balling like a little kid as the emotions brimmed out of me, but I held it together. I swear. Still, I wanted so much to run in there, to pick up the outdated phone that sat on Shelly's desk and an old yellow pages and start calling people. Random people. Telling them about the dogs at the shelter and how much better their lives could be if they got to know one. The adventures they could go on, the way that even on their worst day they could have a companion who would get them through it, even if the world was falling down around them. That the same dog who could help them through it all, was only days away from dying because some punk didn't think they were muscular enough when they had bred them, or some other piece of garbage didn't want to bring a dog with them as they moved. Here that dog was, just waiting for a good home…

But I didn't run in there. And I didn't start calling strangers.

Instead, I got Desmond out of the car and began walking down the same path I had earlier that day, and so many times before, with dogs who were now either stuck alone in a kennel, adopted, or maybe even dead.

Surrounded by their forgotten kin.

We walked to the park, to the garbage covered benches and the neatly maintained hill that overlooked it all. Where there were broken bottles of booze along with the wildflowers that found their way in the middle of a hectic city. Everything about this place was so contradictory; I think that's why I loved it. In one small corner of the world, there were people dedicating hours of their lives to give the dogs a better experience. Yet, in the same spot, some piece of work had decided to abandon the very same dogs only hours before. It all happened there: the good and the bad…

Dogs brought in off the street, who had seen the worst of humanity and had to completely relearn the idea that humans could be good. That humans could even be loving and nurturing and not hurt them. You'd see it all the time, a dog afraid to approach the front of the kennel one week, cowering in fear and bracing for a kick when any person walks by. The next week? Well, that same dog is throwing its body at the front gate in excitement as you approach it with a leash, their eyes filled with pure joy at the thought of being with you.

It all happened in this little shelter, which most people didn't know existed and who, given the chance, would gladly vote for a politician that would slash its budget to shreds and ban the dogs it held.

My heart felt...I guess the only way to describe it is heavy. An electric tingle of sorrow bubbled in my chest and by the time we got to the hill, I needed to sit down, to think and wallow in contemplation. Desmond obliged and plopped down next to me just as he did before, the first day we met.

Sitting on that hill, I forgot about whatever was hunting Desmond and myself, and let my mind drift away as it tried to make sense of everything. I felt that Desmond was doing the same thing. He stared out at the city with those deep, sad eyes that had seen too much.

The world could be so cruel and yet so good. The dichotomy of it all, and how such extremes existed so close together, made me doubt anything would ever get better. Good people were always on the defensive, being responsive to something horrid. The shelter was built as a result of people abandoning and torturing animals, not the other way around. It reminded me of fighting: if you're always on the defensive—even if you're surviving—you're still losing the round.

Then eventually you're losing the fight.

The sky was a beautiful blend of deep magenta, royal blue, and black by that point, with just a trim of the earlier orange striped along the bottom. We sat there in silence and let the night take over, even though I knew the park wasn't safe after dark, I didn't care. It wasn't safe at home either and I just wanted a few more moments of thinking.

After an hour of contemplation, Des and I made our way back to the car. Everything was how I had left it. My tires were all intact, and no crudely done, spray-painted drawings had found their way onto my paintwork.

The universe decided to let me think in peace, I'd misguidedly believed.

CHAPTER 11

Dear Jon,

I hope this email finds you well.

To answer your question, in my research there have been a few key components which lead to the burial practices we discussed. One such component: an early death, or string of deaths—specifically, close to the caves where it was believed these spirits lived. Two: a violent attack, such as a murder or burglary. It's unclear whether it was believed these were "possessions" (i.e. the spirit influencing the event) or a welcoming for the spirit to nest in the village.

In regard to how the villages "knew" they were inflicted outside of those two events, I'd say it's hard to know for sure. This is probably the least understood component of the Himalayan mythology, but there seems to be either a prophetic or "dream" component to their knowledge. I believe it is how they got the concept of the "vampires" (as the English language translates it) as being shadows, or dark entities that would attach themselves to certain carriers.

I hope this helps, but if you need more information or just want to go over a few things then let me know. I would love to meet up over coffee to discuss all of this.

Best,

Christina

I skimmed the email after pulling into the driveway from my rendezvous with Desmond to the shelter. It stated, more or less, what I expected, and the Nepalese seemed to mirror most mythologies that I was familiar with. Still, any little bit of knowledge could help.

The stoop light was on, which illuminated the front door with enough light to see a few giant bugs that buzzed lazily about it, but other than that, the house seemingly sat still. I had turned off the car and silenced everything so that I could focus on the email, hoping there was a word or sentence I had read too quickly to really understand the significance.

As I reread the email for what felt like the hundredth time, I noticed out of the corner of my eye that Desmond had perked up in the seat next to me. He quickly scrambled to a seated position and his ears shot up like two antennas as he traced some barely audible noise. Intrigued, I turned my complete attention to Desmond trying to read his "tells" the same way one might read a weathervane.

Storm's coming…

Desmond began to growl. The quiet, but guttural sound filled my small car and I felt my stomach drop.

It would be one of those nights.

I watched for any sign of movement praying my house would suddenly fill up with a burst of light so I could at least *see* what I was about to walk into. As if some sick and twisted genie had been listening to my thoughts, a small beam of light flashed across the front bay window. There was somebody in my house with a flashlight.

It briefly crossed my mind to call the cops, but some small voice in the back of my head convinced me that they'd just be walking into an empty house, that whoever was in there would have already escaped, or worse, and perhaps more likely, the shadow would appear out of nowhere and attack the cops as they entered and I'd somehow be blamed.

It might sound a bit paranoid, but I'd seen enough horror movies where the hero ends up blamed for some grisly crime that I didn't want to risk it happening to me.

There was something else too.

Now, hindsight is 20/20 and looking back, I *should* have called the cops to have them take care of it, but, after seeing that flashlight beam, I figured that whoever was in my house was likely human…and that was when I got a little angry.

Ok, really angry.

I started thinking about what might have happened if this dirtbag had broken in when I was out, and it was just Desmond? They could have let him run out or worse. I decided that whoever was in there was going to pay. I might not have been able to punch the shadow but I sure as hell could hit whatever asshole had broken into our home.

I left Desmond in the car (AC running with lights off, don't worry), as I was afraid he may get hurt in the impending altercation, and made my way to the porch. The door was unlocked and slightly ajar; the burglar must have picked it to get in. As soon as I stepped in, I saw the intruder standing in the hallway. For a brief moment, the outline of the burglar was just a shadow and I felt my heart begin to do backflips, but slowly, the moonlight behind me filled in his features.

He was human. And he was also screwed.

The burglar hadn't noticed me sneak in through the front door somehow and he appeared preoccupied by something in the kitchen. I decided not to give him the chance to realize he wasn't alone. I ran at him before he could react.

He managed to turn around to face me when I was a foot away from him, but it didn't matter at that point. A left hook slammed into his temple and he instantly dropped to a knee with a startled grunt. The punch vibrated up my arm, which was a good sign he wasn't probably feeling too great.

As the burglar stumbled, trying to figure out the world around him, I had a brief moment to look him over. He was dressed head to toe in all black; he looked comical, like a cartoon drawing of a burglar. The only thing he was missing was a pale green knapsack with a dollar sign drawn on it.

Anyways, the hook dropped him and while I didn't see a gun on him, I decided not to take any chances and slammed a knee into his face. The knee landed with a dull thud and spun him around. Despite the fact the knee should have put him out, when he landed belly down on the floor he scurried forward into the kitchen before I could grab him.

I'll give him props, he was still sort of with it. The later blood work that would be done at the police station would reveal that he was hopped up on a cocktail of illicit drugs, which might explain why he was still conscious despite the knee.

I flicked on the kitchen light and the burglar shielded his eyes like I had just opened the Ark of the Covenant in front of him. He was definitely concussed.

As I walked in, he cowered back to the ground with hands raised in front of his face. But it wasn't me he was hiding from. Unfortunately, after the light had been flicked on, I too realized we weren't alone. The kitchen walls were alive with silhouettes from the great unknown. The one closest to me disappeared as soon as I saw it.

It was like there was a spinning lamp in the center of the kitchen with shapes cut into its shade, whirling around and covering the walls with a shadowy wallpaper from a horrible nightmare.

I stood in the walkway and tried to figure out my next move…

…and that was when the burglar stood back up.

There was something different in the way he carried himself as he purposefully found his way to his feet. In a matter of seconds, he had transformed from a slinking coward pawing at his rearranged face, to a confident killer. He stood there quietly, swaying ever so slightly. In fact, we both stood there for a moment.

Staring.

"You're a dead man. If you just give in, it will be painless. If you fight…well, you'll beg for death."

As he spoke, the whites of his eyes were swallowed whole by the darkness of his pupils. I was no longer staring into a man's eyes. Instead, I was staring into two black pinpoints that could trace their roots back to some cavern in the Himalayas.

"You're a dead man…" it whispered again, and this time it sounded like it came from several sources. I was done listening though. I was still running on pure adrenaline and rage, too pissed at the break in and now the intrusion on my revenge by the shadow to really think things through.

"Go to hell," I said, my voice steeped with pure vitriol before I continued. "A dead man wouldn't have made it this far. You've sat licking your wounds in my cellar for the past few days…you know as well as me that you're all going to be sent cowering into the dark again. Or maybe next time I'll let Desmond finish the job," I spat back.

I hated the shadow thing as much as I hated the body it had occupied. And it would have been my pleasure to beat on both.

The voice shot back a high-pitched cackle. The rest of the shadows still prancing around the kitchen walls seemed to join in the laughter. Blood was pouring from the mouth hole in the burglar's mask and as he spoke it sprayed around the room in a maroon mist.

"What do you think happened to that beast's last family? We slaughtered them. All of them. Their skin peeled back oh so nicely. Oh, how their blood rained, and their weak cries filled the air."

The possessed man paused for a moment, as if deep in thought then added:

"That mutt can't save you."

It was the first time the shadow didn't whisper when it spoke. Its voice was hollow, void of any emotion or humanity. The deep treble seemed to rise from the deepest depths of Dante's Inferno, and by the way those dead eyes stared at me, I knew it was meant to send me running in terror. Instead, a cross smashed into the face of the burglar/shadow. I felt soft cartilage collapse underneath my knuckles as the sound of a sickening snap filled the room. Underneath the burglar's mask I could see the man's crooked nose as I pulled back my fist, and blood gushed from beneath the mask in heavy waves.

"You think you can—"

A three-punch combo answered the question before it could even be asked. The last punch buckled the man's knees just the slightest as screeches from all around filled the kitchen.

"...kill him..."

"...feast. Your blood will..."

"...roast the dog over the same fire we use to peel your skin..."

I was used to fighting and listening to voices flying from all corners from my past life. Hell, competing in an event where I didn't hear someone in the crowd calling for my untimely death would have been strange. As such, the threats had the opposite of their intended intent. I felt emboldened.

"You're not going to do shit," I replied to the latest round of barbs, then summoned the cockiest, most obnoxious smirk I could manage.

While the possessed body seemed able to take a beating, whatever was controlling it seemed unable to launch any offense. A herky-jerky lunge towards my direction seemed the best it could muster in the present circumstance. It shot a pawing hand out towards my face that

I quickly slipped. I fired back another cross into the temple of the bloodied would-be burglar.

"There's nothing you can do. There's an army of us. We'll keep coming until your screams fill the air. Dead man."

With that, the burglar's body dropped like a marionette whose handler's hands had been severed, and the yellow kitchen walls broke through the dark mist. A gust of wind whipped through the room as the basement door slammed closed, sheltering the shadow's escape.

The burglar, who must have come to as his body hit the floor, began moaning and begging for mercy.

"Don't kill me," he sobbed, writhing on the ground as tears began to pool in his swollen eyes. He slowly crawled to all fours as blood fell in giant droplets beneath his face. I wasn't in a very forgiving mood, but I also didn't want to hurt him anymore.

"Shut up."

That seemed to do it and he collapsed down to the prone position. The fight, if any had even been there to start, was drained from him. I plugged those three numbers into my phone, and soon, my house was filled with blue and red lights flashing through the front window.

***

The next morning, I awoke feeling the full effects of the fight. My knuckles were filled with a slow, throbbing pain that extended all the way up my forearms. Light from the outside world had just barely begun to fill my bedroom and my alarm clock read 6:09 a.m.—a time I'm pretty sure I'd never seen on a Saturday.

Desmond was curled up on the bottom of my bed, though his eyes were glued to me as he watched my every move. After the cops had finally left the night before and I brought him in from the car, he'd refused to leave my side as I cleaned up the mess and eventually passed out. He practically leaned on me throughout the whole process as I mopped up the droplets of blood that were scattered throughout the kitchen's painted wood floor.

I rolled over and grabbed my phone. Des stood up quickly when I moved and only settled back down once he realized I wasn't leaving the bed. The notification of a missed call was on my lockscreen. Once I opened it, I saw the call was from Chuck, which let me know that the responding officer had followed through with his promise and had contacted him like he said he would.

Turns out Chuck had used a faulty, discontinued (and banned in my county for renters,) lock set-up on the front door to save a few bucks. A look of disgust had been plastered across the officer's face when he inspected the lock and muttered about "slumlords" trying to save "a quick buck."

The faulty lock explained how the burglar had been able to get in so easily, despite the fact they only found a rudimentary pick set with him that shouldn't have been able to open anything more than a bike lock. After inspecting the shoddy lock, the cops had started to question the burglar as he sat handcuffed in my front yard. He was concussed pretty badly though, so when the officer started asking questions the man seemed unsure of the events leading up to him entering my house. Realizing that he had got the worst of it, an ambulance was called which got the burglar zipped away quickly. As mentioned earlier, I'm certain the toxicology report found a plethora of illicit chemicals in him which was used in court to push for rehab instead of jail time. I barely followed the case to be honest.

The fact that Chuck called me that morning, especially *that* early in the morning, let me know that he was aware of how badly I could rake him over the coals for this. I really hoped the cop tore into him when he gave him the report. A boy can dream.

I decided not to call back, at least for the moment, to let Chuck sweat it. Besides, I realized it would take me an hour or two to think of the demands I was about to drop on him. It was then that I remembered that my parents were coming over later that day, and I had to continue tidying the place up to make sure everything looked normal.

I hadn't told them about the break-in yet, and truthfully, I hadn't decided by that point if I would. I'd have to cut out a huge portion of it anyways and give them the same abridged version I had told the cops, so I figured I might as well just forget mentioning the whole thing. My parents had enough on their plate as it was, they didn't need to add any more worrying about me to their laundry list of concerns.

It was still too early to start my Saturday, so instead of jumping up and diving headfirst into my day, I sat in bed for a moment. I looked down at Desmond who met my gaze with eyes full of frustration.

"Sorry bud, I didn't know if he had a gun, or…"

His stare back still seemed filled with distrust. It seemed to say:

Hey! We're a team, jerk. And this is the second time you've locked me away as you rushed into something you didn't understand…

He was right too, that being if my anthropomorphic interpretation of his gaze was accurate. Looking at him, it reminded me of what the possessed burglar had told me the night before.

The dog can't save you…we slaughtered them…

While it came from an untrusted source, I doubted that particular statement was a lie. With how they had found Desmond already so well trained, it was clear he'd had a family who had to have cared for him in the same way Desmond cared for them. And no doubt the shadows had something to do with whatever led to Desmond being without them. They had followed Desmond here, after all.

Lying in bed I grew more and more angry; I shuttered in rage as I thought about the fact that Des had been through something like that. It called into question the fairness of the universe. That the shadow things were real called into question so many of my beliefs already. I mean, if these *things* were allowed to wander around, what else was out there? And what did that mean about the afterlife? Were those the only evil things prowling about, or was I just scratching the surface of a floodgate I really didn't want to know existed?

And to think that the shadow would be allowed to torment an innocent animal—it was too much to bear. I closed my eyes in an effort to calm myself, but waves of frustration still rushed through my body and seemed to fill every square inch of me with seething anger.

But there Des was still resting at the bottom of my bed. His only apparent concern was my well-being. The past, as far as I could tell, had been left far, far behind him. Somehow, he was able to brush it all off so easily.

It made me feel guilty for getting wrapped up in a moment of pity. Of course life's not fair; some people are born into families with more money than they could spend in a lifetime, or IQ's so high they're basically computers, while others are born into situations so wretched it'd keep Lovecraft up at night. That's just the way the cookie crumbles and how the wheels keep turning. I knew that.

All I could do was to deal with the problem in front of me and keep fighting alongside Desmond, while trying to give him the best life possible. Who knew where we were heading, or what troubles (undoubtedly) waited on the fog dusted horizon? All that mattered was that we refused to give up and were ready to meet whatever stood in front of us.

I had another realization as I laid in bed, still refusing to move from beyond the tight embrace of my comforter. It was obvious, but those things were afraid of Desmond. Real afraid. I didn't know why, and I didn't particularly care for that matter, but those things stepped lightly around him, no doubt. Maybe they had followed him in a "keep your enemies close," type of plan. Or maybe, in an act of fairness, despite what I had just been complaining about in my mind, that when something *that* evil exists, there has to be something equally *good*. Something that made evil watch its back. Kind of in a weird, symbiotic relation.

Who knew?

I stayed in bed for another hour reading a collection of Bradbury's short stories and trying to float away to "October Country," although I was already pretty sure I was a tax paying resident. The sun slowly filled the bedroom with bright rays and Desmond began stirring to life.

First, he stood up briefly to stretch his hind legs before laying back down on the bed, which shifted underneath his weight and forced me to adjust. Then, apparently ready to get a start on the day, Des began climbing down to the floor and started stretching again. The tap of his nails on the hardwood floor sounded like the plucking of guitar strings.

He had made it clear it was time for both of us to meet the day. I put the book down on my pillow and led Des downstairs. As we walked down the steps, Desmond still hugged my side. He stared up at me as he gracefully went down the steps, his tail wagging happily. The loud creak of the stairwell underneath our weight, paired with the rays of sun filling the area, seemed to bring the house alive.

It seemed as though the nightmare that had happened the night before was exactly that, a nightmare with no basis in reality. There was no way a break-in, let alone a possession, could have taken place in this quaint little house that seemed to radiate in the glow of the morning.

The recently cleaned floor sparkled in the sunlight as we moseyed about the kitchen. I started the slow-drip and poured Desmond's food into his silver bowl. I swear, even the birds outside began chirping a happy melody like I was living in some Disney movie. It was the perfect morning.

The scent of coffee soon filled the kitchen with its heavy, rich aroma as Desmond excitedly attacked his food and I began cleaning dishes. It felt like something normal to do, and for a bit, all I wanted was mundane. To just be a normal guy, with a normal dog, doing normal people stuff. Dishes, cleaning, and maybe talking about the weather, or those jerks in Washington.

That's what people are supposed to worry about, right?

When we were done, I made breakfast. I realized when I was about halfway through frying some eggs and bacon that I should have done the dishes after, which was a normal person problem. I chuckled softly, but soon the thought of my mistake almost sent me into hysterics.

Did the dishes? Before cooking and making more dirty dishes! What a regular ol' klutz!

It wasn't that funny, or funny at all for that matter, but it felt good to laugh. Desmond stared at me like I was losing my mind, which I promise I wasn't. I guess I just needed to laugh. Maybe it was my brain's way of getting some oxygen flowing back to it, or a pressure release from everything that was building within.

After I was done laughing at stuff that wasn't funny, I managed to finish cooking breakfast without going insane. When I sat down with my eggs and bacon, Desmond watched me patiently. He was waiting for food with eyes as big as the plate I was eating from. I, as any dog owner would do of course, gave him a generous portion of my meal. Despite how impressive Desmond was, he was still a simple dog at heart. His eyes lit up like he had won the lottery as he munched softly on the bacon I handed down to him.

Once we were finished eating, I stood up and poured myself another cup of dark coffee. I had been generous with the grounds when I brewed it earlier, and the pot seemed to contain something that more resembled jet fuel than coffee. That was perfectly fine by me, though; I had found that since the strange happenings had started my caffeine dependency had developed into an all-encompassing addiction.

As I drank the coffee, I remembered Christina's offer of meeting up for coffee sometime. It seemed like that was an eternity ago. With everything going on, perhaps meeting up with a normal, non-robber, actual person was a good idea. I made a mental note to email her back, which was one I was pretty confident I would remember to follow through with. Even though somebody had just been possessed in my house, thoughts of Christina had still managed to drift across my mind in the brief moments of peace I'd been afforded. A meet up with her would no doubt be a good idea.

I spent the rest of the morning cleaning. Desmond scampered around merrily whenever I brought out a new piece of equipment designed to make the place a little less dingy. He pawed at the vacuum, straight up attacked the broom, and tried to turn the duster into a chew toy. The whole process was just one big game to him. He was having the time of his life, and just as I was beginning to think the house was present-able, I heard a soft rap on the door.

Desmond scurried up excitedly. He had returned to the couch after I had switched to boring ol' cleaning wipes, but when he heard the knock, he sprinted towards the door so fast it rattled the house. When he arrived at the entrance, Des plopped down as a giant grin made its way across his monstrous head. I could hear my parents talking from the other side of the door.

"C'mon in. The door's unlocked," I hollered from the back of my small living room. Truth be told, I could have whispered it and I'm sure they would have heard. The door opened, and Desmond took a few shuffling steps back to let them in.

"What a handsome boy!" my mom exclaimed, as she held her hand down for Desmond to sniff.

Desmond shifted his weight back and forth, side to side, and his tail whipped back and forth like a sidewinder. From behind where my mom was standing in the entranceway, the door opened once again, and my dad appeared. Desmond jumped towards him in a flurry of energy that caught everyone off-guard, most of all me.

"He must remember you from the shelter!" my mom said, while Desmond jumped up on my dad to lean on his shoulder. It made it look like Desmond was standing on two legs like a person.

"I don't think I walked him…" my dad answered. "I'd remember a dog like him."

"He got in right after you left for vacation," I reminded him. "He's really friendly. Really well-behaved too. He was already leash trained when I first met him."

"Maybe he smells the other dogs from the shelter," my mom added, still trying to piece together Desmond's excitement at seeing my dad.

My parents stood in the living room playing with Desmond for a bit, the whole time cracking jokes about how great it was to finally have a grandchild. As Des and my dad rough-housed with the long knotted rope toy I had bought Desmond, I noticed my dad still had the same dark bags under his eyes that he had when I last saw him at the shelter. It made him look older than normal, more disheveled.

When Des finally gave him room to breathe and went to see my mom, I asked, "Still having trouble sleeping?"

"Yeah, I still don't know what it is. Just a lot of weird dreams. I don't feel sick until I go to bed. I'll swing by the doctors eventually to get some sleeping pills or something if it gets any worse."

As we spoke, Desmond jumped from the floor onto the couch next to my mom and soon he was curled up by her on the small loveseat.

"He's been saying that for the past week. I keep waking up to him talking to someone who isn't there. It's *really* creepy."

As she said it, I thought back to Christina's email about how the spirits would attack whole tribes and communities. There was the dream component to it all as well. It certainly would explain the dreams I was having, which I had written up to that point as being due to my fixation with the subject. But if my dad was having them too…

My train of thought was interrupted by a loud *clang* which rattled through the small house.

"What was that?" my mom asked, while I began having flashbacks to the night before.

What if that asshole had friends? Friends who would probably be pretty pissed their buddy was spending the night/day getting his jaw wired back into position, then getting dragged away to the clinker…

Rational thought took over after the initial burst of fear, and I remembered it would be all but impossible to get into my house without going through the front door. The basement door had a hefty lock on the side of the kitchen entrance, and the windows that were littered throughout the first floor were much too small for anyone to squirm through.

Desmond's head had perked up while I weighed the possibilities, and a worried look flashed across his wrinkled face. He darted up, then slowly trotted into the kitchen like a wolf getting ready to finish off its prey, shoulders lowered to the ground and ready to pounce.

As I watched Des disappear into the kitchen, I remembered my mom had asked the question I'd been internally mulling over for the past minute.

"Oh, uh…there's a vent in there, and sometimes it'll knock over a plate or a tray or something. Happens all the time. I'm going to go grab Desmond, though."

I rose quickly, worried that perhaps the noise had been something worse than another burglar, and my parents settled into the couch and began talking about one thing or another. Their conversation became background noise as my ears were beginning to grow flush. I had a horrible suspicion about what might be in the kitchen, but Desmond wasn't growling, which could have been a good sign or a really, really bad one.

When I turned the corner past the stairs, and the kitchen opened up, I saw Desmond sitting, confused. He was staring up at the wall above my sink, and at his feet was a beer mug that had miraculously survived the fall from the counter. Before I could see what Desmond was looking at, I noticed the basement door was wide open. The empty space leading downstairs was pitch black, and those damn soft whispers began echoing from the pit of darkness like the doorway was a foul, cavernous mouth.

So much for the lock...

My thoughts were soon interrupted by a familiar, unpleasant voice. "...Dead man..."

"What was that?" my mom hollered from the other room. Even though the shadow had spoken quietly, the voice carried through my small house.

"Nothing! Just cleaning something up quick. I'll be right back in!" I shot back quickly. I sprinted over and slammed the basement door closed. I made sure to lock both the bolt and the doorknob (though clearly it didn't matter) and walked back towards Desmond.

He was still staring at the spot above the sink intently. This, of course, made me a little curious and concerned about what was drawing his attention. I had to work up the courage to see what was there. It was like looking at an injury for the first time, the way you have to will yourself to look down at whatever you heard snap or pop to see how bad it *really* was. But I finally managed to slowly look up from Desmond to see for myself.

The sink was normal, cluttered with beer mugs and half washed dishes, which was *status quo*. So, I looked a couple inches higher.

Again, nothing out of the ordinary. Nothing but a few inches of uninterrupted ugly yellow paint, which I'm sure Chuck got at a discount rate due to both its horrid color and the amount of lead it likely contained.

So, I willed myself to look a few more inches higher…and that's where it was. Smeared in the blood-red dish soap across that god-awful yellow backdrop.

"Dead man."

The writing had already begun to drip, which made it look like the wall was hemorrhaging blood from a particularly nasty gash. I stared at it for a moment in disbelief. For some reason, that particular attack pissed me off more than any of the earlier ones, possibly because my parents were in the next room. It took everything in me to not sprint down to the basement and start throttling something.

Luckily, before I could enact my ill-advised impulse of revenge, rational thought took over and I grabbed a wet dishrag and wipe off the message.

I heard footsteps approaching.

"What took you so long?" My mom stood in the entranceway of the kitchen and looked around the room to make sure I wasn't living too slovenly.

"That vent knocked over that mug, and then I noticed a stain on the wall as I cleaned it up," I replied. I scrubbed furiously at the little message, which by then had transformed into a wall of foamy suds.

"Dish Soap? Why didn't you use a wipe?" my mom said gesturing to a roll of wipes sitting right next to the sink.

I shrugged, as if to say: *I'm just a man-child living on my own, I don't know about all this fancy cleaning stuff.*

The shrug apparently conveyed the message, and my mom began to laugh.

"You kill me sometimes, Jon. Just like your father."

Speak of the devil, and he shall appear. As soon as my mom mentioned him, my father appeared in the narrow doorway. Desmond, who was no longer occupied by the death-threat from the basement, scampered over to my dad. As he did so, I noticed my dad looking all around the kitchen as if he was searching for something.

"Fire alarm's right above you," I said, assuming that's what he was worried about.

"It's not that…I just swear, one of the dreams I had was in your kitchen. I didn't remember it until, well until I was staring at it, I guess. But I guess I did have a dream about your kitchen the other night. It was one of those nightmares I keep having, and I was either asleep, or here in your kitchen…and your basement…"

He eyed the door with distrust for a second. Then, as if coming to his senses, he shook his head and changed the subject.

"Have you changed the batteries in the detectors yet?"

***

After my parents left, I went and re-read Christina's email. I scanned over it again and again, one part stood out.

```
"…but there seems to be either a prophetic or
"dream" component to their knowledge. We believe
it is how they got the concept of the "vampires"
as being shadows, or dark entities that would at-
tach themselves to certain carriers."
```

What if that was the reason my dad was having nightmares? Maybe since I was being attacked and had started having the dreams as well, the rest of my "village" was brought into the mix.

It didn't provide an answer as to why my mom wasn't having similar dreams, but it did seem to explain some other things. At least the mystery was partly coming unraveled.

As I thought about it, Christina's comment also helped answer how Desmond might have become involved in all of this. Before me, he was part of someone else's community and, maybe, his former owner had those things attached to them somehow. Whatever happened to them, (I shuddered thinking about it) meant that Desmond for some reason inherited it. Only thing is, Desmond was apparently too wily for them and now he had formed a new tribe. One that included me and my family.

"Well crap," I said loudly to myself as I stared at the computer screen, and things began to become clearer. Desmond tilted his head as if he was trying to understand me from his perch on the couch.

"Oh...nothing..." I said, for some reason explaining myself to Des, who, while bright, certainly didn't understand me. He slumped down from the couch, slowly moseyed over to me, and collapsed at my feet. Apparently exhausted from the trek between the two couches.

After watching Desmond's strenuous journey to my side, I sat with the computer on my lap and finally worked up the balls to email Christina back with a time and date for coffee. I tried not to think about it as I typed, since I knew the second I stopped to read what I had written I'd hate it and the email would never be sent.

Once the email was sent, gone with the wind and out of my control, I closed my laptop and prepared to call Chuck. Before I did though, I said to no one in particular:

"Well, at least I keep my circle small, and there's not a lot of people for them to mess with."

Maybe it was to convince myself that everything was ok, or maybe it was a challenge…

Whatever the reason, they were famous last words of an idiot.

CHAPTER 12

I'll spare you all the gritty details of mine and Chuck's conversation, but I'll let you know this much: I never cleaned a pool for him; I had a free pass to have as many animals as I'd like on his properties; and I got a new regulation lock installed the next day from an actual contracting company. All in all, I made out like a bandit for the impromptu sparring session with the burglar.

The rest of that weekend went on without a hitch. The day after my parents visited, Desmond and I drove out of the city to go on a hike. We spent the day parading around the woods without a care in the world. I also got an email back from Christina confirming our plans to meet up at Java's. Life was going pretty swell all things considered.

Of course, the other shoe was about to drop as it normally does when things start to look up. This specific shoe fell on Monday when I returned to work.

"Rick, you look like sh–you look tired. Everything alright?" I had asked as I strolled into the break room.

Rick was sitting with his head buried into his bony folded arms. He was wearing a flannel, which wouldn't have drawn my attention had it not been the dead of summer in a museum with no air conditioning. Even with his head tucked away it was evident he was feeling sick, and his ears were a flushed molten red.

"Just not feeling great," he mumbled, and he burrowed his head further into his curled arms.

"Why don't you take off, I'm sure me and Samantha—"

"She called in. Sick as a dog too. It's just me and you, and I don't think I'm going to be much help today. I think you're on your own for tours. Sorry man."

"Not a problem." I shrugged.

Truth be told, I preferred giving tours over office work any day of the week. It makes the time go by quicker; and besides, it's a nice reminder that I work in a museum. Sometimes when I'm stuffing away invoices and order forms into the crap-brown filing cabinet in my tiny office, it's easy to forget what a cool place I work at, but when I'm guiding tours, it's hard not to find myself in awe of the museum and all the curiosities within.

"Feel better man," I said quietly. I grabbed my coffee and went to drop off my backpack in my office. Behind me I could hear Rick make a pained grunt that sounded like a thank you...I think. It was hard to tell.

When I got to my office, I could already hear a group of visitors murmuring in awe as they explored the displays in the waiting area. The intercom line on my phone lit up before I even had time to check my email. It was the volunteer—which one in particular I couldn't tell over the cackling intercom—at the desk who informed me of the group's arrival. I quickly threw on my nametag, grabbed my walkie-talkie, and made my way to the waiting area.

"Is everyone here for the ten o'clock tour?" I asked as I arrived at the gift shop. Soon, a group of four nodding visitors formed a slightly-too-personal half-circle around me. As was usual for the morning tours, this group consisted of two retired couples, who (based on the graying hair, fanny packs, water bottles, and the travel maps that they clutched like treasure maps) were on a day trip to Buffalo's cultural sites.

"Hi everyone. I'm Jon," I continued, "and I'll be your tour guide through the museum."

I went over the rules, some of the things they could expect to see, and then told them briefly about the museum's history. Once that was all taken care of, I led them into the first viewing room, which was the tavern's parlor. I won't bore you with the historical trivia—if you want that, you'll have to book a tour ticket—but basically the parlor served as the nineteenth century introduction to the family that one was visiting. For the purposes of the museum, the parlor was where we would introduce the visitors to the historical figures they'd be learning about.

The room consisted of a few odds and ends Smith had collected during his world travels: a giant 1850's Steinway piano was stuffed in the corner, and there were several painted portraits of his family and other important figures of the time scattered throughout. There was also a small Chinese tea table and a Swiss wood carving of a cougar.

The portraits are really the talking point of the room, though. Of particular interest to several of the Museum's visitors, is a silhouette image of Smith's family that he had commissioned towards the end of his life. It's the piece we close the room out with since it does get so much attention.

"Smith would go on to travel the world with his inheritance but would continue to run his tavern."

The tour group stared in wonder and snapped pictures of the portraits with their phones. Behind them, and above the entranceway to the library, the silhouette drawing sat hanging on top of the doorway. When I was done talking about the paintings and other knick-knacks littered throughout the room, I gave the group a moment to take pictures before I planned on using the silhouette painting to segway us into the next room.

The four tourists were all gathered around a painting of Andrew Jackson that Smith had bought somewhere with their backs turned to me. I turned around to lead them towards the library, but before I could open my mouth to prod them along, I noticed something strange. A soft ripple across the family silhouette drawing…like the piece of art was a puddle, and a drop of rain had fallen and broken the calm surface.

Not here…not now…

I stared at the picture in horror, knowing I was caught pissing with my pants down.

Please not here.

But my call to the universe would go unheeded, and a small, dark shadow seemed to grow from one of the silhouettes in the drawing. The way that the shadow scampered off mischievously would have been funny in any other situation, however, I knew the 10 o'clock tour had just gotten a lot more complicated.

Behind me I could hear one of the husbands in the tour begin spouting off random facts about Jackson trying to impress everyone, which bought me a few seconds to think. I had lost sight of where the shadow had disappeared to exactly, and for all I knew, it could be waiting for me at every turn for the rest of the tour. Despite this, I decided to get the tour moving to the next room without mentioning the silhouette painting in case it wasn't done spawning.

"Uh…if you'll all follow me to the next room."

I led them into the library slowly, my heart pounded while I braced for an unseen attack. As I stepped into the room, I expected books to be flying from shelves all helter-skelter, but everything looked normal. Still, there was a tense energy in the library which I'd never felt there before.

"This is, of course, the library," I said while gesturing around the room theatrically. The four surrounding walls were covered floor to ceiling in leather-bound first editions. The group oohed and aahed at the sight of all the old books, their rich smell filled the small space with the aroma of spices always attached to libraries.

As the visitors' eyes shifted around the room looking at old classics, my eyes darted frantically around, and I inspected every nook and cranny in the room…looking for where that thing might have gone. The library was dark and only a few decrepit lamps provided any sort of light for the dimmed room. The inkiness seemed to make the smell of ancient books hang even heavier in the air, and the marble busts scattered around the room seemed to glare suspiciously at me in anger, as if to say: *How could you let that thing in here?*

"The collection, of course, includes the classics; however, being an avid traveler, Smith also has a large collection of travel memoirs and local lore as well."

I knew the tour had to go on like normal…well, as normal as it could with an evil shadow sprinting around my place of employment. I figured the thing was trying to torment me, to force me to make a mistake, or to wear on my nerves until it drove me to the edge of acting irrationally, to make me mess up and do something the shadow could then capitalize on.

I had to stay focused and try to ignore the attack as best I could, but it was at that moment that I realized that Rick and Samantha's sicknesses weren't random occurrences. I remembered from Christina's email that in the English translation the shadows were considered vampires because they were said to drain the life from a community. This was them branching out their attack.

I managed to calm myself down but almost as soon as I had braced myself in the library, I saw the shadow sprint across the wall above the tour group. They were too busy admiring the books to notice the evil spirit prancing about the wall by them. The shadow stopped above the group for a moment, the outline of its head peered down at where they stood as if it was trying to figure them out, then it disappeared as quickly as it had appeared. I knew the shadow was mocking me, forcing me to watch it parade around while there was nothing I could do but stand by helplessly and hope things didn't escalate.

"Dead man," I heard whispered from somewhere behind me.

"What was that?" one of the husbands on the tour asked, apparently remembering I was in the room with them. All four of them were wearing some form of hearing aids or another, so I wasn't all that concerned that they had actually understood the threat.

"Oh, I saw you were looking at our first edition copy of *The Water-Witch*. Smith was also a fan of popular fiction during that time."

As I spoke to him the man's body seemed to go rigid in a violent, brief spasm. It was a subtle transformation, but he was no longer hunched over in the manner he'd been the whole tour leading up to that point. Instead, he stood tall, with his hands opening and closing as he balled them intermittently into fists, like he was figuring out the mechanics of a human body for the first time.

"Are there any books about Nepal? Or better yet, the burials there?" he asked as a wicked smirk grew across his weather-beaten face.

It was no longer the tired face of an old man staring at me, there was something else pulling the strings behind a mask of benevolence. His wife and the other couple with them were, of course, oblivious to what was happening, so I decided to keep my cool.

"Books? Well, I don't know. But we do have some artifacts we just found. An especially dangerous-looking stake that was, for some reason, a part of the burial…but I don't know much about that."

The man still smirked, like he knew something I didn't. His eyes were the same engulfing black pits that the burglar's had stared back at me with. The rest of his party briefly looked up from the shelves and nodded in appreciation at my answer. Still not noticing the change in their friend, they swiftly went back to looking at the books.

"I've read a bit about those burials. I think you should too." The man's voice was cold and empty. He looked at me with dark, hollow eyes that were lacking any semblance of humanity. They were so empty, they could have been the pit I had seen in my room a week prior.

He continued, "Many times, when they'd find them recently dug into cliffs, there'd be no evidence of anyone in the area. Seemed like wherever those graves were, somehow the whole town would find their way into them, almost like the whole village was destroyed and buried…with no survivors. Not even animals. All dead and destroyed with no sign of who did it."

"How morbid!" his wife said, coming to his side and grabbing his arm. As she yanked at him, the man's shoulders dropped back down as if the unseen puppeteer had released the strings, and a look of confusion flashed across his face. The surprise only lasted for a moment, and soon, he was back with his group looking around the library mumbling about random titles.

I let them wander around the room unheeded as I processed the last few minutes. They were perfectly distracted enough, and for the first time since I had encountered it, I was beginning to feel like I understood the thing that was attached to Desmond. Well, maybe understood wasn't the right word…but I knew what it was capable of at least.

I knew it seemed to have the ability to briefly take over peoples' minds but not enough horsepower to manipulate the body into a real threat. I mean, when I pieced together the burglar, I might as well have been fighting a punching bag with how little the possessed man resisted. It seemed to be limited in who it could take over too, for whatever reason. I theorized that it only targeted those it knew it could manipulate. I was also beginning to suspect that the various shadows were just a tool used by the black pit I had first encountered. That there was one big bad, and that all the others were just the minions. That the pit or main shadow was the real evil, and that was where the thing's real power was.

I watched as the group moved about the library, staying close together and whispering amongst themselves until one of the women saw something on the opposite shelf that caught her eye. Watching as she broke away from her companions, another thought hit me.

The pit, well that part of it seemed less mobile than the shadows it sent out to handle its light work; and it appeared that the thing preferred the underground—which is why I probably hadn't seen it much. Then there was that dream where I had seen it in the cave. I was pretty confident that the main shadow would only leave its lair for a guaranteed kill. Or maybe the shadows would bring its victims to it. Something awful like that.

There was a lot I didn't know (and still don't for that matter). I hadn't figured out if there was any rhyme or reason as to who it targeted, or why some people got sick, while others had dreams, and some seemed completely unaffected. Or why Desmond mattered so much to it.

There was definitely more that I didn't know than I did, but I was getting somewhere.

"If you'll follow me into the next room…"

The rest of the tour went on without a hitch, which I figured would be the case after the shadow got its say in. The old guy with the drooping shoulder even took out a membership to the museum before leaving, which was the least he could do.

As I stood in the gift shop and watched them file out after thanking me for the tour, I came to another realization. Des, the shadow, and me, we were in a stalemate. We were stuck staring at each other from our separate corners of the ring, posturing and trying to force the other to react. I was stuck in my house, which was now an ever-evolving battlefield between the two sides, while the shadow was a little more mobile in its attack; the further away from the cellar it got, the weaker it seemed to get as well. It was attached to Desmond, but still needed to find a suitable environment to fully function.

So, there we all were shaking our fists at each other, and digging in our trenches a little deeper each day. I knew, even then, it would take something drastic to force a direct confrontation. I also knew that direct confrontation was in the not too distant future.

Standing in the museum, watching those people leave—last of course, being the hunched over old man who had somehow found his way into this story—I felt myself shudder at the thought of what would cause the unavoidable encounter. And how it would all end.

***

"I'm glad you could meet me," I told Christina over the background strums of an acoustic guitar. We were at some hipster coffee shop we'd decided on meeting at, and she had apparently beaten me there.

After the weird day at work, Christina was a sight for sore eyes. She was sitting at a table that looked like it was made from a piece of driftwood and had a large manilla folder in front of her. As I settled into the chair across the table from her, she peered over the brim of her glasses with a look that could have knocked me dead.

"Of course; it's not often I get a chance to talk Himalayan mythology with someone who isn't a professor," she said, shifting in her seat. A waiter appeared and took our orders before I even had a chance to make myself comfortable.

"That's why I like it here," Christina informed me, after he had left. "Most coffee places take *forever* to serve you. This place doesn't mess around."

I was beginning to get the impression that Christina didn't put up with much bull—a trait I certainly respected. I tried to relax in my seat, and soon realized I was about to spend the rest of the date feigning ease and comfort.

I nodded as if I was impressed with the coffee shop's efficiency, and I was about to start making small talk about the driftwood table, but Christina spoke up, thankfully, before I could get my lame comment out. She was apparently ready to get down to brass tacks and had flipped open the folder to thumb through the contents.

"Your email got me thinking about the origin of our sources—"

The waiter dropped off our coffee, which barely elicited a response from Christina, who was too focused to break concentration. Her green eyes seemed to become electric as she began talking about her research.

"—and how limited they are. They're mostly archeological and anthropological interpretations, after all. So, I went to hunt for a *primary* source. Now, obviously, there's not likely going to be any remaining texts from those early villages due to the dates we're talking about, but maybe an oral tradition that was passed down, that a later missionary might have taken the time to record. That was what I was hoping for. Something to put us a little closer to them."

As she spoke, a giant grin grew across Christina's face. Apparently, she had been conducting some research since the last time we spoke and had found what she was looking for. And judging by the intensity of the smile, it was something significant.

"I found it! It wasn't even in a Tibetan or Nepalese historical archive, weirdly." Christina shook her head almost in disbelief at her own achievement. She scrunched her face and closed her eyes as she nodded, and a cluster of sun freckles seemed to gather around her nose. "A European historical archive of all places," she continued, "I think I was the first person to access it too."

Christina was fired up, and I was literally on the edge of my seat, eager to see what she had found. I tried not to appear too antsy, but I found myself taking rapid, small sips of my coffee. It was an effort to keep my hands from reaching out and snagging the folder between us; but the sudden burst of caffeine only made me more anxious and on edge to see the discovery.

"It's the closest thing we have to a primary source! Recorded by some jerk of a European missionary in the 1400s who visited the mustang region. Most of it is just chastising the locals—but there is one mention of the cliff graves, a local legend about a hero, and I figured you'd want to see it. I'm including it in my dissertation, and it might be a big discovery, so if you could keep it between us…"

It dawned on me that Christina was taking a bit of a personal risk showing me this document. I mean, she had stumbled upon a historian's dream—it was a niche topic, sure, but I'm positive any student of Asian history would give their first born to include *this* source in a thesis. And she was just letting me see it the second time meeting face-to-face.

"Of course, I won't tell a soul. And thanks, it means a lot that you're letting me see this." I looked across the table at her with the sincerest expression I could muster. Christina met my gaze, and I saw the right corner of her lip curl up in a knowing smile.

Without breaking eye contact, she closed the folder and slid it clumsily across the uneven tabletop, like a KGB agent secretly turning over private data to a US informant. Once the folder sat in front of me, she leaned back in her chair with her arms crossed and waited for me to read.

I opened it slowly. The folder was filled with pages of printed text, all of which had scribbled notes written in the margins in blue ink—presumably from Christina. The original text must have been in pretty rough shape too, judging by the long blank spaces which were filled only by the blocky "indistinguishable text" marker.

Of the locals, not much can be said that hasn't been detailed by my predecessors. A simple, backward lot. Void of the (knowledge) of our lord and savior... (indistinguishable text...) Legend of (the) locals regarding death and (indistinguishable...possibly afterlife,) leads to burials high in (the) cliff walls of the surrounding area. The natives believe they are haunted by spirits of deceased (indistinguishable text...) burial involves desecration of the (corpse.)

I have met with a local leader...Remain unreceptive of the (gospel.) (...indistinguishable text.) Over our meeting, he told me stories of a recent village (they had) discovered empty. Animals all slaughtered or cut (loose.) The cliff by the abandoned village was filled with recently dug graves. The locals refused to investigate, but I convinced them to bring me to the site. (...indistinguishable text.) will follow the river.

(New entry. No recorded date.)

...tale of a hero who battled the (...indistinguishable text...) The confrontation took place inside a grave. (I) was told this story as we moved toward the abandoned village. The man's village succumbed to madness inflected by the shadows, which resulted in his following battle. Porter describes the man fighting his tribe, who had become the shadow. In the crypt the man confronts (...indistinguishable text...)

(New entry. No recorded date.)

We have arrived at the village. Sitting at the base of two cliffs. Dead animals lay scattered around the empty village to the banks (of the river.) No (human) life. Porters refuse to move toward the cliffs. All appear recently dug. (…indistinguishable text…) Signs of a major struggle…

"Whoever transcribed the journal left a lot out," Christina said with frustration dripping in her voice when she saw me look up from the text.

"It was probably in bad shape and they probably didn't think anyone would be reading it," I replied, for some reason sticking up for the anonymous grad researcher who had been left to transcribe the old journal as busy work.

"Yeah, I guess," Christina said, clearly disheartened. "It's just frustrating: I can't track down *who* transcribed it, and when I called the library it was supposedly housed in, they had no record of where it went. It's probably sitting in some professor's personal library, collecting dust forever. Luckily for us, some student was forced to transcribe it before they retired and took it home with them."

We sat there drinking our coffee, both lost in our own thoughts. I'm sure she was thinking about ways to locate the rest of the journal, while I was thinking about how the new information could prove useful to my current situation. Unfortunately, I was drawing a blank.

I mean, supposedly there was someone who fought the shadow…but the ever important how, and the outcome, was lost with the rest of that journal. To make it worse, the transcript described the shadows driving a whole village to eat itself alive. I mean, a whole town of slaughtered animals and recently dug graves? With that on top of all that I had seen, I was beginning to doubt my odds.

"You know, I guess I owe you for getting me to look into it from a different direction," Christina said, breaking the silence.

I shook my head violently.

"Trust me, it's me who owes you. I can't believe you'd include me in this amazing research—you're doing groundbreaking stuff here. I'm just thankful I got to see a bit of it. I mean, look at this!" I said, and for some reason I waved the manila folder she'd given me. "You just made this appear out of nowhere, based on some nobody's random email. I'm amazed."

I tried to reel myself in, but I really was impressed. Christina had basically gone out and discovered a new source based on some lame question I asked her to help my ghostbusters quest.

She smiled at me.

I thought back to my graduate history classes, and realized that Christina was the first person I actually enjoyed discussing history with. I mean, here I was, sitting in a coffee shop with some evil shadows patrolling my house, and for the first time I was enjoying having a conversation about a topic I had spent thousands of dollars to study in a field I now work in. There was something almost poetic to it.

We talked for another half an hour before I decided I needed to get back to Desmond to make sure he was alright.

"This was really fun," I said as I stood up to leave. I wanted to say something smarter that she might remember, or something to thank her for all the information that would undoubtedly help in the future, or for taking the time to show me her findings…but the words wouldn't come. I felt frozen.

Luckily, Christina was a cooler customer than I was, or that might've been our last meeting.

"Fun, I agree," she said with a smirk. "It was so fun, in fact, I think we should do it again…maybe over dinner?"

I nodded stupidly, and she let out the softest laugh I'd ever heard in my life. It sounded like chimes fluttering in the breeze, I swear it was musical. Her eyes seemed to sparkle at the same time, as if those same chimes were made of some rare gem that had caught the sun's rays *just* right…

We planned to meet each other for dinner later in the week. In my bumbling exit I forgot to grab the folder that contained the transcripts, which would lead to our next encounter being much earlier than we planned. The dinner date scheduled for that week would never happen...but that's for later.

CHAPTER 13

"There's my boy!"

Desmond greeted me at the door in the same way he had every day since I had adopted him. A goofy grin was spread out over his boxy face; it was as if the sly dog knew I was getting back from a date.

"Yeah, yeah, I know," I said as I bent down to scratch behind his ears. His grey eyes lit up as I stooped down, and Des buried his massive frame into my crouched body as if to say *I missed you.* He looked up at me and slumped his burly head on my knee; as he did so, his face seemed to smush into a bundle of wrinkles. I stayed there petting him for a good while. It was nice to be missed.

I could tell the extra hour apart had thrown Des off, and who could blame him? He was used to our normal routine; a walk, then I'd leave for work, back at lunch, and once again at exactly 5:15. My coffee with Christina had clearly made him worry that I wasn't coming back.

"C'mon buddy, you know I'd never leave you."

I couldn't tell if he understood me, but I like to think he did. I also like to think he still knows I mean it.

Damn do I ever...

I brought him on a walk that night. It would be the last walk for a while, and I wished I had just kept walking with him. Just disappeared out of the city, and then into the country until we ended up wherever we were meant to go. The coast somewhere, where the bitter salt air would be too far removed from the cold winds of the Himalayas, and the shadow would be forced to quit its pursuit of us. Or maybe to another country; some log cabin or small apartment amidst a place too serene for anything bad to ever occur.

But that's not what happened.

We walked for a bit and returned to the house, though my mind had drifted to those places far away. Des and I stayed up for a bit; me reading, him cuddling up next to my leg on the couch. Any other night, and the memory of reading Bradbury with Desmond would be a perfectly suitable retreat into my mind.

I mean, it was just so normal, which is why when I remember it, the memory hurts so much more. The next few months would be hell, which I mean in a very literal manner. To have that night be so mundane fills me with a regret so deep, I doubt there's a way to remove it outside of a complete lobotomy.

Hindsight's a bitch, huh?

Reading must have tired me out because I passed out early that night. Another dream kept me tossing and turning all night, which probably didn't help the events of the next day, but here's what I remember from it:

No fancy fade-in from the darkness; no slow immersion this time. I was dropped right into that cave in a *whoosh* of disorientation. The second my surroundings became clear, my ears were filled with sharp, horrifying screams that ripped across my mind like the retort of a gun. I tried to scream, but the sound would just die in my throat before it managed to escape.

The noises were amplified by the walls of the cave, and no matter how hard I tried to cover my ears or bury my head, they made their way through. The screams were everywhere, coming from all directions and shooting through me like lightning.

I could feel the tears beginning to pool in the corners of my eyes. Not from pain or sadness, but it was like my eyes were trying to clear themselves as best as they could before I was going to see whatever lay before me. My body seemed to be making me ready for the next step.

The screams began to die out, only to be replaced by two voices from somewhere deep in the cave. I knew one immediately; that soft dull hiss would be familiar to me anywhere. The other voice was too distant for me to make out. It sounded so familiar. There was a tone to it I knew well. I just couldn't place my finger on it.

I began walking forward, because I knew I was supposed to see whatever was before me. I figured that's why whatever was controlling this sent me here, after all; to see why these dreams had become a regular occurrence and had already begun to infect my village. It was not to hide in the background, but to unravel the mystery. And to face whatever was there in the cave.

So, I moved forward in the pitch darkness. Each step sounded with the crunch of gravel as I made my way further down into the cavern. As I progressed it became clear that I was walking into the sight of a complete massacre. A sole torch seemed to appear from nowhere, partially lighting the way.

In the light, I saw the blood was smeared on the uneven walls of the cave. The glistening liquid was so abundant that it looked like it had come from the cavern itself, as if it was hemorrhaging. A particularly gruesome red handprint was pressed into the wall beneath the crudely mounted torch.

It had been dragged down the wall, and a copper tinted trail was all that was left behind. It was as if the unfortunate victim who left the morbid cave art had thought that reaching the torch would be their escape, only to find themselves pulled back into the darkness. I shuddered thinking about it, then turned quickly to meet the shadow in its throne room. If I waited too long, I feared I might lose the nerve to find out what was waiting for me. Still, I paused for a moment outside to gather my courage.

You can do this. You have to do this.

I braced myself to confront whatever lay in the cavern, but before I could burst through the opening to face the shadow, along with whatever it was talking to, something stopped me in my tracks. Blocking the way into whatever hell was beyond the entrance, was the most beautiful woman I'd ever laid eyes on. She had appeared out of nowhere and was resting still against the base of the opening. Despite her beauty, I knew she was dead, there was no questioning that, but she looked at peace, save for the slightly unnatural tilt of her long neck.

She was calm, serene, and beautiful.

A single trickle of blood escaped the corner of her mouth, and I remember kneeling down next to her praying there was something I could do, that maybe it wasn't too late, maybe she could be brought back to life. But as I gently lifted her head forward from the jagged cave call, what I knew all along was reinforced: it was much too late. Her cold skin burned my hands as if I was touching dry ice, but that didn't stop me. I slowly moved her to a more relaxed sitting position against the cave wall, trying to find some way to make her neck support itself as it would in life. As I did this, I discovered what had extinguished this beautiful woman's life.

Centered midline of her body, just below where her throat ended and her sternum began, was a clean puncture wound. It was so perfectly circular it looked like she had simply fallen underneath an industrial-sized hole puncher. But I knew what it was.

A wound from a stake.

I turned away, more furious than I'd ever been in my life. The thought that for some reason, some cruel and meaningless reason, this woman had been a victim of the shadow made me angrier than when I had seen the burglar in my house. It made me hate whatever god, whatever deity, or whatever *thing* allowed the shadow to spawn, and hadn't in all its infinite power snuffed the shadow's life before it could start. I was filled with pure vitriol, and all I wanted to do was hurt mine and Desmond's arch nemesis.

I planned to charge in all gung-ho. To do what exactly, well, I had no plan…but I was filled with venom and something had to pay.

As I stood up, I felt a pair of ice-cold hands grab my leg, and I was pulled back down to stare into the eyes of the dead woman. Those kind eyes that should not have been as flat and glossed over as they were.

"It's started again…" she whispered. Her hands were holding my face, her thumbs moved gently as if they were wiping at tears beneath my eyes that weren't there. The pallid look of death crept from her eyes, and a twinkle seemed to return as she spoke.

"He killed it, but it's back. And you'll have to finish it. You will have to see things that will hurt you, but you must kill it. It's the only way to save him. He did this to me, but he had to. You'll have to, too."

"But how?" I asked, knowing exactly who she was talking about saving: Desmond and *my* village.

My voice cracked as I stared into those eyes that had seen death, the worst death, but were now, somehow, full of life and goodness.

She didn't say anything, she just looked at me, like she was evaluating whether I could *actually* succeed. I didn't know who she was, or to whom that second voice coming from the cavern behind her belonged, but I felt that if I could find that out I would be on my way to ending this.

"Who are y—"

beep beep beep

The shrill sound of the alarm ripped away any hope of discovering who she was. I stared at the blurred grey and red neon block like it had betrayed me in the worst possible way. So close…

"So, this is *all* your place?"

141

I couldn't tell if Christina was impressed that I lived on my own, or amazed that I was living in what could be considered a "little house." Still, there she was, standing in the doorway being greeted by Desmond, who she happily threw her arms around.

"He's so precious!" she exclaimed as Des coated her with kisses. Truth be told, I was a little jealous of the ol' dog who was in all his glory as Christina heaped attention his way.

Now, it might seem peculiar that Christina was showing up at my place the day after a first date, especially when we had scheduled to see each other a little later on, however, I had texted her the night before (right before I nodded off in fact) when I realized I had forgotten to bring the folder of transcripts home with me. So, seeing as it was the weekend, she had graciously agreed to drop them off so I could continue my research.

"Thanks so much for dropping them off. I could have picked them up and saved you the trouble."

She shrugged, as if it was no big deal, and Des pranced around her.

"I was doing some running around anyway and I'll take any chance I can get to see a dog! My landlord won't let me get one."

Desmond had (naturally) come up at some point as we had gotten coffee the day before, and it was evident even then that Christina was a dog lover. As Desmond crawled all over her, she didn't do so much as flinch at the 70lb pit bull's complete and undivided love. In fact, Christina returned it.

"He's just a big ol' lovebug!" she said in baby-talk as she grabbed Desmond's jowls in her hands. Des was hamming it up, and his head rocked back and forth gently in her grasp.

"He's a good boy…" I said to no one in particular, as I might as well not have been there. The two of them were much too busy to pay attention to little old me. I took the folder Christina had given me and tossed it on the couch.

"My notes are in there; hope you don't mind. I copied it after I got your text, and of course read it again. I still can't believe I found it!" Christina made her way over to the opposite couch, where she was closely tailed by Desmond who hopped up beside her. "I mean, a complete narrative referencing a local oral tradition—one that we didn't know about on top of that. I can't wait to write about it."

She seemed more relaxed. Maybe it was because she was with a dog, or maybe it was because she was dressed in a T-shirt and yoga pants. Whatever the reason, seeing her relaxing on a couch with Desmond cuddling up next to her made me hope there might be future lazy days. I pictured us sleeping in, then taking Desmond on walks; or maybe reading books together or listening to Christina discuss her research while we were both still in sweatpants. That was all I wanted at that moment. I was about to ask her if she'd like coffee before I got lost in my daydream, but she continued:

"I mean, even the priest who didn't believe the story said they visited an abandoned village where something happened. I wonder what it was. Probably another village attacked. I wish we had the full account of the hero who fought this thing. I mean, what it could tell us about these early communities; what they valued and feared."

Me and you both.

Christina brushed her flowing red hair from in front of her eyes. "We don't have any further transcripts about what the priest sees but that's ok. I think I can run with what he gave us. Maybe focus on how the early settlements were in a constant state of flux, or how this new tale proves they had developed a cosmos beyond what we knew. I mean, I'm sure as they were traveling, these early settlers often stumbled across other abandoned villages, so maybe this tale was a way to explain away the very real threats of disease and warfare."

Christina was monologuing at this point, which was fine by me. I knew she was just trying to flesh out her ideas before she put pen to paper, and with me being the only person who likely knew about her research, Christina had to take this opportunity to hear her thoughts out loud.

"It did say that he—I mean the hero the priest briefly talks about—was forced to kill his village that was overrun by the shadow before killing the shadow itself. It's really a tragic story," Christina said with a sigh.

Her sigh was barely audible over the other sound though. It started immediately as she finished her previous statement, and it filled me with a deep sense of dread as soon as it made its way to the living room.

It was the mention of the man who killed his village that would finally bring the confrontation to a head. Maybe whatever happened that day had left a bad taste in the shadows' mouth; or maybe the mere mention of it set the shadow into action. Whatever it was, the shadow had decided there was no time better than the present to get violent.

A soft, slow drumming made its way up from the basement. Desmond's head perked up, and I knew something wicked was afoot.

"Uh, it's been really nice having you here," I stammered, feebly trying to kick Christina out before anything could happen. "I have to get to a mee—"

"What's that noise?" she interrupted, ignoring my desperate attempt to get her out of the house, to go far, far away and forget about me. She looked down at the carpet beneath her and tilted her head in curiosity, the same way Desmond did. "It sounds like it's coming from somewhere below us. Like there's *something* below us…"

Not for long.

I tried to gesture her to the front door, but Christina wouldn't budge. She seemed intrigued at what was happening.

"Sometimes you can hear the trucks going by outside," I lied. It sounded good, and for a bit, it seemed like Christina believed that passing trucks were the cause of all the commotion. For that fleeting moment, I almost believed I would be able to get Christina outside before she saw anything.

The basement door slammed open violently, and any hope at explaining it away disappeared into thin air. A look of surprise was plastered across Christina's face as she looked into the kitchen from her seat on the couch, and I could tell she was trying to figure what the slamming noise of the door opening could possibly mean. The look of shock quickly transformed into a look of concern, and I swear, in that brief half-second, it almost looked like Christina had figured everything out: why I had contacted her, why the transcript was so important, and why I was so interested in the topic. All of it.

"You need to go upstairs," I said frantically, as Desmond stood up and began pacing back and forth like a boxer in his corner in front of the still seated Christina. He had begun to growl, and it was evident that he knew as well as I did that the game had just changed. No more posturing. No more feints.

Something was going to get wrecked today.

By now, the kitchen was alive with the sound of evil whispers and pans clattering with the wicked wind it brought with it. I chanced a look inside from the doorway and saw an army of shadows prancing along the wall, but more concerning, was the pit of blackness that had located itself into the top corner of the room.

I hadn't seen that dark, cavernous opening which led to the void since the first night I'd brought Desmond home, and seeing it again filled me with the morbid realization that I was probably going to die that day.

I stood watching the shadows overrun the room. They filled it with a darkness so complete, so empty and evil, it was all I could do to not just break down and weep. To beg for a quick death, or at least, a death that would take me someplace far, far away from all of this. What could I possibly hope to achieve against this monster? These vampires that had drained whole villages of life.

At least you can save Desmond and Christina...

In the face of such an ancient evil, one so engrossing it had even begun to permeate my dreams, the thought that I could do at least *some* good helped me gain my composure.

As if to remind me I wasn't alone in all this, I felt Desmond's presence next to me. I didn't hear him, didn't see him as I focused on what was in the kitchen, but I knew he was there next to me. Something was radiating from Desmond that for some reason I was picking up. The best I can do to describe it is as an energy that seemed to clash with the aura of death in front of us.

I heard Christina come up behind us too. I couldn't make out exactly what she was saying but I'm sure it was utterances of complete disbelief as the army of shadows catapulted around the small room, and the cursed ringing of the abyss filled the tiny house.

The last thing I remember is Des's bark.

Everything faded to darkness after that.

PART II

"I am going far away to the land of robbers and ghosts."
– Hutter, *Nosferatu* (1922)

CHAPTER 14

The pinpoints of bright colors fluttered through the blackness. Accompanying them were beams of light, which cut through the melancholy backdrop like puncture wounds.

What time is it? Am I dead...again?

The blurred landscape slowly filled in around me. Soft, mysterious edges soon emerged from the dark, and became the clear lines of a windowsill. The bursts of bright color were transformed by contrast into prayer flags, which danced across the alleyway outside the window of the teahouse. The hum of gathering crowds in the small marketplace below drifted up, and a particularly shrill voice of one of the local sellers seemed to rise above the surrounding commotion.

Nepal. You're in Nepal.

Waking up had been difficult since that day in the kitchen, when everything had gone up in flames. Even then, two months later, I couldn't remember what happened. Every time I tried, and trust me I really did, I would come up with nothing but a splitting headache and frustration.

Luckily, Christina was there and boy, did she remember everything.

I woke up two days after her visit to my house. That's the first formed memory I have at least. Christina, who despite barely knowing me, visited me during my stay at the hospital; she said I would wake up during those two days screaming out gibberish. I'm glad I can't remember those dreams.

The cold, sanitized lights of the hospital, shining down on me from above the gurney, that's the first thing I remember—though at the time I had no clue where I was.

The sickening taste of copper filled my dry mouth as I came to; the trace of blood was still there even days after. I remember looking up at the light radiating from the ceiling and wanting to shield my eyes from its white glare, but as I tried, I realized I couldn't. I was stuck, too entangled in the jungle of tubes and IVs that wrapped around me like vines, to move even the slightest bit.

The pounding light from above filled the room. It was blinding, and it took a moment for the figures around me to reveal themselves. For that brief, horrifying second, I was sitting in the unknown surrounded by shadows. I was too disoriented to put up a fight—to do anything for that matter—and I resigned myself to the gruesome fate I was no doubt about to suffer.

Those figures slowly gained contrast, and soon, I realized it was Christina, my parents, and an especially young-looking Physician's Assistant standing next to me.

Hospital...I'm in the hospital.

It slowly began to make sense to my fragmented mind.

"Des..." I managed to get out. Apparently, the IVs weren't working that great, because along with the taste of blood I was also suffering from the worst case of cottonmouth in the world.

"Oh good, he's up," the assistant said. His voice was high pitched and pierced through my pounding head like a knife. It made me want to bury my head into the cement block of a pillow I was laying on even more than the light did. But I was strung up by those awful tubes, unable to escape any of it.

Desmond...the shadows...kitchen...

That was all I had, just being in the kitchen, resigned that I was about to die, and then somehow, I was at the hospital.

As I tried to piece the world together, I saw my parents approach my hospital bed.

"Why didn't you tell us your house was broken in—" my mom started, before she cut herself off. I'm sure my face was plastered with a look of pure confusion, which caused her to pause. "Christina helped file the report," she continued once she realized I was still trying to figure out which way was up. "The police seem to think it's a revenge thing. Maybe a friend of the original guy who broke in. Thank God Christina was there to see him hit you from behind and call the police. Otherwise who knows…"

Her voice trailed off, and for a brief moment, I allowed myself to think I'd imagined it all. It was the sweetest relief I'd ever felt.

Of course, there's no shadow, you've been unconscious and had some bad dreams. Nothing weird went on at all. You jacked up this guy's friend, and he ambushed you. Probably happens all the time.

But then I saw Christina's face, and any false illusions were shattered. She was about four feet away, sitting in an especially worn hospital chair and looking as pretty as ever. Her eyes though; the dark bags underneath those pretty greens let me know Christina hadn't slept much since what she'd seen in the kitchen. A particularly squinty look cast my way was followed by a long exhale and was clearly meant to tell me that she'd fill me in later.

"I'm sure they'll find the guy even though Christina said she didn't really get a good look at him. It doesn't matter. Anyways, we're so glad…"

My Mom continued talking for a bit, but it all faded to the background. I noticed my dad was standing there silently, and next to Christina sat a pile of books so large that the side table they rested on seemed to bow in the center.

None of it mattered though.

C'mon buddy…you know I'd never leave you.

Nobody answered my first question. I was with it enough to know that. Which meant something bad had likely happened to Des.

And, if that were the case, then something *really* bad was going to happen to that thing.

***

I sat up and quickly checked the base of my bed. My backpack was there, it hadn't walked away with some other traveler. Some of them have sticky hands, despite being here for some undefined spiritual quest that their yoga instructor back in the States told them to undergo. The bag was overfilled, near bursting, and seriously old. It sat at the bottom of the bed, slumped against the frame.

That's where Desmond should be sitting.

I stuffed down the overwhelming rush of emotion that washed over me like an electric surge and began getting ready for the day. The early morning light was pouring in from the window, and the smell of bread and spices drifted through the opening in intoxicating waves. All around me fellow backpackers were beginning to stir, and the clamor of the morning slowly filled the overcrowded room, eventually overtaking the stir of the market beneath us.

If you strained to listen as everyone got going, you would hear at least a dozen different languages being spoken in the small hostel I was staying at, but as beautiful as that might be, I didn't care. I wasn't there for sightseeing, or to quench some underlying sense of wanderlust, or even to climb for that matter. Well…I wasn't there to climb *recreationally…*

I was there to fight. To fight something that had hurt me and had taken someone good from the world.

152

After my parents left to get something to eat, it was just me and Christina sitting alone in the dreary hospital room. There was a moment where we just stared at each other, neither knowing where to jump into the whirlwind of a conversation that needed to be had. The whirring of various machines pumping me full of pain killers provided a weird, sci-fi backdrop to this talk.

"That was one of those *things*, wasn't it? That's why you were so interested in the history of it." She spoke softly with no anger in her voice. The way the words trickled out, it seemed like she was still unsure of what she had seen or hadn't had the chance to say the words aloud. The certainty with which she normally spoke was nowhere to be heard.

My head still pounded and was propped up in a wildly uncomfortable position by some strap I couldn't see, but I managed a slight nod. "I told the cops it was a burglar. I knew they wouldn't believe me if I told them the truth. I guess the other burglar made it a pretty bulletproof story." She nodded her head in disbelief at the fact the lie had fallen into place so nicely. "I don't know if I believed it, at first, but I *know* what I saw. Why didn't you tell me?" Christina pleaded, still shaking her head in frustration.

"Nobody…would…believe…" I managed to get out, though my throat felt like it did after a night of throwing up cheap vodka. The deep acidic burn made each word seem like a ball of razors as it climbed up. I saw Christina's face soften; she knew I was right, that if I had told her before she had seen it, she would have thought I was crazy.

Still, I couldn't blame her for being angry at me. I wished so much I could go back in time and tell her to just bring the transcripts to dinner, not drop them off. I wished I could've kept her from seeing the shadow, but there was another thing I wished I could have prevented even more. A thing I knew I couldn't avoid anymore. I braced to hear the inevitable.

"What happened...to Des?"

We were alone, and there was no skirting away from the question.

Christina's face softened even more, and I could tell she was trying to figure out how to tell me, or if I was even ready to hear it yet.

"Please." It was me pleading now.

She looked at me with a truly sympathetic look.

"I don't know exactly what it did to you. I was there behind you and the whole kitchen was filled with those...those things. Desmond sprinted past you, and you went after him. I...I didn't know what to do. And then the dark spot...I don't know how...but it was on you. All over you like a blanket. You disappeared, and the whole kitchen was empty. Just Desmond standing in the middle of it, barking and crying, but then you were back, and there was blood coming from your mouth, your ears. I thought you were dead."

Christina looked down for a moment. I could tell she hated remembering what she had seen, and I hated making her relive it. But I had to know.

"Des..." my voice was cracking, and not because it was dry this time.

"When you came back, the whole wall was filled with that...the pit. I was trying to drag you back into the living room. I don't know why, but I thought that would make us safe. Desmond..."

I could feel the hot tears rolling down my face. My eyes stung worse than any pain I'd ever felt before. The last thing I wanted to do was cry in front of Christina, but I couldn't stop it.

"He just stood, staring at that thing. He wasn't even barking. I mean, it sounds stupid to say out loud, but he seemed...I don't know, resigned? At peace. The last thing I saw was him moving towards the pit. Then it all disappeared. Everything. All the shadows, that god awful noise…and him. We were all that was left. They said without a witness the case would go nowhere."

We sat there in silence, both of us lost in our own thoughts, and while I can't speak for Christina, I know what overpowered my mind.

Vengeance.

"Jeez, is all you do sleep?" Sajit asked when I finally made my way to the small cafe located next to the tea house. Both served tea, but one was basically a house open to tourists that had meals, beds, and everything you could need to make it home for a night, while the other just served the drink.

"It was six hours; I think I'm allowed that."

He shrugged, as if to say: *Your life you're wasting away,* then took a long sip of the foggy tea that filled the gold rimmed glass.

Sajit was one of Christina's connections in the area, and he'd been my guide while I was in Nepal. Having someone who knew the area was a godsend from the moment I touched down. When I'd landed in Kathmandu, I had no idea which way was up, let alone how to navigate the chaotic city. Luckily, Sajit was there outside the airport with a sign bearing my hastily scribbled name to save me from becoming an aimless drifter, lost in the backdrop of the tiered city.

We had taken another flight to Jomsom soon after, which was a much smaller city than Kathmandu, which was where we were drinking tea that morning. We'd almost not made it to Jomsom. The plane ride from Kathmandu had been an absolute nightmare, almost derailing the quest before it could start, with an overbooked flight, fog making the runway dangerous, and basically everything that could go wrong. But eventually, through some stroke of luck, we made it. The plus side was that waiting for the flight gave Sajit and myself a few hours to get to know each other.

Sajit was funny, even in the face of danger. He'd been cracking jokes the whole flight as the plane tossed and turned dangerously while everyone else seated around us seemed somber and resigned to death. He was unbelievably smart too, and seamlessly answered every obscure question about the Mustangs (the area we were headed) and Nepal that I asked as the plane finally landed.

Christina had initially put us in contact with each other and had described him as a local fixer and historian when we were planning this excursion. He was clearly well-versed in local mythology, and it influenced his understanding of the Mustangs, which was good, because he wasn't so stuck in rigid academic disbelief as to turn down an offer to kill some evil spirit with me. In fact, as I came to find out, he believed every word of mine and Christina's story when we told it to him over email a month before I arrived. I couldn't believe Christina had been so forthright as she emailed him, but as she typed up a quick synopsis of the evil shadow in my basement, she had assured me he would be on board. As I should have expected, Christina was right.

Sajit had travelled all over his home country of Nepal and the world during his life, studying, researching, and most importantly, talking to people. It gave him insights into beliefs and experiences most other people refuse to acknowledge he told me. During that plane ride he told me about conversations he'd had with people who lived on the outskirts of Gettysburg and what they'd seen, and about researching local legends of Europe. It was fascinating, but as I came to find out, his true love was always the country he'd been born in, which is why he'd returned.

"Today will be a good day to head out and see them. We'll follow the river for as far as we can, since our porter thinks he knows where we're heading. The valley, the river, the tombs—his eyes lit up when I mentioned it. I'd have sworn that description would've been no good, but he knew just what we were looking for," Sajit said as he peered at me from over his still steaming glass with a glow of excitement in his eyes.

Today was the day. We were finally set to see the cliff tombs.

"You're lucky he did too, we'll be passing thousands, you'll see, which would have made searching all of them…well, impossible. But this guy seems to know of a smaller group much further north that matches the description you gave me. He doesn't think any outsiders have seen them before either. I think most of the excavations have been towards the southern end of the region."

Sajit had worked magic as a fixer. He'd gotten us the all-but-impossible permits that allowed me to travel through the Mustangs. I'm telling you, these things are *hard* to get; archeologists would have given their first born to have the permit that Sajit had managed to bribe and finagle his way into.

"Well," Sajit said, rising from his chair, "let's get going."

***

You're probably wondering how I ended up in Nepal. My little stay in the hospital (along with the injuries which the medical team didn't *really* understand, based on the story of being brained with a lead pipe) earned me about three months where I wasn't supposed to do anything.

And I mean absolutely zip. The docs said I had a mild concussion (which made me pretty spacey for a week or two, I'll admit) but the medical team was worried that any stress might make it not-so mild. So, any light from computer screens was a no-go, which meant no work, no TV; "straining myself" was out too, so no work outs, no runs around the park. Not that I'd want to go out now, anyway. Not without Desmond.

I was supposed to be completely bedridden, basically lost in my own thoughts and guilt as if I had never woken up. A catatonic cocoon of self-loathing and helplessness. Which, well, obviously was not going to happen, but my state did earn me short-term disability pay, and some downtime to plot. Samantha had even promised to save my job for me while I recovered. So, there I was with three months of no work, no responsibility and nothing to do…except dwell on that bit of good ol' bitter rage to fuel me. Because that thing had to pay for taking Desmond.

It had to die.

I had enough money coming in from the temporary disability checks to survive, and enough saved up for the trip itself, so the only thing I had to do was formulate the plan and then *make* the eventual trip when my body was up to it.

The whole "no computer screens" was a real bummer for scheduling the plans; and it really hurt my efforts to research and set up the excursion. Luckily, Christina promised to help. Something about seeing the supposed early myth she'd spent much of her professional life studying made her (almost) as determined as me to see it extinguished. Probably because Christina knew how horrid the thing actually was, and what it was rumored to be capable of, even beyond the firsthand knowledge she'd acquired in my kitchen.

So, with her help, connections (she had already been to Nepal through her studies, and knew a ton of people who would help me get there) and just general support, Christina helped me get ready to leave. The only problem was, we didn't know exactly where I was headed, or had some great plan of action once I found it for that matter. I mean, I figured I'd have to use a stake at some point, and we knew the general vicinity of the cave tombs…but that was all. For a little bit, it looked like the trip was going to be a real crapshoot of me wandering aimlessly through Nepal poking things with a sharpened stick.

Enter stage right, my dad.

About a month into planning, just when Christina and I were beginning to hit a wall and some (more) doubt about the whole plan was
beginning to rear its ugly head, my dad called me. He said he wanted
to talk but was pretty cryptic about what.

We met at a bar near me and, to boil down a two-hour conversation to a few paragraphs, he told me about a dream he had the night
Christina, Des, and I were attacked. He remembered it quite vividly.
He said somehow, when he woke up, he knew there was about to be a
phone call about something bad happening to me.

After he explained it, I realized my dad's dream was basically a
continuation of the last dream I'd had. The one with the pretty, dead,
talking lady. As he spoke, the gloominess of the dive bar seemed to
magnify the memory tenfold.

Apparently, had I been able to continue into the cavern uninterrupted by my alarm clock, I would have seen the man responsible for
the past confinement of the shadow. A Nepalese man, clothed in a fur
overcoat and drenched in blood, my dad told me, was screaming as
the whole cave seemed to come alive with shadows and wind. He said
it was like the cave was a vortex of some awful storm, one that erupted
from deep in the earth.

My dad couldn't remember exactly what the man was yelling as
he confronted the shadows, but he could remember small tidbits.
Things about being forced to kill "the whole village," or how he was
"here to end it where it started."

All around him were bodies and signs of a struggle. I remembered
the smeared bloody handprint I had encountered in the dreamscape,
and realized why that priest from Christina's transcript had found such
a desolate town when he first visited the tombs: that man had to kill
them after the shadow took over.

I listened as he continued to tell me how the man battled through the army of smaller shadows that attacked him, before finding himself in front of a giant, dark figure. As the cavern grew louder with angry screams, the wind blowing furiously at this point, the man thrust a sharpened stake into the wretched body. As he did so, the cavern seemed to collapse in.

Complete darkness.

"But then there was a peak of light shining through," my dad continued.

Instead of waking up at that point, the dream went on, and as the world seemed to shake around him, my dad remembered a gloved hand reaching through the pinpoint of light. Soon, the whole world was a burst of white light.

"For a moment, I wasn't me; I was that thing that got stabbed. The dream gets blurry here but, I swear, I remember that gloved hand and a man's face. Then more faces. Then Desmond."

He paused and took a long drink from his glass.

"I don't know why I'm telling you this anyways, Jon. I mean, the dreams have stopped, but I can't stop thinking about that one. And that call about you...I just thought you should know."

I thought he was done, but then he said one more thing.

"I remember a river. It split this huge valley where the cave was. I don't know... it was there when the dream started."

We finished our beers that night, and talked about the shelter, life, and upcoming fights—normal stuff—trying to make small talk. The entire time, it took all of me not sprint out into the streets thanking whatever gods exist for those directions. The truth was finally beginning to emerge through the fog.

***

The rigid landscape was somehow softened by the long wisps of grass that covered it, which seemed to ripple across the winding walkways with each soft gust of cold wind. Sajit was in front of me, walking slowly with his head tilted up to admire the surroundings. Every once in a while, he'd stop, peer up at the encompassing cliffs, and whistle. For a moment, the high-pitched noise would echo around a bit and stir up some distant birds who would shriek back, annoyed at the disturbance. The whistle would slowly die down, and the birds would forget what had bothered them, then we'd be back to walking in silence again.

"I've never seen them before," Sajit said from in front of me. A touch of awe and wonder seeped through his voice, which hung softly in the mountain air. "To think they were able to survive here…to trade and thrive. My People!" Another pause. Another whistle.

The surrounding cliff sides seemed happy to respond to Sajit. All around us, the towering walls of ancient stone returned the high-pitched tone, bouncing the noise back and forth between each other.

The cliffs were a site to behold. Greys, browns, and everything in between made up the pallet of colors that seemed to engulf the horizon. Even the colors of the plants in the area seemed dull, like the tombs had somehow seeped into everything living and had changed their colors to match the landscape.

"I mean, think about how hard it was to get here in a jeep!" Sajit said, bewildered. "They walked here. Can you imagine? I mean in a jeep it was almost impossible."

His long, stark black ponytail was whipped about by the cold mountain winds as he peered about his ancestral homeland with the same amazement that I, too, felt. Any human who could survive the trek here on foot, much less make this their home, deserved nothing but complete reverence and respect.

That the trip was almost impossible was not an understatement either. It had begun as soon as Sajit had finished his tea and had lasted the better part of an absolutely grueling twenty hours.

Roads, when there were some, were uneven: carved from jagged gravel that jerked and pulled us every which way as we slowly progressed down treacherous slopes. The passageways were barely wide enough for the jeep; luckily, we hadn't run into anyone going the opposite way on what was essentially a one-way, or somebody would have been backing up for miles, and miles, and…

To top it all off, there had been a few times when I was all but certain we were going to flip the jeep upside down, as one side rose dangerously towards the tipping point. But every time when all hope seemed lost, to my amazement, our driver would manage to right the sinking ship, at the last moment. After each brush with death, I would glance over at Sajit in bewilderment; only to see my guide casually reading from a hunting magazine, or even dozing off in one particularly dire instance.

Even without the (very real) possibility of dying, the herky-jerky nature of the trip made my head swim. There were a few times when I would begin to feel nauseous, which was a lasting effect of whatever happened in the kitchen. When this happened, I was forced to have the driver pull the car over so I could lose my breakfast real quick before we'd start back up.

We crawled over streams that trickled down from the ancient mountain tops that surrounded us, passed paths carved by countless goat farmers heading to and from market, and further away from the hustle and bustle of the towns, which became few and far between, the longer we went.

It was so beautiful and so sad at the same time. I felt the same melancholy I felt outside the shelter months before. But this time, I felt like I was trespassing on something that wasn't supposed to be seen by humans.

Maybe this was the original Eden? I mused as we drove towards the cliffs. I was feeling extra wanderlusty that day, I'll admit. You can give me a break though, I was pretty sure I was going to die in the not-so-distant future, and there was something so wild and uncontaminated about it all. We were far, far away from any major city or town, and outside of a few farms we passed intermediately, it seemed like we were returning to a world without humans.

The way the cool, crisp air nipped at every piece of exposed skin made me feel more vulnerable than normal. And the deep sadness that had been in the pit of my stomach since I found out what happened to Desmond grew with each kilometer we drove.

How much death did those early villagers, the ones who first settled this beautiful place, see? Why would they stay?

The snowy peaks of the surrounding mountains towered over us as we made our way, apparently unmoved, or unbothered at our advances. They stood above us like ancient gods, who looked down at the small specks slowly moving in their direction without concern.

Onward we moved.

We passed farmers herding their goats, who watched us with only slightly more curiosity than I had imagined the mountains did. We were far away from Everest, the major money maker in the area, roaming where tourists rarely went. Still, the farmers seemed impartial to our existence as we passed them.

Towards those damn tombs.

That night, we sat around a fire quietly. It was just me, Sajit, and Betsa, a porter who normally brought yuppy tourists up Everest, but who was now bringing a yuppy tourist to see some tombs. It was a slow climbing season (later, Sajit would inform me that a recent accident had caught some international air time, and had briefly culled the average CEO's will to climb Everest) so Betsa was offering his services as a driver and jack-of-all-trades. Eventually, we would need him to help us climb into the caves, which would require some serious technical skills that I obviously lacked. That is, if everything went according to plan on the way.

So, there we were, watching the brightly colored flames kick and crackle against the frigid mountain air. We were sitting at the base of the all-encompassing cliffs, which strut from the ground all around us. The veil of smoke from the fire seemed to wrap around our huddled figures, and I'm sure if there were any spectators, from a distance we'd have appeared more fog than human. But we were alone.

Sajit hummed softly, which gave the night an eerie sense of foreboding; almost like the slow musical build up before the big reveal in a horror movie. Betsa sat carving a small figurine from a piece of driftwood that had washed up on the bank of the river we had followed to the cliffs—the same river my dad had dreamt about. I was sitting in silence, taking it all in.

There was something so sacred about the area. Maybe not in a religious sense but there was certainly something special about it.

The overpowering cliffs around us were formed as the earth shifted and changed in a timeframe that would boggle my mind if it was possible for me to truly appreciate how long it took. And there I was, a blip in a timeline that would make those cliffs look like spring chickens. It was a thought-chain that was both depressing, and freeing at the same time; beneath a black ceiling that swirled with pinpoints of light as the chaos of the universe unraveled overhead, I felt serene for the first time in months.

"Why do you want to see them?" Betsa asked, cutting off Sajit's humming in the middle of an especially somber note. He rested his knife and figurine on the ground next to him and leaned forward. His brow was furrowed as he stared at me with the same intensity that an interrogator might stare at their culprit.

I could tell by the tone in his voice that I should tread lightly with my answer. Outside of Sajit, I'd been extremely tight-lipped with my purpose. Not least of all because I knew the site I hoped to use as a sacrificial chamber was of serious historical significance. Very little was known about the genealogy of those early settlers, but there's no doubt they left an important cultural legacy behind. With all the hassle and hoops that we'd needed to jump through to get where we were, I doubted that an experienced porter like Betsa didn't already suspect some underlying reason behind my interest in the site.

"I want to see them…to see where it all began, I guess. Most cultures only have a few cave paintings to mark where they started. There's so much more here. The museum I work at had some artifacts from the area…and I guess I've just been interested in the sky graves since I first heard about them." I realized Betsa might be concerned that I might be trying to steal something from the important site, so I continued, "I know how amazing they are. *That's* why I want to see them."

It was as close to the truth as I planned to go that night.

Betsa grunted and appeared satisfied with the answer. But before Sajit could begin humming again Betsa spoke again: "You know what they say about that place, right?"

I shook my head and tried to appear curious as I gazed at Betsa through the smoke. I'm sure I failed at looking quizzical, and probably appeared to be on the verge of pissing myself; acting was never my strong suit.

He took a moment to think. I could almost hear the gears turning in his head as he weighed his words carefully. English was a second language for Betsa, but it was a tongue he spoke fluently after all his experience dealing with tourists. In the short time I'd know him, I already knew it wasn't like him to take this long to answer.

"They say...they say the place is alive. That the caves hold dead who have not been properly passed on."

He was referring to the modern practice of sky burial, where the body was de-fleshed and cut into bits, then fed to the local scavenger birds. It was a local belief inherited from Tibet Buddhists that a body had to be completely destroyed from the current life to reincarnate in the next one. Before you pass too much judgement, remember most other cultures dress dead people up and parade their corpses in front of their loved ones. Every culture has a death ritual that might seem strange to outsiders.

As if reading my mind, he continued: "No...no, not just that. I remember when I was a child when I first heard about the place." He closed his eyes, as if he was transporting to that very moment again. "My grandfather said that when they—my people, our people—first found the place, they knew it was one of evil. He said that my great-great grandfather was one of the people who first visited the tombs. Who stopped them from ever rising again...who made sure it was finished."

Sajit had been silent the whole time, but he interrupted here.

"Phurba?" he asked. Betsa only nodded, while I sat there confused.

"Dagger...uh..." He stumbled thinking for a moment to find the right word.

"Actually, I think a stake would be a better translation," Sajit finally said.

"Betsa is saying that his great-great grandfather went into the tombs and staked all the bodies to the ground...just to be safe. With the mountain spirits and all." He shrugged as he said it.

Believe it or not, outsider.

"Most of the bodies had already been staked, but there was one in particular, one *specific cave*—" He hissed those last two words; they were much too sinister to say in a normal cadence, apparently. "My grandfather would never talk about it. The most I got out of him was that...well, he said the other caves were just normal burials. But not this one. They were all staked, but they went through again to be sure...*Narasanhāra*..."

"Massacre."

I could feel Sajit's eyes on me as he translated the word muttered by Betsa's grandfather. *That's the one.*

The one that Betsa's great-great-grandfather had visited, who knows how many years ago, to stake some haunted corpses, that's where we were heading.

CHAPTER 15

Like every other morning I'd had since arriving in Nepal, the one after our little ghost story started early. The sun peeked through the channel of cliffs running along the river and flooded the ravine with a startling burst of bright light. The glaring sun filled my tent and made the idea of falling asleep again all but impossible. It was time to get started.

I could hear Betsa and Sajit rummaging around outside, as cooking pans clashed loudly against each other from somewhere beyond my tent flap. The noise filled the valley with a shrill echo as they clattered together like bells, or in this case the world's most obnoxious alarm clock. I peered out from the flaps of my tent and saw the two of them stirring up the embers of the fire from the night before. Hovering above the rapidly growing flames was a tin tea kettle, which had already begun to hiss with steam.

"Coffee?" Sajit called from outside the tent, as I fumbled through my stuffed backpack to find the portable French press I'd lugged along.

"Hell yeah!" I yelled back a little too enthusiastically. There was no way I'd be able to handle whatever was ahead of us without my daily injection of caffeine, and Sajit and Betsa's tea didn't cut it. It was strong, sure, but not what this lil steamboat needed to get his engine revving.

Christina had made fun of me as I packed the coffee maker (something snarky about being a stereotypical millennial, or hipster, or whatever) but staying caffeinated was in-tune with staying alive at this point. Plus, it helped with the headaches which hadn't completely subsided after the kitchen debacle. However, that morning my head felt as clear as the glassy blue sky that hung above us.

I quickly dressed in my hiking gear and made my way outside. It was October, and the cold morning air was refreshing as I emerged from my stuffy sleeping quarters. The day before, Sajit had informed us that it would be relatively cool until the afternoon, when it would warm up slightly for our stay in the Mustangs—perfect weather for the excursion we had planned.

On that day, we were heading to the base of the cliffs to pin down which specific cave we'd be heading into first. Most of the sky graves were fairly small in size, around ten feet by ten feet, but we knew we were looking for one that was significantly larger. Christina had informed me as we researched and planned together that most of the tombs seemed to be carved out by hand; but based on what we knew about the size and dimensions of the tomb we were looking for, Christina and I figured the one I was interested in was most likely a natural phenomenon. A cave or cavern that had been formed by nature, rather than created by humans.

Betsa's story from the night before only helped further my belief that we were headed in the right direction and that, for whatever reason, the dreams were all connected and not, simply, a coincidence. The dreams were a real concern that had kept me tossing and turning in my bed more nights than I care to admit, especially as my dad was having them too.

I might be heading towards my death…but least I'm heading towards something.

Coffee and tea were brewed, steeped, and poured as we braced ourselves for the day. Staring up at the cliffs made the mission seem even more daunting than it ever had before. Their rugged fronts were littered with an innumerable amount of small, black openings that were no doubt cliff graves on the stone facades which seemed to stretch on forever. The river and meadows that somehow managed to snake through all this were dwarfed in magnitude by the surroundings.

And there we were, three small specks drinking our breakfasts, and peering up at the stone gods all around us. If there was anywhere for an evil entity to be spawned, this was it.

I wish Desmond could see this.

The thought made me choke on my coffee. Betsa raised his eyebrow at me, but thankfully didn't say anything, because I wouldn't have been able to answer without sobbing. As I sat there on a piece of driftwood which served as a makeshift bench, I felt that hollow feeling expand in my gut; the coffee became tasteless.

Truth be told, I hadn't really come to terms with what happened to Desmond. Instead, I'd just been stuffing the feelings of complete and utter sadness deeper and deeper down, waiting to unleash it on the cause. The thought of his last moments entrapped in that thing— all to save me—was enough to make me want to hurl myself off one of the conveniently located cliffs.

I blamed myself for the whole ordeal. Sure, the rational side of my inner psyche could argue all day that I did everything I could, that anyone else would have abandoned Des long before the kitchen, but that didn't drown out the other voices of doubt and blame, which reared their ugly heads a little too frequently.

You couldn't save him then, and you won't be able to get your—

The internal voice of self-doubt was cut off by an outside one before it could get too self-deprecating.

"So, you and Christina think we're looking for an actual cave?" Sajit asked, his eyes tracing the fragmented cliffs for any irregularities that might hint at something beneath it. I didn't have the heart to tell him we were looking for a needle in a haystack, though I'm sure he knew.

I nodded in response, trying to regain my composure. I think if I'd spoken then, my voice would have cracked worse than it ever did in middle school.

"Why are you looking for this specific one?" Betsa asked, curiosity rising in his voice. I had forgotten he was under the impression I was just here to see some tombs.

I managed to shake it off, and answered (without my voice cracking I'd like to point out), "The museum I work at has some artifacts from this specific tomb, I wanted to photograph it for them while I'm here, so they can use the pictures in an exhibit."

The answer seemed to satisfy Betsa, who went back to packing for the day. From what I could tell, Sajit had not told Betsa anything beyond what I had mentioned around the fire about the real aims of this trip. Which was good, since based on the story he told about his grandfather, I doubted Betsa would be on board with bringing a tourist to his probable death if he knew the truth of our venture.

I made a mental note to ask Betsa to return to camp once we found what we were looking for, so he wouldn't get wrapped up in all this. There'd been enough innocent bystanders dragged into this already. No need for one more.

As for Sajit, I doubted there was enough money in the world to convince him not to enter the cave with me. He seemed *excited* about the whole thing if you can believe it and carried himself throughout the trip with a bravado that would have put a prime Rambo to shame. Even from our brief time together, I could tell Sajit had a bit of a wild streak; which, coupled (and probably quelled) with his spiritual beliefs, made him gung-ho for the chance to kill some shadow vampires that haunted his people's land. Every time I'd mentioned the shadow to him, his eyes lit up with a devilish sparkle.

The three of us quickly packed up the gear we might need for that day as the coffee and tea disappeared. We left most of the camp intact since we planned to return later that night. All in all, it took less than a half hour to get ready.

We planned to use the current setup as a sort of basecamp. It was close to the river and on fairly level ground. Everything one could ask for when camping.

We started walking towards the closest cliff wall, which, despite filling the landscape, was still a serious hike away. The three of us crossed the river holding the gear above our heads while we waded slowly through the rushing waters. Two months earlier this little soak would have been all but impossible, since it would have been during Nepal's monsoon season, which would have made the river much too deep to traverse. In October, though, the water had subsided enough to allow us a freezing, but accessible passage to the other side.

The walk across the river sapped my energy, and I found myself dragging-ass less than half an hour into the day. Still, work needed to be done, and I bit down on my metaphorical mouth guard and plunged forward.

Sajit and Betsa were both uncharacteristically quiet. I think the otherworldly landscape demanded their respect. I know I certainly felt like my words would only pollute the pure surroundings. Layers of browns, purples, and every color in between peaked through each layer of the higher altitude, giving the skyline a never-ending base of majestic stripes beneath the empty sky.

As we moved away from the river, we trampled through the lush foliage of plants that had set their roots as close to the nutrient rich riverbank as they could. The further and further from the river we went, the more the dulled green at our feet seemed to give way to a variety of brown and grey. It was a place teeming with life, but also death.

A perfect duality.

I don't know how far we walked (not to be melodramatic, but it felt like forever) before we came to the base of the first cliff. I turned to see how far the camp was in the distance and I could just make out the three, barely visible small points of white that were our tents.

"Here we are," Sajit said, finally breaking the silence. His tone was somber, and reverence practically radiated from him as he pressed one hand against the cliff wall. He reached out so slowly, so tentatively, it was as if he expected to be shocked once he made contact with it. No sparks flew, however, so he leaned all his weight against the granite wall and looked about.

"Look here!" I heard Betsa say, before I could ask a million questions about how we planned on scaling this thing.

Sajit and I walked over to Betsa, who was staring in disbelief at the rocky, fragment covered ground.

"Is that...?"

Betsa slowly nodded.

At the base of the cliff, less than a foot from Betsa's worn trekking shoes, was a broken piece of a human jawbone. The sun had bleached it, and the majority of the teeth were missing, but there was no doubt we were ogling human remains.

"It must have fallen in a landslide," Sajit said quietly. The jaw poked out of the gravel like any other stick or piece of debris might, but this had been part of a human at some point. Now, it was strewn unceremoniously on the rocky ground. And it was, in many ways, a sign of things to come.

We looked around the area and found an array of human bones scattered around the base of the cliff. Landslides and mini earthquakes were common in the area, and like Sajit had guessed, it was likely that one of the two had been responsible for sending the contents of a grave tumbling down the cliffside.

Along with the bones there were a few rusted copper artifacts mixed in with the gravel. They seemed to be mostly trinkets that were buried with the dead above us, and their new home in the dirt made it difficult to tell what any of them were as the chalky grey dirt made them unrecognizable.

We left everything as it was. Well...almost everything. The only artifact laying in the gravel that was even remotely identifiable was a particularly sinister looking phurba, which Sajit pointed out. It was sticking handle up out of the ground as if someone had stabbed it into the ground and walked away years ago.

I didn't say anything when it happened. As Betsa and I went back to surveying the area around the stake, I saw a quick flurry of movement out of the corner of my eye: it was Sajit, who picked the weapon up and swiftly tucked it away in his backpack. I knew it wasn't exactly kosher archeological practice, but it was on the ground, and it was his peoples', so who was I to say anything?

Besides, that quick snag is, in part, the reason I'm alive today typing this.

After we'd gotten our fill of the macabre, we began mapping out how we were going to get into the tombs. Looking up, I counted at least four entrances to caves on this cliff wall. It was no doubt a difficult climb and all eyes were on Betsa, the climbing expert.

"I think we have to go up, then down."

The plan was to walk along the cliff until we found a path up. Then, once we were on the platform above, we would climb down. It would be safer, since there would be less of a chance of a landslide, and it would make Betsa's job of bringing two inexperienced climbers with him much easier.

As we walked along the bottom of the cliff, I remembered Christina telling me that it is theorized the tombs were built by tunneling from the top of the cliff down. So, in a way, we were following in ancient (and successful) footsteps.

My mind drifted back to Christina during the trek. I'm sure it'll be of no shock to you, observant reader, that we were dating by this point. I'd officially asked her out about a week before leaving for Nepal, but even before that, we were dating in all but the most official sense. Part of me felt a little guilty leaving her for what was potentially a suicide mission, but she seemed so confident that I'd return, that it rubbed off on me a bit.

Maybe it was a moment of selfishness, but I couldn't leave Christina without allowing her to make an honest man of me. It was very 'kiss before shipping off to war,' asking her out and all, but the heart wants what it wants, I suppose. There was a moment too, that I was worried she was going to try and join me on the trip. I couldn't lose her and Des, I couldn't...

Luckily, she was preparing for her doctoral defense and couldn't bail on that. Christina was smart beyond the academic world and I think she knew this was something I needed to do alone.

So, there I was, with Sajit and Betsa, my girl halfway across the world. We walked for what felt like an eternity, though could really have been minutes. I was too lost in thoughts of Christina's electric emerald eyes and fiery red hair (two things I was certain I would never see again) to keep track of something as pointless as time. My mind was beginning to drift to other parts of her that I'd never see again, when a sudden holler brought me back to the real world at the base of the cliffs.

"Path!" Betsa hollered in excitement, ripping me from my daydreams as he pointed to a narrow space leading up. It was a trail in the most liberal sense of the word, and in no way deserved to be described as a path.

"It's straight up…" Sajit said, and he wasn't wrong either. The path jutted up like a stairway to heaven…well probably not *heaven*, but definitely up to somewhere metaphysical. The only difference between the supposed path and the rest of the cliff face was that the spot where Betsa pointed was smooth. Without him, I would've walked right past it without so much as a sideways glance.

"Ancient goat path. Doesn't look like it's been used in a while. Probably because of this area's reputation. We'll follow it up, it must lead to the top," he said. He was being concise, clearly reinforcing the point that this was the *only* way up. If we wanted to see the damn thing, we'd shut up and listen to him.

And we did.

The trek up was slow and grueling. I mean, it was ten rounds of sparring with a fresh opponent coming in every round to make you beg for mercy grueling. There was no daydreaming of Christina's kickin' body, or anything for that matter, since every ounce of my being was concentrated on surviving the climb. We were essentially bear-crawling up a 75-degree cliff, with few (if any) holds to grab onto.

I'd been last in line on our climb up, and even with the path being smoothed out generations ago by a bunch of goats, rocks and crumbling dirt rained down on my head every meter or so. The silt caked my sweaty face, essentially blinding me to the world above.

"Doing okay down there?" I heard Betsa shout down.

"Peachy!"

Laughter echoed down, along with another wave of pebbles. By this point I was climbing with my eyes closed in an effort to shield myself from the falling debris. With each clumsy, blind paw above my head, I prayed I would find something to grab onto so that I could hoist myself up. And, amazingly enough, I always did.

Every muscle in my body strained as I climbed but my legs burned the worst. Each lunge up the incline briefly allowed one leg to fill with a dull, numb reprieve, while the other side would be filled with a fiery burn that would make a demon sweat. Another push forward, and the pain and numbness would switch sides; I think the constant on/off made it worse.

I could practically hear my heart pounding in my ears as my lungs burned with molten lava…but I didn't dare stop to catch my breath. I knew that if I stopped at this point, I'd be dead in the water, and there would be no further climb that day.

So, I continued to push on.

As I fought to focus on something other than the physical pain, that sweet voice inside my head started offering me a way out, and softly, it made reasonable suggestions.

Who are you kidding? You'll be no good when you get there, you'll be too tired. Why don't you tell them you want to go back down and rest? Hell, while you're at it, why don't you tell them you don't really need to see the caves? Go see some tourist attractions, you're recovering still. You tried. No one will fault you if you don't finish this. You tried. Des would understand…

It was so tempting. I mean, nobody *would* fault me, especially since nobody really knew why I was even in Nepal.

But I couldn't give up. I promised myself that my body would have to go before I allowed myself to quit.

And it almost came to that. My forearms were just about to give way. They felt like balloons that had been blown up too full and some idiot was about to deliver the balloon-popping gust…but then I heard Sajit and Betsa laughing ahead of me. I gritted my teeth so hard I could practically hear my jaw screech like the brakes of a train trying desperately to stop, and I clawed furiously into the dirt path. I forgot about the heavy lead weights in my arms, legs, and every inch of me for that matter. I forgot about the dry dirt caked into my fingernails, which made my hands feel as dry as a mummified corpse.

Almost there. Almost there.

I repeated those two words in my mind *ad nauseum*. I knew that if I let any other thoughts cross my mind, that voice of doubt would become overpowering.

Almo—

There it was. A bright blue backdrop replaced the earthy brown that had dominated my blurred vision the whole way up. I felt two pairs of hands grab each of my shoulders and hoist me up as my legs became suddenly lighter.

When it all came to, I was standing in an open vista that was surrounded by more mountains, but that were too far away to be intimidating. The ground we had been on hours before was hundreds of feet beneath us.

As my blurred vision slowly began to gain focus, I noticed that even Betsa looked tired.

"That was steep," he finally admitted after we all caught our breath. There was a moment of silence, where I think he expected to be chastised for prodding us up the path; it never came though. For some reason, hearing Betsa admit that the trail we took was steep was the funniest thing I'd ever heard.

A soft chuckle soon turned into a deafening howl. It was a laugh so aggressive it would have fit right in at an insane asylum and it would have been embarrassing if I was alone.

But I wasn't.

Betsa and Sajit were doubled over, laughing just as maniacally as I was. Had someone asked, I doubt anyone of us would have been able to explain what was so funny. Nevertheless, something was, and we laughed and laughed until tears streamed down our faces.

I think it was Sajit who stopped first. After we had all finally managed to regain control of ourselves, Betsa spoke.

"We'll rest here for a few moments. Then, we will enter the first tomb."

I dropped down where I stood to rest. My body was completely numb, but already I was beginning to feel rejuvenated as a slow and steady pump of adrenaline surged through my body.

Go time.

CHAPTER 16

I always hated feeling claustrophobic. It was probably programmed in me before I was little more than a bundle of growing cells. Maybe it was genetic, or maybe I had some horrific experience I couldn't remember.

Who knows?

What I do know, however, is that there was always something about that feeling that the whole world was crashing down on me that was tough to stomach. I hated that creeping sense that I was about to be so compressed that the very air would be sucked from my lungs as the free space about me slowly shrunk, until eventually, there would be nowhere to move in a vacuum of darkness as I collapsed into nothingness with a *pop*.

Small spaces just gave me the heebie-jeebies something fierce.

Yet, there I was about to slowly begin wiggling through the entrance of a small, dark opening in the cliff side. As I stood, well, *hung* there rather, in front of the pit's opening, I stared into the deep cavernous entrance.

There was something so *familiar* about it.

That's when I remembered it. The broken jawbone we had found on the ground somewhere hundreds of feet beneath where I was.

It's like entering the black, glaring mouth of a skull. One that's smiling with sinister intentions as my miniscule self dangles helplessly in front of it. A mouth that leads down. Down to twists and turns that'll bring you into the belly of the beast. I'm just an appetizer to this thing.

The voice of doubt from earlier became the voice of the skeleton who I'd envisioned being engulfed by. The dry voice somehow became even more hollow and soulless than before, which must have been a difficult task.

C'mon stupid! it jeered with a cackle. *What's the worst that can happen in a claustrophobic grave, ten stories in the sky? It's not like those things are ten nightmares wrapped into a big bundle of screw you. Sheesh, you thought the basement was bad; boy, oh boy, do we have something for you!*

Scattered boulders and rocks that rested along the bottom of the tomb's entrance gave the opening a row of bottom teeth. I kicked at one, and heard it bounce somewhere into the darkness. The *clitter-clatter* of the rock echoed deep in the unseen, while the sudden movement of the kick also sent me swaying weightlessly in the air. Above me I heard Betsa yell down.

"Jon! What are you doing down there?" An almost paternal worry seeped into his voice. I'm sure he was just worried that a climbing accident here would not bode well for the tourism industry Betsa's livelihood depended on.

Though, maybe by this point he was coming around to me. I guess I had shown some good ol' fashioned gumption when I insisted on being the first one to descend. I wanted to make sure that if anything happened to me, Betsa (who had been brought in under false pretenses) was able to escape. It was the least I could do, after all.

And maybe Betsa was impressed a bit.

"Checking to make sure the mouth…eh-entrance…was stable," I hollered up. It was a pretty solid lie to come up with on the spot. Plus, it sounded a lot better than "kicking a pretend skeleton in the mouth."

A grunt from the heavens let me know Betsa thought it was a good idea to check the spot that I planned to land on. Better safe than sorry; it certainly didn't hurt to make sure the hovering ledge wouldn't give way the second I dropped my weight on it. I slowly applied my weight

181

to the floor of the cave's opening, and I did so with a soft, tenderness that would have led you to tears, dear reader.

I started with the very tiptoe of my trekking boot and slowly applied more pressure until eventually I felt the harness begin to go slack behind me. By this point, I was completely supporting my own weight on the ledge in a wildly uncomfortable crouched position. I was also trying to ignore the (horrifying) distant pitter-patter of loose gravel somewhere far down below.

As I adjusted my footing, I took a deep breath that had been stuck somewhere in my chest during the whole climb down. The smell that drifted up from the cave, and I know this will be hard to believe, was *not* unpleasant. With the wind whistling behind me softly, I was reminded of when I was younger and would open the cupboard in the kitchen to steal some chocolate chips. It was that same burst of the smell of dried spices and the old wood of the cabinet that drifted up from somewhere deep in the cavern below.

I flipped on the switch on the headlamp I was wearing. The dark, serpentine tunnel immediately filled with a burst of light, but even with the bright beam shining in, darkness blurred the edges of my field of vision. I felt like I was a deep-sea scuba diver who was about to disappear into a murky abyss. Into a void filled with the monsters that hunted ancient sailors and haunted the mind of Lovecraft; I could practically see the tentacles slowly emerging from the depths to grab me.

"Good down there?" Betsa called, clearly anxious about my lack of movement.

"Never better. I'm going to move in slowly while you land. The ledge seems fine, but I wouldn't recommend doing any jump squats on it."

My voice sounded strange as it echoed in both the cave and through the open emptiness behind me. Apparently hearing a human voice in the area was a rarity, since behind me I heard a group of birds screech loudly as they flew away from the sound. Their shrill caws only added to the unsettling atmosphere that had led to a light tingling coursing through my veins. As the adrenaline rush washed over me, I had to bite down hard to stop my teeth from chattering, the noise of which would have been amplified a hundredfold in the tunnel.

There was a soft rat-a-tat of feet behind, and I turned in the tight space to see Sajit staring at me, well, past me, I guess. Without warning, he flipped his headlights on much the same way as I had when I first landed.

"Hey!" A blinding ray of light sent me scurrying to cover my face.

"Sorry."

From the crook of my elbow, I saw the area around me darken once more. As I looked up and through the flurries of fireflies dancing around my vision, I was slowly able to make out Sajit's outline again.

"It opens up a few feet down, we'll all be able to fit," I informed him, as he crawled forward to give Betsa a spot to land. As we waited, I heard soft *clings* echoing above.

"Anchors for when we go back up. He's putting them in as softly as he can so as not to disturb anything. Don't want a...well, you know." Sajit was looking past me still as he spoke. There was a look of awe gleaming across his face.

"Yeah, a cave-in would not be ideal." I paused. "Do you have it?"

He looked at me confused for a moment, and then a sheepish grin slowly crept across his sweat glazed face.

"You saw?"

I nodded in confirmation.

"Well yes...I do." He patted his thigh. Then he asked, "Do you have yours?"

I too patted my leg. When I applied the pressure to my thigh, the cool, metallic press of the spike was applied to my leg muscles that were still screaming in agony. The long metal stake felt like the best ice pack that ever existed.

"Good. I think we're gonna need them."

The stake, or *Phurba,* had been my first purchase in Nepal. After meeting in the airport, Sajit and I had spent the night in Kathmandu before making our way to Jomsom. While there, Sajit had introduced me to a seller of…well, peculiar items are what we'll call them. I hadn't been able to justify taking the one from the museum, dire as my situation was; it just seemed dirty. Which is why I was on a mission to get one while in Kathmandu.

"You're going to need something special," my new friend informed me as he led me past a maze of booths that were filled with delicious smelling food, climbing equipment, and other various trinkets meant to draw in travelers such as myself. The outdoor market was bustling, and as we cut through the chaotic scene my first impression of Nepal was that it was overwhelming.

Not like New York City overwhelming, where you feel like the city might engulf you and you'll disappear forever if you don't stand your ground…but overwhelming in the sense that Kathmandu seemed to be alive. It was a living organism, composed of sights and smells that were so different, but so pleasant too. And humans were just a small part of this thriving, living entity.

I listened to merchants haggling with college-age kids (all of whom were rocking a Buddha necklace of some sort), watched as serious-looking climbers moseyed through the streets like gangs of soccer hooligans, and was completely taken aback by the vibrant colors that seemed to decorate every square inch of the space. Nepalese children scooted about playing a game of soccer that included walls, bystanders, and any obstacle that might emerge, but no one seemed to mind.

Laughter, voices, music; all these human noises floated like butterflies through the corridors of trade. It took everything in me to stay

184

disciplined and follow behind Sajit, and not just slowly disappear into the backdrop. To become a part of everything that was happening here.

"He'll have it. If anyone does, it's this g—" Sajit's voice cut in-and-out, overpowered by the smashing *cling* of cymbals that some patron was testing out enthusiastically before purchasing. I got the gist of what he meant.

We eventually ducked down a side passage, and the crowd that had submerged us in a sea of humanity became a thing of the past. The walkway was narrow, and the two of us walked single file as prayer flags fluttered in the space above us.

And though I didn't know it at the time, the grey front of the store and apartment walls that made up the alleyway had a startling resemblance to the cliff graves I'd soon find myself in.

"Here we are!" Sajit said from a few feet in front of me as he suddenly disappeared into a doorway which looked the exact same as the hundreds we had passed on our way over. I followed him into the white framed archway and was immediately awestruck by the shelves of items that filled the small room.

A cabinet of curiosities.

The bright glisten of shiny trinkets contrasted with the dull texture of ancient ones. Each rested on wooden shelves that seemed to have grown out of the concrete walls on their own. It was cluttered, no doubt, but there was a strange sense of order that prevented it from being overwhelming. Instantly my eyes fell on a row of books towards the back that made my heart flutter in excitement. I stepped in their direction but forced myself to stop. That's not why you're here.

"Thomson! Thomson!"

Sajit was yelling towards two doors located behind a small counter that contained nothing on it save a dated cash register. The doors he hollered at belonged in an old west saloon. They were parted in the center and made of the same wood as the shelves. They looked as though a gunslinger was about to bust in and stir up some trouble.

"He'll be right out," Sajit turned to me and said, though I hadn't heard anyone reply to him.

As we waited, I looked around the shop that was little more than one room, though a room stuffed to the brim. I felt like a kid in a candy shop or, perhaps more aptly, a spectator in Indiana Jones' dreams. Clearly, this was a shop meant to appeal to western tourists chasing a sense of adventure, I realized.

Surrounding me were artifacts that belonged in museums. Some of the items were clearly from Nepal: ornate Buddhas and other items cluttering the overstocked shelves which gave me flashbacks to that old box I had wrangled down from the Museum's attic, but there were other things too. An old suit of knight's armor stood in the corner of the store like an outdated security guard who was keeping watch on the joint. I also noticed a real, honest-to-god Sioux peace pipe on another shelf amongst ancient Ottoman weaponry. It would have been easy to miss, seeing as it looked like a weapon itself, but wasn't. The dark, glazed wood piece was no doubt original. It wasn't like those bedazzled, overly ornate pipes sold to ponytail rocking white guys who claim to be "two percent Cherokee." No, this was real, and how it ended up in Nepal was a mystery and a half on its own. I felt a twinge of guilt, seeing it for sale in a shop and suddenly wished I hadn't.

This stuff shouldn't be for sale.

"Sajit, seriously, what is this place? Are we *in* the black market?"

(I know the black market is not a physical location; but it was either that, or I'd stumbled into the Nepalese version of "Needful Things.")

Sajit laughed. "It's just a store. Promise. Thomson has traveled the world. I think he was in the Peace Corps. I know it's not great, but…"

Sajit looked around for a marketing sign, or something to explain what this store was. When he realized there wasn't anything except for the items, he shook his head like a dog drying off, and continued his explanation.

"Anyways, he did *something*, and as he traveled, he bought or traded things. Then traded some more…and some more. Now, I think he mostly buys stuff decommissioned from museums. Don't you work at a museum?"

I nodded but was too distracted by a pair of dueling pistols to answer with anything more than an amazed mumble.

"Sajit, you fiend! What the hell are you doing here this early? I expected you to tumble in five minutes before closing."

"Thomson! You still look like hell; how's it going old friend?"

The two men laughed, then shared an awkward embrace over the glass counter case that was filled with even more collectibles. They were polar opposites: Sajit wasn't tall by any means, but still he towered above the short and stocky Thomson. Sajit was athletic, while it was evident by the slight beer belly hanging over Thomson's belt that his was a sedentary lifestyle. His pale white skin seemed to further acknowledge that Thomson did not get outside much, especially when compared to Sajit's sun-darkened skin and stark black hair. While they both had ponytails, Thomson's was grey.

Still, despite how different the two men were, they shared a similar electric energy. The same energy that filled the warm-up room before a kickboxing fight. A feeling of excitement, of the potential of something explosive happening. And that energy was rippling through the store in waves.

"Well, my friend here is looking for a thing. A thing I think my other friend might have a few of. A few he's looking to get rid of too," Sajit said.

Thomson stroked his goatee and leaned forward on the glass barrier.

"Well don't keep me waiting in suspense, what's the man looking for?"

They were speaking as if I wasn't in the room, which might have been annoying in another circumstance, but I was too enamored with Thomson's merchandise to really care.

"Nothing too big…just a few daggers. Stakes, rather."

I had drifted over to the counter by this point, seeing as it was *my* vendetta that was the reason we were all gathered together.

Thomson scrunched his wildly unkempt grey eyebrows quizzically and dropped one elbow down on the counter. I could now see that the viewing glass of the counter (that was now supporting all of Thomson's weight) was in desperate need of a wipe down. Smeared fingerprints and smudges streaked across the dull glass, making it a muddled grey color.

With Thomson posed like the western bartender those swinging doors behind him deserved, I decided to speak up.

"I'm looking for something that would've, or could've I guess, been used ceremonially. In a ceremony to be specific."

"Of course! Of Course! Ceremonial weapons. Hell, we've got a whole damn bundle. Why stop at a stake? I mean, have you ever seen a ceremonial axe, kid? We got one lying about here somewhere. Just let me find it!"

He spun around and began rummaging before I could respond. With his back turned to me, I noticed a long, jagged scar that ran down his neck until it disappeared beneath his flannel. I imagine collections like his don't come together without some close encounters.

"Don't need an axe. A stake will do," I said. I looked towards Sajit for backup, but I could tell by the look on his face that he had wanted to see whatever a ceremonial axe looked like.

"Suit yourself. I'll be back in a jiffy!" The saloon doors were swinging back and forth before I had even looked back from the disappointed Sajit.

"I told you he'd have one. He's a cool cat…weird, but definitely cool. And he's got a lot here in this store." Sajit now leaned forward on the glass counter the same way Thomson had only moments before. "You think a stake will work? I mean you saw the shadow, right? Can a stake *really* kill it? Can it even die?"

As he asked, he stared a little too intently at an old map hanging behind the counter. He was purposefully avoiding eye contact.

It was the first time since we'd met that Sajit had mentioned the shadow. Sure, he had emailed us about them, but I could tell by the way he was avoiding eye contact that he was either genuinely concerned, or thought it sounded stupid to say out loud.

Or maybe both.

"It's as good a guess as I've got. It sure seemed to recoil the first time it saw me with one." I was going to leave it at that, but a little sliver of guilt made me keep talking. I couldn't lie to Sajit if I planned on dragging him along with me. "But I don't know. It might be impossible to kill. We're in uncharted territory here if I'm being honest, and I get it if you don't want to—"

He cut me off before I could finish, shaking his head back and forth, and slowly waving his hand in the air to let me know he didn't even want to hear it. He knew the risks and he was fine with them.

"I think the stake will work. I bet it will." He sounded like a man who was putting the last of his chips on black twenty-one and who enjoyed the finality of it more than he feared the risk of losing it all.

"Here you are, my young friend!" Thomson emerged holding a blood-red silk wrapping, which draped over a long, skeletal shape. For a fleeting moment, I half-expected him to pull the covering away to reveal a contraption of loaded springs, which would send out a wave of paper mâché flowers or snakes. The whole presentation seemed like a magic act with Thomson transformed into the lead performer.

But no snakes or flowers showered me, no magic wand appeared to amaze the audience. Instead, a long copper rod emerged from behind the maroon drapery. The handle was ornately carved with the powerful wings of a hawk, and the sharpened, serrated tip would have made Queequeg smile with delight. Seeing it I had a flashback to the museum's attic, where I had found the stake that would lead us to contacting Christina.

The hawks…they were hawks, I thought, remembering that when I had held the museum's stake, I hadn't known what the design was. I realized the stake that I held in my hand was an almost exact replica to the first one I'd seen, just a little nastier, and a little more ready for business.

"Won't tell you how I got it. Never do. Company policy, you see."

A magician never reveals his trick…

I shook my head vigorously to let him know I didn't care how he got it, though that twinge of guilt hit again, this time a little harder. Sajit wolf-whistled at the inanimate object beside me.

"How much?" I asked curtly. My funds were running dangerously low at this point, but I knew this was as important as the plane ticket here. I needed that stake.

I won't bore you with the haggling process, but I didn't need to sell my soul or anything like that. The price we settled on was fair for both the buyer and the seller, and after the deal was done the two of us shook hands.

"Pleasure doing business. Sajit said you'd be here for a few days. Swing by again before you leave—new inventory shipment coming in, I'd love to show it off to somebody."

I smiled and nodded. I didn't have it in me to tell him I likely wouldn't be walking through those doors again.

"Watch out!"

Sajit awkwardly waddled forward, which forced me deeper into the tunnel. Behind me, the *thud-thud* of feet let me know that the three amigos were back in business.

Without saying a word, the three of us began to move in unison. The climbing gear temporarily disappeared, and beams of headlights and flashlights cut through the darkness. When we were ready—well, as ready as we could be—I took the first step forward. Then another.

We slowly sunk into the darkness. The headlamps and flashlights seemed to be an effort of futility, as their puny beams were engulfed by the all-encompassing shadow.

And we were swallowed by the pit.

CHAPTER 17

"What do you see?"

It was a fair question. I mean the tunnel was only big enough for one person to squeeze through at a time, which meant even my small frame was certainly obscuring Sajit and Betsa's view into the cave.

"About as much as you." It came out snarky, but I swear it wasn't supposed to. The truth was I couldn't see much at all. Even though Christina had warned me that the cave tombs this far north were unique, I still hadn't been prepared, and was just then beginning to realize how different these graves really were.

Most of the cliff tombs in the Mustangs (especially in the more accessible areas closer to Jomsom) were real, honest to God caves. And by that, I mean in the way I pictured caves before this trip based on the caveman cartoons I used to watch every Saturday morning. These easier-to-reach tombs had wide openings and were more similar to rooms carved into cliffs than they were tunnels. They were big enough to house multiple people at once and, as Christina had informed me, one that had been excavated contained the remains of at least thirteen people. They were pretty cavernous in design.

This was *not* the case for the area we were exploring. The entrances were much smaller, but they led to a series of connected passages and rooms once you managed to squeeze in. In many ways, it was like a hidden city beneath the wall of a cliff. The closer to Tibet you got, the more this shift in the sites was noticeable, and we were about as close as you could get.

"It'll open up. You wait. It will." Sajit's voice filled the tunnel with confidence, and I knew he was right.

The few excavations of this area had revealed some extremely well-preserved Buddhist paintings and shrines lurking within. The present problem, however, was finding these hidden rooms in the dark. As we slowly bumbled forward, I mentally ran through the checklist of everything I knew about what we were looking for.

The entrance we're in looks like it wasn't man-made. It was certainly by erosion.

This checked out. From the dreams, I knew I was looking for a naturally made cavern, not a finished room like we might've found in another area. Besides, it just made sense. Wherever the shadow spawned from, I doubt it would be a place that a human would want to spend any amount of time in.

You're looking for the site of a massacre.

That much was evident from the dreams and Betsa's story. I needed to fill in some gaps, but I was pretty sure I knew what happened. After the villager managed to stake the original entity, he had either died or offed himself. Leaving the place frozen in the moment of the tragedy. Which is why Betsa's great-great-relative had visited the site along with the condescending missionary. The fact that he had most likely killed himself was understandable too, given that he had to kill his entire village and all.

That was about the extent of my excavation plan and what signs I was snooping for. Looking back, it wasn't great, but you gotta start somewhere.

As Sajit had predicted, after a few more feet of slow, crouched progress, the tunnel transformed into a cave. Standing up was a sweet relief for my cramped lower back and legs, which were still in pain from the climb up only hours before.

I glanced around and let the head torch bathe the area in light. As it filled nooks and crannies that hadn't been seen by human eyes for hundreds of years, I heard Betsa and Sajit gasp in awe behind me.

"Look up, Jon…"

I glanced up slowly as an explosion of nerve endings somewhere deep in my gut made me feel as if I was floating: my body was preparing me for the fight. A wave of anticipation and excitement hit me like a fifty-foot wave crashing down from above.

Could it already be time? Could it already be here? You've been waiting for this since you woke up. It's almost over. It's almost over.

"Jon, look!" Sajit said. Sharper this time.

I jerked my head up and let the light beam do the rest, ready to see whatever waited. The light revealed a smooth dome that had been carefully carved into the top of the room, which gave it a cathedral feel. Scrawled across the spherical ceiling was a colorful mural of Buddhist imagery that filled it completely in rich hues of blue, gold, red, and dull yellows.

"Do you think anyone's ever seen this before?" Sajit asked.

I was too lost in amazement to immediately respond. An image of the Buddha practically filled the entire dome, though he wasn't alone. Elephants, tigers, and other obscured animals paraded across the colorful backdrop in harmony. It was at that moment I remembered the Buddhist belief system and their views on humane treatment of animals. Dots started to connect.

Maybe that's why the shadow hated Desmond.

It evolved and witnessed a culture that revered them and being the antithesis of what is right and good in this world it quickly grew to despise animals.

Betsa's voice cut me off before I could explore my idea any deeper. "There weren't any signs of recent climbers on our way down, and looters would have made a mess of this place."

"Thank God no looters got to this," I murmured. My voice sounded small, like it was a hundred miles away while I relished in the discovery. I was completely awestruck at the cave painting's beauty and thankful no tomb raiders had rooted through this place. It's an unfortunate fact of history and archeology that those who would look to preserve a site are normally a step behind those who would look to profit off of it.

I finally managed to peel my eyes away from the artwork when I realized that the drawing almost guaranteed this wasn't the tomb we were searching for. Somebody had spent a lot of time here creating the mural and it was likely an important site to the ancient community that visited it.

"Crap," I whispered.

"What's wrong?" Betsa asked, hearing my frustration.

"Nothing. Let's just push forward a bit and see what else is here."

The three of us continued exploring the maze of rooms.

Most of them were similar to the first one we had stumbled upon, with artwork on the walls and not much else.

I can't stress enough how huge the cave complex we were in actually *was*. Each room was big enough to hold several people at once, which made the connected underground structure seem like we had stumbled into the remaining city of a civilization that operated completely underground. We were basically walking around a slate stone maze. It was overwhelming to think there were more tunnels like this one, but even then, I knew the show must go on.

We made our way down the steps into a funnel that led us back into a narrow, sandstone ravine where the walls closed in. Each step forward seemed to kick up more dirt and disintegrated stone. Soon, the clear walkway that had been in front of us was swirling in hazy fog.

The headlamps barely managed to cut beyond a few feet of ancient soot.

"Don't breathe."

I couldn't tell who was speaking at that point but either way it was sage advice. There was no telling what kind of bacteria had been growing in the air here for the past hundreds of years. I remembered the foldable respirator I had stuffed into the front of my cargo pants, and after a moment of searching various pockets I managed to get it in place. As the mask closed out the world around me and blocked my peripheral, that earlier feeling of claustrophobia seemed to hit me like an uppercut.

I tried to ignore it. I reached out blindly and pawed at the wall of the tunnel to get my bearings as I heard Sajit gasp loudly in front of me. This time I knew who it was because whatever had caused him to gasp also caused him to stop moving, which resulted in me crashing into his backpack.

"What—" before I could finish asking, I saw it.

The dust had finally settled down in the small opening, revealing a carved cubby in the wall to the left of us about knee high. The crevice had run directly next to us the whole tunnel, and we had just walked a good fifteen feet next to it without any of us realizing it.

But that wasn't why Sajit had stopped. It was what the shelf contained: human bones were scattered atop the carved-in recess the whole way down as far as the eye could see. There was no rhyme or order to it either. It looked like several skeletons had been spread out, then smashed together in a concentrated effort to make it as helter-skelter as possible. The piles of bones just went on, and on…

I was instantly thankful for the respirator I had hated only moments before. Without it, I'd be breathing in the dried up, floating particles of the decayed bodies.

"Did looters do this?" I asked.

"Too deep. And we'd have seen signs of them earlier. Earthquake, maybe?" Betsa guessed. His voice sounded muffled, and I realized he had put a respirator on as well.

"Definitely, look here…"

Sajit shined the flashlight he was holding through a partially exposed ribcage that was sticking halfway out of a layer of soot. The beam of light caught a golden reflection of something in the ribcage. Even beneath the dust and grime, whatever it was still glimmered.

"No way a looter would have left that behind; way too valuable."

That was what I realized what I was looking at. I leaned forward to look at the phurba, which was by far the most decorative I'd ever seen. It was tough to tell in the dark, and with the dirt it was encompassed in, but it looked like there were jewels pressed into the hilt.

Sajit added: "That's not all, either."

Sajit was a few feet down from me. As I looked down the row of skeletons to where he was, the glisten of more copper and gold items seemed to follow his flashlight.

There were decorative bowls, statues, trinkets. Basically, anything you can imagine.

"There's so much here." Sajit's voice quivered in excitement, a feeling we certainly shared. It was an amazing sight to behold; the remnants of an almost forgotten culture that had fought to survive and thrive in such a treacherous landscape.

As I stood there in the dark, I closed my eyes for a moment and thought back to mine and Desmond's second walk at the shelter when it had been closed for the night. I remembered those thoughts I had about the shelter, about all the potential for life and death, all the stories that could be made, or extinguished, and realized I was standing in a similar space. Life can be beautiful, and it can be cruel; sometimes it takes an animal shelter or an ancient burial site to make you understand that it's what you do in those realities that matters.

Eventually, Betsa suggested we turn around and call it a day. Neither Sajit nor I argued.

As we retraced our steps, a flutter of hope filled my gut.

No looters were here. This is far enough away where no one would visit it. You're on the right track...

The thought would keep my spirits up throughout the difficult trek back.

CHAPTER 18

We opted to set up a new camp for the night. By the time the tents were up, and the fire was roaring, the sun was barely hovering above the mountains to the west. The decision not to return to the original camp was made in an effort to save some time and, more importantly, energy. Betsa found some flat ground above the tomb we'd explored that was ideal for our new home—good news for my aching body.

Truth be told, I doubt I could have made it down to the original camp that night. Getting out of the tomb and climbing up had been bad enough. Luckily, Betsa planned to return to the original camp the next morning to grab the rest of our gear, allowing me a few more precious hours of sleep and rest.

As night set in around us, we sat by the campfire again and each of us retraced our earlier steps into the cliff grave in reflective silence. Both Sajit and Betsa were staring into the fire, their mind's lost in thought of the caverns we had just wandered, and the early people who had built them.

I was feeling a weird mix of emotions as well. As I tried to untangle my thoughts against the background noise of the crackling fire, I realized that whatever *I* was feeling, Betsa and Sajit were likely feeling tenfold; they had much clearer ties to what we'd seen after all. To whatever degree, I knew we were all feeling a mix of awe, reverence, and truthfully, a healthy dose of fear of what we'd just seen. We had just been involved in a truly amazing discovery.

But still, it was difficult not to be frustrated that we hadn't found the shadow. The likelihood of finding its origin was deteriorating, and my disappointment was growing. There were so many tombs to explore, and as I had just learned, it wasn't as simple as rappelling down and looking into each one. Each small entranceway would need a thorough walk-through before we could know what it held. The undertaking of such a venture could last several lifetimes.

As I slumped closer to the fire in defeat, a voice in my subconscious began speaking up; only this time, it wasn't the normal thoughts of doubt that typically haunted me:

You've made it this far and you found the valley from the dreams. Why would you think this is where it ends? With you going home empty handed. Clearly, something you can't comprehend wants this thing dead.

You'll find it.

The sudden burst of confidence took me by surprise and sent a wave of energy through my tired body.

"We'll find it," I mumbled to no one in particular. But when I looked up from the fire, I noticed both Betsa and Sajit were nodding in agreement.

The wind beat against the canvas tent, sending ripples up the loose material. The tent I was sleeping in was a backup emergency tent, since the other one was still set up at the base of the cliff. Still, the inside was warm enough to promote a night of good sleep, which is exactly what I was having until something had startled me awake.

I blinked my eyes rapidly and found myself wide awake. No groggy start: no, I was as awake as I'd ever been. The wind was blowing so wickedly, I noticed it carried a shrill whistle with it. I figured that the noise of the wind was what had caused me to wake up.

I curled up into a ball and tried to fall back asleep. My body throbbed with dull muscle pains, and no matter which way I twisted or turned, I couldn't rest.

And that whistle of the wind...

When I finally gave up trying to fall asleep, I laid on my back, feeling every protruding pebble and stone underneath me, and stared at the earthy brown canvas ceiling above me. The wind set it alive with each gust, causing waves to rise and fall. The screech of the wind paired itself with the movement of the tent, crashing down onto my ears.

I sat up abruptly, deciding that some fresh air was what the doctor ordered. The only animals I'd seen in the past few days had been goats, so I wasn't too worried about running into any predators all the way out here in the dark. I plunged through the tent flaps into the outside world and was immediately greeted by the bitter night air, which all but guaranteed I wouldn't be going back to bed anytime soon.

The cosmos above me seemed to be in a state of war as the swirls of distant galaxies were ambushed by bright points of light. The never-ending battlefield filled the night sky completely. I stood for a moment admiring the vastness of it all before I began to shiver. The fire was barely burning by that point, but I hurried to it hoping the glowing embers would still produce enough warmth for me to cling too.

As I squatted down by the dying fire, the wind picked up in a sudden fury that almost knocked me down. I barely caught myself and as I found my footing, I realized the whistle of the wind had changed. It was higher pitched now. No longer shrill, but...sweet. Almost musical.

I listened to it and peered out into the dark night, hoping to find the sound's origin. There was no doubting it, the wind was carrying a woman's voice with it. A soft, beautiful sound that sent more shivers running through me than the frigid air had managed.

"Who's there?" I whispered, not wanting to wake either Sajit or Betsa from their much-deserved sleep. I couldn't be completely sure the sound wasn't my mind playing tricks on me, or that I was just imagining things from the high altitude, but I longed to know.

There was no reply. Only the soft hum of the woman's voice which filled the empty night with an eerie undercurrent.

I continued to listen, too afraid to call out again and potentially scare the mystery singer away. As I perched over the fire, I understood how the ancient sailors who described the sirens must have felt. There was a soft pull that would never stop as long as the song continued. I needed to know where it was coming from.

I stood up, about to head in the direction I thought it was originating from. Before I could make it to my feet another blast of wind came, another crescendo of song, and another realization.

It's coming closer.

The melody grew louder. The song was a blurred string of melody sung in another language, with its soft rises in pitch being too subtle for my unfamiliar ear. Above the wind it sounded like a soft, sweet hum that, for all I knew, could have come from the cliffs or mountains themselves.

I stayed sitting in what felt like a trance. I don't know how exactly, or even when, but the next thing I remember is the blurred, out-of-focus silhouette of a woman approaching me. The soft moonlight bathed her in a pale shroud, and she moved so gracefully it was as if she were floating.

"I know you…" I mumbled in a daze.

It was the woman from my dream, whose dead eyes had stared up at me. As she grew closer the same features that had enamored me in my dream grew clearer, and clearer. My mind was in a stupor. I couldn't run away, and although I wanted to, I also couldn't begin rapid-fire questions. The only thing I could do was watch.

You are close.

Her mouth never moved, and she never spoke. But somehow, I heard her.

You must follow my husband's footsteps to kill this demon.

She took my hand and led me to the edge of the cliff.

Beneath us, you will find it.

I woke up in my tent the next morning with no memory of getting back to the campsite. I stumbled out to the fire, which had been replenished with some dry pieces of wood and noticed a pile of gear stacked neatly near it.

"Betsa was up early; climbed down and got all this. Only took him two trips. I swear he might be the best climber I've ever seen," Sajit mused.

I mumbled something that even I couldn't understand, and then dove for the French press that was balanced precariously on a gear bag. As I held it in my hands like a new father might hold their first child, my eyes scanned the campsite.

"Is there boiling water?" I asked with the same concern that an alcoholic might ask a bartender for just *one* more drink before closing time. Sajit nodded towards a tin teapot that was resting in the outside ring of gray coal surrounding the fire.

A few moments later the coffee was made, and I sat down to talk to Sajit. As I mentioned before, Sajit was a variable mix between local historian and spiritual wanderer, and at that moment, I had questions that required a solid understanding of both. I didn't know how to gently introduce the topic, but I figured he was already all the way out here based on my story, so I opted to dive right in.

"I think I saw a ghost last night...I'd seen her before too."

I went on to tell Sajit about the dream, about seeing her corpse sprawled out in the cave we were looking for, and how I now knew it was her husband who had first imprisoned the shadow. The whole time I spoke Sajit listened intently, holding his chin in his hands and staring stoically into the fire.

When I was done speaking, I followed his example. The flames were a blend of orange and yellow, and the bright colors seemed out of place against the surrounding backdrop of earth tones about us.

"I think..." Sajit started, "I think we have been chosen. No, that's not right. Maybe we just stumbled on it, and since we've been recruited..."

He stopped to mull this over for a moment, shook his head violently as if to say, *Doesn't matter,* then continued.

"I think whatever is talking to you knows that we can end this evil. Your dog probably hurt it. That's why it's left you since, and now it is time to finish what was started."

It was reassuring to hear that Sajit had no doubt I had seen something and didn't think I was losing my mind. It was also comforting to think that Desmond had hurt the shadow. He was a brave boy and I knew wherever he was, knowing he had taken a toll on his arch nemesis would make his tail wag.

Before I could respond, Betsa's distant bellow interrupted us. He was too far away to make out what he said completely, but a few sentences managed to travel to where we sat.

"There must've been an earthquake...new open cavern..."

Sajit looked at me with a knowing, somber glance, and I felt a fire light in my gut that would put the bonfire next to us to shame. She had led me to it last night.

The entranceway was open.

It was time.

CHAPTER 19

When you're a kid, you always think you're destined to do something special. You have this feeling that you're unique and meant for greatness or something. That, for some inexplicable reason, you're different from the millions of people who toiled, dreamed, and died on this green earth. I think everyone, whether they'll admit it out loud or not, thinks this way.

I know I did.

If I'm being honest, it was probably that unjustified sense of self-worth that propelled me forward on the trip to Nepal. Sure, a big part of it was getting revenge for Desmond and that emptiness that filled me since I found out about what happened to him, but I'd be lying if I said that was the only thing that sent me into these caves. Or at least, provided me with some confidence that I had a chance to succeed in my crusade.

Something deep inside my (possibly twisted, self-absorbed) psyche told me I was supposed to do this. That I was the one meant to destroy the shadow, even though everyone else before me had failed. It would be me, Jon, the knight who would ride through a foreign land and execute this mythological shadow, which had destroyed whole villages before me.

And when I heard Sajit echo a similar sentiment when I told him about the vision, I felt like it was all coming together.

Destiny. *My* destiny.

From our spots around the fire, Sajit and I listened as Betsa, who was little more than a speck on the horizon, hollered about the new cave entrance that had somehow opened the night before, and that toxic feeling of certainty reared its ugly head. Everything was as it should be. I should've known it was too good to be true, but even Sajit excitedly rubbed his calloused hands together as he listened to the distant shouts. It felt like the universe was serving us this thing on a silver platter.

Out of breath, Betsa finally arrived at the campsite. He tossed down a canvas bag carelessly and the clinking ring of pots echoed across the empty space. Sajit and I leaned in to hear what he had to say, as Betsa struggled to find his voice.

"Normally...normally I'd notice a quake. Would have cleared us out to the valley below to be safe. But it must've been a small one." Betsa was still catching his breath and speaking in short bursts. "It was big enough to change the cliff though...there's a new cave. Big one. Must've been blocked by debris that spilled out last night...it practically splits the cliff in two." He sat down and finally took a long draw from the tin canteen that dangled like a revolver at his hip.

I didn't even bother asking Betsa to describe it. I knew what it looked like. We'd found exactly what we'd been looking for.

This was the burial site, the site of the massacre, where that thing had been trapped.

It should be noted that until this point Betsa had been the voice of reason the whole trip. After all, his reputation as a porter hinged on successful trips, and exploring a recently revealed sky grave that could be unstable was not exactly a safe venture. I expected a long drawn-out conversation with some begging and pleading to get him to lead us there, let alone to let Sajit and myself explore it.

I knew Sajit and I couldn't get to or in the cave without Betsa helping us, but at the same time, I didn't want him to go in with us. I couldn't have it on my conscience if something happened to him because I hadn't been completely forthright with what the real goal of our little trip was. Somehow, I would have to explain this sudden change in the plans to Betsa without alerting any suspicions. To be honest, I was worried that Betsa would think we planned on stealing from the important cultural site.

As I prepared my words carefully, I noticed a glint in Betsa's eyes that slowly transformed into a wide, knowing grin.

"Sajit told me before the first cave, while you slept. And…and I saw her too, last night. She spoke to me and…I won't go in, but I'll lead you there, and get you both inside."

And that was that.

We barely spoke as we marched towards the cave, there was something ceremonial about the walk, which made me feel like I was in a funeral procession. In many ways, I believed it was exactly that.

I found myself taking deep breaths of air as we walked, as if my body wanted as much oxygen as it could get before we entered the unknown. Those longing breaths came with the startling realization that I might never do so again.

No more Mom or Dad. No Christina. No more books, or museums, or hikes. All those things you love, those die with you. You'll never get to see them again. It might be complete darkness, or it might be worse.

I tried to force the dark thoughts away. The price of doing something great might be steep, but I was prepared for that. Besides, after all those other lives extinguished by the shadow, most importantly to me being Desmond's, it would be an act of pure cowardice not to confront this thing while I had the slight upper hand.

I stared down at my feet as I stepped and understood what a final walk to an executioner's chambers must feel like. There was a sick sort of elation in it all. As much as the prospect of losing the things I loved filled me with sorrow, the thought of never having to get up early or having to watch a loved one die before me, overwhelmed my sadness. Despite the fact I was certain I would die within the day, I felt invincible.

Before I knew it, we were there. Standing on a drop off that stood hundreds of feet above the ground beneath it. It was the perfect vantage point to view the landscape. The mountains seemed to ripple along the never-ending horizon while the river below cut across the ground, almost as if we were a dividing line letting us know we were standing on the edge of the world.

"Here we are," Betsa said matter-of-factly. His voice was confident and focused on the task at hand, as always.

Betsa hurriedly unpacked our climbing gear. As he laid everything out on the ground, he informed us of his plan.

"I'll wait at the camp for two days. If I've not heard back from you, I will report your location and a cave-in when I return to Jomsom, and an emergency team will come find you."

Sajit and myself nodded appreciatively, and when everything was all set up, I found myself tongue tied. I wanted to thank Betsa for everything he'd done, but the words wouldn't come out. Instead, as I approached the rope line, I finally managed a thankful pat on the shoulder. Looking back at it, it was a pitiful gesture towards a man who had traveled countless miles with us, but it was the best I could do. He looked at me as I stepped forward and nodded.

The simple gesture sent me back to what felt like another lifetime before. A quick nod was the same gesture my old kickboxing coach would make before I stepped into the ring, and for some reason that subtle acknowledgement was better than any long-winded goodbye could have ever been.

Sajit, on the other hand, grabbed the porter in a giant bear hug that was so forceful it lifted Betsa off his feet.

"I expect dinner to be ready when we get back," he laughed, "something with some kick, for once, you bastard."

With that, we secured ourselves to the ropes, stepped into our harnesses, and checked to make sure all clips were where they should be. Betsa watched our every move like a hawk, and I found the technical procedure of preparing to descend helped distract me from the task on the horizon. When we jumped, I did so without thinking. No big, deep breath, no mental psych up. I knew any hesitation might be the end of it all, so I just went into the darkness.

CHAPTER 20

The cave's opening was somehow darker than the first one we explored. In fact, it was darker than anything I had yet to see in my life. My headlamp was all but useless, barely casting a sliver of light within the engulfing blackness that seemed to extend to the ends of this earth. I knew that Sajit was behind me somewhere when we landed and started pushing into the cavern. It was comforting knowing I wasn't *completely* alone as we wandered into the dragon's lair with little more than a few ceremonial daggers to do battle.

Behind me I heard Sajit begin to hum. I thought about telling him to be quiet, that he was going to ruin our element of surprise, but I realized that, of course, this thing knew we were coming. This was its realm, and nothing we could do would catch it off-guard. So, the humming continued; floating softly down the long tunnel we plodded through.

The phurba was held out in front of me. The gilded metal glistened majestically in the light of the headlamp and the hawk, which was carved in the weapon's hilt, seemed to come alive with the imminent bloodshed on the horizon. With each step forward I felt a closer connection to those echoes of the dream that had taken me down these walkways before.

When something is taken from you violently, cruelly, you make the guilty party pay. That's as old as time itself.

That ghost of the past, the stranger who had his whole village taken from him, had tracked down the shadow to its cavern to punish it for the villagers. For his wife. Now, it was my turn to avenge an equally innocent soul who had been taken needlessly by this monster.

The scattered piles of bones around me almost went unnoticed as the task at hand dominated my thoughts; however, the crunch of a femur beneath my foot brought me back to reality. As I looked down, I saw a row of skeletons lining the floor of the cave. The headlamp illuminated the grotesque queue. Despite being ancient, the dirt covered bones glistened back against the light as if they were covered in fresh blood.

They were different from the ones inside the tomb we had been in the day before. These skeletons had managed to escape centuries of earthquakes and landslides unharmed. Still, there was no neatly carved shelf prepared for these dead to rest on. Instead, the staked bodies lay strewn in hastily, yet organized, lines.

Seeing the line of bodies helped me realize my walk was a little different than he who came before me. The village man had been forced to lay waste to his village below, then somehow drag their bodies up here after the deed was done.

I stepped more carefully, not wanting to disrupt another eternal rest. I took another gentle step forward, then a soft *snap* sounded to my left, and then quickly to the right. We weren't alone.

With the sound of that soft click, the tunnel ahead was suddenly illuminated on both sides by torches that ran along the walls. I heard Sajit gasp as the ancient torches came alive from nowhere with the burst of fire. Each torch seemed to cackle and snarl menacingly, daring us forward. I looked momentarily at the closest one, which was welded into the wall of the cave the exact same way as they had been in the dreams.

The first domino was tipped, and we were being summoned forward. The walkway began to turn into a void, and it wasn't long before the whispers started.

"I let you live…why are you so desperate to die?"

"The same fate as all of them. When I'm done with you, your family will be next."

The torches provided the necessary backdrop for the shadow figures to begin their hideous appearance. Soon, the whole wall was a warped mural of featureless figures pawing their way towards us. Dark, soulless beings from some sinister beyond finally finding themselves released.

I can't explain it, but for some reason, there was a feeling of complete serenity in that moment. I knew the attack was nothing more than an intimidation factor, and that the real battle was still somewhere down the road. So, I stood as straight as I could manage, and walked forward trying to purvey the calmness I felt. As I pushed forward, I ventured a glance back at Sajit, who was slowly stumbling behind as he stared in awe at the chaos surrounding us. When he noticed me looking back at him, Sajit visibly bristled at having been caught slightly unsure. He regained his composure almost immediately, then he too stood up straighter and marched forward with a renewed sense of purpose.

The whispers continued to berate us from all sides with taunts from several languages. There was a veritable demonstration of multiculturalism in the dark tunnel as the entity made sure to provide us with examples of its far-flung reach. A reach that contained knowledge of many cultures, some still around and some extinguished, which the shadow had drawn blood from and outlived.

Still, we walked forward.

The fact that we refused to back down seemed to evoke more vitriol from the army whose midst we paraded through. Louder, more guttural howls boomed like thunder through the bone filled passage. Ahead of me I saw a dark shadow leap towards the remains of a former person in a dark haze. As we walked past the grime covered skeleton, the skull's eye sockets filled with the shadow's murkiness while the hinged jaw slowly managed to open and close with the threats it uttered.

"You'll beg for your death. It always wins. The darkness always wins."

I was tempted to send the skull flying down the tunnel like a football through the uprights, but then I remembered that the poor soul whose body was *again* being desecrated by the shadow deserved to remain intact. Against every fiber in my body telling me to strike out, I managed to keep moving.

Soon we approached a familiar sight. The tunnel had come to an end and before us and through an assuming natural doorway, waited the cavern where the shadow spawned from. But also, where it had been hurt before, and where Sajit and I planned to end it forever. I stopped for a moment as I scanned the base of the tunnel and looked for the spot where she had fallen in my dreams.

I inspected the crumbled remains that coated the walkway, and the malevolent whispers seemed to fade to the background. They knew that their job was done, and that they were no longer a part of the drama that was about to unfold.

"Keep moving!" I heard Sajit holler, but I knew I had to find her before I continued.

For some reason, something within me begged my conscience to find her, since that part of me *knew* the memory of her remains would come into play.

I finally found her skeleton slumped against the wall of the pathway. She could have blended in with the hundreds of other bodies littering the floor, save one tell-tale sign that let me know it was her.

Within her ribcage a small group of flowers had bloomed. It filled the normally cavernous space with a burst of majestic purple, and even the sinister, flickering light cast from the torches couldn't take away the beauty of it.

I felt Sajit's gloved hand grab my shoulder to prod me forward, but at the sight of the plant he too stopped in his tracks. There was something special about the flowers that demanded our complete, undivided attention. The many layers each flower possessed seemed to be carefully wrapped in silk, as if by some divine being, and the sudden discovery of such natural beauty amongst so much death made it all the more powerful.

"The whore couldn't save him...he killed her." I ignored the whisper from the doorway and moved towards the remains.

"That's Ambition Himalaya," Sajit said from behind me, identifying the flower that had somehow taken root in the deep recesses of the tombs.

I carefully reached into her sternum, making sure not to accidentally disturb the body, and plucked a sole flower from the bloom. As I backed away, I placed the single flower into my shirt pocket. I don't know why I did any of it, but for some reason, having that flower close made me feel better.

I was about to charge forward when I noticed Sajit. He too tucked a flower into his pocket, I realized that for the first time since the torches had been lit, the whispers had stopped completely. There were no more shadows in sight for that matter either.

"Think they're regrouping?" Sajit asked.

"Who cares?" I asked back, trying to sound confident. The truth was, I really did have some concerns about what lay ahead, but fake it till you make it, right?

A little slower, we moved into the cavern. Each step filled me with flashbacks to my dream, and as we entered, I expected to see a giant iron throne in the center of the room.

214

But it was completely empty. No ornate seat, no cloaked demon summoning me forward. There wasn't even a torch. The cave was empty, save the two beams of light from our headlamps. The two lights bounced around in the darkness like a pair of excited hounds looking for a scent.

Eventually, Sajit's light climbed up what must have been the far wall towards the ceiling. And, like the first time Sajit and I had been in a sky grave, Sajit told me to look up.

His voice was quaking, and when my eyes finally adjusted to make out what we were seeing, I knew why.

Above us was a mural. Not a nice, historic painting like the first one we had stumbled on though. No, this mural was a vivid depiction of Sajit and I suffering all sorts of cruelties and horrific fates.

To make sure we didn't miss any of the scenes of our brutal eviscerations, a flame suddenly burst to life in the center of the room, filling the cavern with light. I was too focused on the depictions above to even bother looking towards the roaring fire when it started; the mural above was that engrossing.

The portraits featured too many gory fates for yours truly to ever hope to record them all. I will highlight a select few though, which even in my state of utter horror I couldn't help but appreciate the creativity put into coming up with those brutal endings.

In one, which looked like it had been finger painted in blood, your wavy-haired protagonist had his stomach slit open with various entrails pouring out every which way. Now, these organs were not simply dangling willy-nilly, no, these were being pulled every which way by a pack of dogs which looked startlingly like Desmond.

Next to it my body sat skewered by a giant stake and was surrounded by the dismembered heads of my family and loved ones. In another, I was a red mass of tendons and muscles that looked like an anatomical textbook, since I had apparently been skinned alive before dying. They went on, and on…

Looking at the mural, a strange feeling of déjà vu crept over me. I began to feel nauseous and my head started to spin. Still, I kept looking, taking in each scene of torture and death.

When I was finally able to pull my eyes away from the gruesome ceiling, I saw that the fire in the center of the room was slowly dying. The flames were fading, giving way to a wispy smoke that hung in the air longer than it should have.

That was when the whisper started again.

"You thought you could come in here and stand against me? You thought you were different?"

As it spoke nausea gave way to a pulsating headache. It was like nothing I had ever felt before, like my head was being filled with a toxic sludge that was pushing the limit of my skull's capacity until it would surely pop.

I gasped and prayed that the sudden influx of air might clear my head, that it might overpower the pain, but it did nothing. I could practically feel my brain begin to hemorrhage and sputter, but still over the pain I could hear that voice. I looked at Sajit who was kneeled over in pain as well, though he seemed to be fairing slightly better than me and was making an effort to grab at his phurba.

"You don't remember. No…but you will."

I traced my pain-soaked memory trying to figure out what the voice meant, trying to figure out what I couldn't remember.

"I let you escape once for the dog. You won't be so lucky now."

And that was when it came back to me. It was such a sudden, violent realization that it almost overpowered the whisper.

The images in the mural were real.

In the kitchen, when I was in the darkness and when I disappeared, I was here. Those brief seconds when Christina said I had vanished were an eternity.

The memories played out, each so horrific they drowned out the headache and bodily pain I was feeling. Then an even worse thought flashed through the memories.

Did Desmond take my place?

The headache was nothing compared to the gut-punch of that thought. My eyes welled with tears as the thought of Desmond suffering the fates above made me double over. Though I tried not to, I felt myself whimper as tears began streaming down my face.

I heard the wicked cackle of laughter and managed to look up. In front of me, only a few feet away was the dark, shadowy pit that was causing all the suffering.

I made up my mind to end it the same way Desmond had, if I could. I crawled forward pathetically, each small increment towards it was a labored motion that took all my strength. When I was finally at the edge of the shadow peering into the abyss, I realized I was not alone. Sajit was by my side, and I felt his hand on my shoulder.

"Would you like me to go first?" he asked.

It was the bravest thing I'd ever heard. Without Sajit I would have curled up right there, resigned to my fate. Instead, I grabbed his shoulder, and again, we went.

CHAPTER 21

The darkness was everywhere. It wasn't like air or open space, no, the black void was somehow thicker than that, with pressure weighing down and wrapping around. We were falling, but it felt more like drifting into the nothingness, where time and thought would have no meaning. We stayed there suspended in the nothing until slowly the background began to seep into the abyss.

As the splotches of color filled the surroundings, and for a brief moment, I had to wonder:

Are we dead?

For all I knew, we had died the second Sajit and I dropped into the pit. But something in me, some small voice, told me this wasn't the case. We were both still alive, at least for the time being, as we floated in a place where nightmares began their germination.

As the world around me formed into strange blocks and landscapes I can't even begin to describe, I finally saw what I had expected to see when I first stepped into the cavern.

The throne.

In it sat a cloaked figure, which I knew was the real evil orchestrating the past few months; this wasn't the minions, nor shadows it sent out to torment us, this was the big bad. The cloaked being sat still, apparently not worried by our presence. Around him, in the sickly, rolling grey hills I could make out the blurry outlines of humans wandering about aimlessly. I turned to say something to Sajit, but he wasn't there anymore. I strained my eyes to see if I could find him amidst the distant beings. Still nothing. Even from the distance I was, I could see the slumped shoulders of a broken population. There was no doubt these were the shadow's victims and Sajit, thankfully, was not among them.

The ground beneath me was a swirling drift of grey dust, which wisped about like smoke rising from the ground. It was the same color as the sky above.

I stopped my steady advance for a moment and gazed out at the never-ending horizon. I hoped to spot Sajit somewhere out there before confronting the cloaked figure. No matter where I looked though, it was only more of the damned.

Convinced I was alone, at least for the moment, I continued on towards the throne. As I walked, I carefully unsheathed the phurba that was attached to my hip in the frayed leather case. If the cloaked figure noticed the weapon, it gave no indication of concern. The hood faced my direction, the empty black opening making it look like some kind of cyclops. With each step I took I began to feel more confident, though something still told me it wouldn't be as easy as it seemed.

When I was close enough to see that the shadow's cloak was embroidered in grey stitch-work with a language and alphabet I'd never seen before, close enough to dive and attack it for that matter, it finally acknowledged my presence with a slight nod of the hooded head.

That brief motion might as well have been a gunshot. I froze, and so did the phurba, turning cold in my hand and now feeling useless against such an ancient entity. As I stared into the hooded void where a face should've been, the extent of the shadow's history finally struck me. Surrounding us, across the plains and hills for which there were no worldly measurement to track their magnitude, roamed an army of cursed souls who had crossed the shadow's path. And I had just (literally) dove headfirst into its lair.

The hooded figure stared back at me for a moment and slowly adjusted itself in the throne, beckoning to some unseen spectator in the beyond. As the shadow moved, a familiar pitter-patter of paws filled the gloomy earthscape like cannon fire.

It was Des.

His normally vibrant copper fur seemed as dull as the surroundings, as if the very color had been drained from him. The chalky ground had kicked up all around him, making him seem as if he'd appeared from a heavy fog next to the throne. He looked at me with distant eyes, and for a moment I thought I was looking at the ghost of the animal I loved so much. I was too stunned to say anything, and so, instead, I stood there feeling utterly defeated. In one, subtle move the shadow had seemed to checkmate my attack. Desmond stared back, looking equally defeated.

But then, a slight flicker of something flashed across his eyes, and I knew he was back. Maybe it was just a miniscule scrunch of his snout I'd seen, or maybe it really was some color returning to him; all I knew was that Des was the same as he'd always been.

Perhaps realizing the sight of Desmond that was supposed to permanently unnerve me had suddenly created the opposite effect, the shadow began speaking. The voice was powerful, filling the whole nightmare around us with a thunderous boom.

"This is where I brought you. This is where you saw what lies ahead for the rest of your damned existence. This is where you'll spend eternity in suffering, for daring to challenge me."

As he spoke, a vision smashed into my mind, and I saw exactly how old the shadow was. How it had roamed the mountains of the Himalayas for as long as they had jutted from the landscape. How the shadow had traveled with early warring parties of nomadic hunter gatherers across the world, bringing death and madness as it went. How it had outlived all the societies and cultures that we read about in history textbooks, adding to its collection at each step and with each journey abroad. And how it always returned to the caverns of the mountains it knew and loved after each escapade, to enjoy the successes of its adventures. That was, until the mountains of Nepal began to provide victims and communities for the shadow to prey on without ever having to leave the grounds it called its home.

As the vision played before me the sky changed from a dreary grey to the rich, dark color of blood. I sat close enough to reach out and touch my nemesis, but I was unable to move. Frozen in fear, dread, and a deep self-loathing to wrap it all up with.

"You thought you were enough to stop me?"

The all-knowing, all-encompassing voice rained down from the maroon sky in mocking indignation. The hate seeped down in the voice from above, and all I could do was look down at Desmond in shame.

"I'm sorry. I'm so sorry…" I pleaded, wishing for some sign that he forgave me and understood. The fight drained from me, and the stake in my forward stretched hand dropped down to my side. My arms, hell, my whole body, was a lead weight, sinking down into the watery grave of guilt.

It's all my fault. I dragged everyone into this. I could have ignored it or could have dropped it rather than pursuing it in my sick, twisted attempt at going on an adventure. It was all my fault and it always had been.

The thought ripped through me and hurt more than whatever lay in the future ever could have.

In labored, heavy steps, Desmond walked towards me. I prepared for the end in a wave of cowardice that tore at me worse than anything the shadow could do to me, no matter how long I was doomed to spend with it. As I reached out to pet Desmond in what I thought would be my last act of something that brought me any happiness, I felt a change in the atmosphere. It was subtle; almost too small to detect, but the oppressive vacuum that had engulfed me since arriving in the pit lifted just the slightest.

I was no longer alone.

Sajit was by my side from seemingly out of nowhere, and with him was a burst of energy and confidence that rippled through the dead surroundings. And then Desmond was next to us as well. The three of us faced the dark figure with a renewed sense of purpose. But it seemed to have little effect on our adversary, who rose from his throne. As he stood, the figure seemed to grow and when he was standing completely upright it became evident that it was far larger than a human being should be. It was tough to tell exactly its stature, but the cloaked figure had to be well over nine feet.

"And you bring him? Someone whose people I've hunted for sport?"

The landscape shook all around us, and I had to steady myself by reaching down and posting lightly on Desmond's back. At first, he felt cold to the touch, and I worried that his time spent in this underworld may have sapped all the life from him. My hand stayed on Des as the shadow seemed to grow angrier; its voice raised, and it swore cruel threats at all of us. Along with the threats, thunder roared through the blood red sky above.

If this was how I was going to go, beside Desmond and Sajit, I was okay with it.

But Des wasn't. He lunged first, ripping at the shadow's giant sleeve, which hung down to the poisoned ground. Sajit was on it next, slashing and burying his phurba into the cloaked figure's gut. Finally, phurba raised, I sprinted headlong into the fight, aiming each stab into the same cavernous opening of the hood.

Around us, hordes of shadows appeared from the ground beneath, their screams ripping through the sullen landscape with primordial rage. But their shrieks didn't stop us. In fact, our attack seemed to grow more furious with each wail. The phurbas fell swifter while Desmond practically glowed as his color returned.

The figure still managed to stand its ground.

I couldn't tell if we were doing any significant damage; but in that moment it didn't matter. It just felt good to strike out at this thing. The thunder above soon overtook the helpless cries of the surrounding army, and as a bolt of lightning cracked through the sky, I could hear the sound of rain droplets crashing down.

I looked down at my hand after feeling a warm splash land on it and was surprised to see a trickle of blood slowly running down it towards the dagger. I looked around to see if either Desmond, Sajit, or I were wounded, but another splash hit.

Then another. The blood was raining down from the sky.

Soon the downpour of blood was torrential, covering everything with the seeping, red fluid. We were completely drenched in it. I tried to clear my eyes of the maroon curtain using my forearm, but it didn't matter. By the time my arm left my face another wave of blood crashed down, blinding me once more. My clothes clung to my body as the blood continued flowing from above.

Still, despite barely being able to see, we kept on our attack.

As the blood rose higher from beneath us, the hooded figure began to fight back. It reached out towards Sajit in a slow, calculated manner, the whole time showing no effects of the previous pummeling and grabbed him by his throat. Sajit was hoisted off the ground for a few seconds, his feet kicking like a marionette being swung about, before he was slammed beneath the still rising level of blood.

The thick liquid around him began to bubble like a cauldron. I rushed over and frantically began ripping at the shadow's sleeve trying to sever the arm beneath. The raining blood made the sleeve too slippery to grab, so I began stabbing it with everything I had in me. The thing paid me no mind though, and matter-of-factly turned and told me:

"He's always been afraid of drowning. Ever since he was a child."

Desmond rejoined the attack, ripping at the same sleeve below where I was stabbing. The cloaked figure began to laugh as the flurry of bubbles slowed. He hoisted Sajit's blood smeared face just above the bloodline, allowing him to breathe for a moment.

"Welcome to eternit—"

A dull clunk cut the shadow off. He stumbled back, dropping Sajit in the process. Sajit was on his feet in an instant, sputtering as he tried to catch his breath. The phurba was still in his hand.

As the lake of blood seemed to become choppier with waves and swells slamming against our legs, the shadow's cloaked figure gazed upward, looking for something.

A droplet of blood exploded upward next to us as a rock from somewhere above dropped down. Then another.

Soon, a hail of rocks turned the lake of blood we were wading through into a frothing minefield of explosions. And as the mountain above attacked, for the first time the shadow seemed completely unsure of itself.

The thing backed away from us as its hooded head darted around suspiciously, trying to make sense of it all. Behind it there were no longer any grey hills or cursed wanderers, only the blood-stained walls of the cavern we had first walked into. It had been dragged to the cliff tomb with us.

The cavern was dark, and I could barely make out the outline of the cloaked figure in front of me. I felt my stomach plummet as Desmond was nowhere to be seen. As I watched the scene unfold, I instantly felt a wave of regret at not being able to say a better goodbye to Des, certain he was trapped in the void we'd just escaped, though I prayed he'd been released from shadow and would be allowed a peaceful afterlife, whatever that might look like. The wave of regret was quickly overcome by a concern for self-preservation.

Debris clattered to the floor with loud claps, and I instinctively covered my head with my arms. Sajit was doing the same. However, after bracing ourselves for the sting of the onslaught, we found none of the rocks were hitting us. In fact, no rocks landed anywhere even near us. Instead they were all pelting the giant hooded figure. A dimly lit torch came to life out of nowhere, and I watched as the force of the rocks sent the billowy cloak crashing back down to the ground every time it tried to stand.

Larger rocks soon began to fall. Giant, ancient pieces of the very cliff itself seemed to throw themselves down, in pent-up anger at the ancient evil. With each crash the cavern would shake, and the shadow would seem to take another small shuffle in retreat.

But there was nowhere for it to go. Its back was pinned to the blood-soaked cavern wall, and rocks continued to pile up around it. In moments, the shadow was stuck cowering from the rocks that were pinning its bottom half down. The mountains decided it was time for the shadow to taste a sweet bit of karma.

"Let's get out of he—" I cut myself off before I finished. There was no way I wasn't going to double-tap the bane of my existence while it was a sitting duck. This thing wasn't going to emerge from a pile of rocks as Sajit and I were making our getaway like some eighties slasher flick.

This thing was going to die, for good.

I grabbed a hold of the phurba and prepared to charge, turning to Sajit to make sure he was on the same page. And that's when I saw it.

Well, him rather.

Desmond stalked forward from some hidden corner of the cavern. His teeth bared, with a fire in his eyes that filled me with fear. Real, honest-to-God fear. The same terror cavemen must have felt when they stumbled upon their first apex predator. It was primal, and I was thankful I wasn't going to be the target of Des' revenge. There was something tucked into his collar, but in the dark, I couldn't make out exactly what it was.

As Desmond prowled his prey, he never broke above a slow, determined crawl towards the shadow.

I'll give credit where credit is due: the shadow did not beg or cower as Desmond approached. It sat there unflinching, surely knowing what awaited. As Desmond moved closer, the shadow hissed at the impending doom. His anger almost rivaling that of his approaching executioner.

Desmond lumbered forward, his fur tinted a dark red, his growl practically shaking the cavern, even more than the earthquake. When he was in front of the shadow, Des paused for a moment and stared. His white teeth flashed like daggers, which grew larger as his snarl increased in intensity. It was clear he didn't want to let the shadow off easy. He stayed wavering in front of the doomed evil, savoring the moment.

But the moment of climactic revenge couldn't last forever. In a blur of coiled, copper muscle, Des' teeth ripped into the spot where the dark cloak's throat would be. The sound of his teeth gnashing together filled the cave, and the ground around us seemed to shake as if cheering Desmond on.

I jumped into the flurry of fur and cloth, driving the phurba repetitively into the hoods opening. Sajit followed suit.

As the unrestrained attack, fueled by months of the thing's torment, rained down on the shadow, it continued to screech and bellow threats, but none of its army showed up to defend it. It writhed with each tear of Desmond's muzzle, and shook with each thrust of the phurba.

In the midst of bloodlust, I realized two things. First: tucked into Desmond's now ragged collar, was a bright purple flower. The same kind I had taken from the body. Seeing something so beautiful tore me from the attack, which led me to my second realization: the cavern was still rumbling, rocks were still dropping, and our attack wouldn't be the blow that finished the shadow off; perhaps, that honor belonged to a landscape it had haunted for so long.

There was too much going on to connect the dots then and there, since we didn't have long to get out. The cavern resumed shaking in pure, white-hot rage.

"We need to get out of here," I yelled.

"Not without—" Sajit didn't waste his breath explaining any further.

Instead, he thrust the phurba into the center of the cloak figure's torso, pinning it to the ground. The cloaked shadow convulsed violently, and a burst of smoke billowed from the wound. Figuring the more the merrier, I followed Sajit's example and stabbed the stake down into the cloak with all the force I could muster. As the phurba shot through the cloak, my arm reverberated as it notched into the granite. The shudder was so powerful that it felt like I had swung an aluminum baseball bat against a metal pole.

Once more, the shadow shook violently, and smoke continued to shoot out from around the stakes. Its chest heaved up and down, but it couldn't muster up enough force to escape the anchors that held it down. The shadow wouldn't be moving anytime soon and, with the cascading rocks from above, I had serious doubts that it would ever see the light of day again.

I grabbed Desmond, who let go of the cloak as he seemed to grasp his mortal enemy's impending doom, and we began to rush out the way we'd entered. Sajit was just ahead of us, his sleek frame spinning and twisting as he dodged the onslaught of stones from above.

As I sprinted past the entrance of the cavern, I took one final look at the skeleton of the woman, who I knew I owed my life to, along with the return of Desmond for that matter. No longer a skeleton simply housing a few straggling purple flowers, the spot where she had rested was now an explosion of Ambition Himalayas.

I wanted to stop, to pause, and to take *one* peaceful moment to pay tribute to the beautiful shrine in honor of my suspected savior, but there was no time. Boulders rained down, and the cave shook so fiercely it was a struggle to maintain any footing.

I cast one last glance at the garden of purple flowers that would soon be buried in tons of sandstone and ran for my life. Sajit was slightly ahead, and Desmond refused to leave my side as I hustled forward. He could have easily sprinted ahead to safety, leaving me behind, but I knew he never would. He'd stay right next to me even if it was the last thing he did.

We made our way past skeletons that were exploding into plumes of dust as stones crashed into them, destroying the ancient burial ground in minutes. There was no time to mourn the loss of history, we just had to keep running. Everything was happening so fast that I barely gave a thought as to what we'd do when we reached the mouth of the cave. It would've been a tough ascension with just Sajit and I, and with the third member of our party (who by this point in the story, I'm sure you realize, I wasn't going to leave behind and lose again) a difficult climb would be nearly impossible.

But that seemed like a distant concern as I felt a piece of granite dig into my shoulder with a thudding impact, which sent me spinning momentarily. I managed to get my feet under me at the last second and avoided toppling over, and Desmond slowed down next to me, only resuming pace when he had double-checked to make sure I had as well.

Somewhere in the distance, a small splotch of circular light appeared in the darkness, offering a teasing chance at escape. It was so far away, but its mere existence meant that we could all somehow escape.

What about Desmond? How will he escape?

Somewhere deep within, the voice of reason began to cast doubt on the plausibility of survival. I ignored it. What did reason think it was doing rearing its ugly face? I was running through a crumbling cavern that only moments before had contained an ancient evil shadow bent on killing me, and to top it all off, I was reunited with my dog that was presumed dead (hell, he might have been, who knows?) dashing off to possible safety.

Reason be damned. Planning and worrying would do no good at this point. We were going to live, or we were going to die, and either way, I couldn't do much other than run and hope I was still in good with the gods of the mountain. It all came down to instinct and luck.

The pinpoint of light grew larger. And larger. Until…

A burst of fresh air filled my burning lungs. I could practically feel steam rising within my chest as if the air was water hitting scolding embers. Until that moment, I hadn't realized how thick and heavy the air was within the tombs, how stale with the smell of death it was. The mountain air was sweet and promised a chance.

Sajit stopped for a moment at the edge of the cave. I heard him yell something, but the sound of the mini earthquake muffled his shout to an indiscernible murmur. His shadowy outline was completely encompassed by a ring of light that gave him an ethereal appearance.

For a moment, it was only him basking in the promising light of day, but, with another incoherent shout, a shadow dropped into view.

Betsa.

Even in the state of complete disarray I was in, my fried mind was able to put together that Betsa had heard the ground shaking beneath him and rather than stay put, as he had said he would, he had decided to join the fray.

When Desmond and I were at the edge of the cliff, I saw Betsa's eyes light up with excitement and relief. He hoisted the dog up in his arms (an impressive feat on its own) and began climbing up.

We were flying on autopilot now. Somehow, I was in my harness, then I was in the air, and then again, I was at the top of the cliff with the group. We quickly moved away from the edge at Betsa's prompting.

"Remember those bones from the first night, the ones that tumbled out?" he asked, not really wanting an answer. "Those were too close to the edge of a cliff during a tremor and look where they ended up."

The memory of the shattered porcelain bones was all the convincing I needed.

We made our way back towards the camp in silence. There was nothing we could say that would convey the array of emotions we all felt. So instead, silence reigned supreme. For my part I let the overwhelming rush of happiness seep into every ounce of by being, as Desmond trotted by my side without a care in the world.

I decided to enjoy that feeling, rather than the sense of accomplishment I might've felt for playing a part in the demise of the shadow. Truth be told, I knew my role in the drama was miniscule compared to the efforts of all the other parties involved. All that mattered during that quiet walk back to camp was that Desmond was next to me. His tail swayed back and forth happily, despite the fact he had just essentially returned from the grave after staring down an ancient evil face-to-face. I decided to follow his lead as I let all the stress, anger, and uncertainty wash away.

I mean, in the grand scheme of things, is there anything more important than enjoying a walk with your dog?

EPILOGUE

"I can't wait to see the two of you tomorrow. Des is all excited too, especially since it'll be your first time seeing him since he got found. Anyways, love you, and see you tomorrow!"

It was late so I hoped the answerphone wouldn't wake my parents with its shrill tones, but I wanted them to know I was thinking about them. I really was excited to see them, to have a bit of normal back into my life after such a crazy time recently. I smiled at the thought of my normal life returning, and walked into the living room where Des was cuddling up with Christina on the couch.

"I'm glad you thought of the stranger finding him and dropping him off story," I said as I settled in next to them. When there was no reply, I realized Christina had dozed off with her head resting on Desmond's belly.

I really was thankful to her for the cover story; there was no way to explain how Des ended up in Nepal if I'd been forced to explain. Following the logistical nightmare of getting a dog through customs at several stops, (let's just say some palms got greased, and the last leg of the trek was on a particularly sketchy container ship that could have been delivering a doomsday device to Gotham for all I knew) eventually we made it back to the States. To protect all parties involved I won't mention the exact port where Des and I found ourselves dropped off. However, luckily for us, there was a pretty redhead who was there to pick us up.

As Desmond slept in the back of the car, I had told Christina everything that happened in Nepal. I mean, I told her *every* small detail I could remember. I told her about how Desmond, Sajit, Betsa, and I had packed up our camp immediately after escaping the cave-in. Then I told her about how we had walked back to Jomsom through the night in silence. And finally, how when we arrived in the city, we had dropped our supplies off at a hostel then beelined for a bar.

With a few drinks in us, the dam of self-reflection bowed to the increasing pressure to talk, and the whole story spilled out. Sajit had seen different things then I had and Betsa had heard things coming from the cave that we hadn't—it was how he knew to be ready for us.

Desmond sat at my feet sleeping during that strange breakfast of chyang and beer. The rest of the day was a blur as we drank and ate, and drank…it reminded me of the day after a fight, where the weight of worry had finally been hoisted off, and the need to celebrate was overpowering. Or maybe it was like attending your own funeral, who knows?

Sajit and Betsa had helped me get to Kathmandu and had put me in contact with several people who helped me along the trip back to the US. When it was time to say goodbye, the moment was surprisingly short for all that we had endured. I think everyone had come to a mutual understanding that we'd be seeing each other again. I mean, I had fallen in love with Nepal, and with Christina's research…well, there was no doubt I'd be back and wanting to adventure with the two of them.

The car ride home with Christina was a blur of cities, passing lights, and the soft sound of Des snoring in the back seat, while I talked non-stop for close to the whole ride. It was so freeing to just talk about what happened while also trying to flesh out the unknown parts with Christina. I think that was where the seed of an idea to write down the story was planted. It was also where Christina had the idea of telling my parents that, as luck would have it, after pulling in from my trip abroad to forget a miserable few months a kindly stranger had been waiting with Desmond, who knew where to drop him off thanks to his collar. The idea that he'd survived on his own for a few months after going missing while trying to chase the made-up burglar wasn't all that far-fetched, and I certainly couldn't craft a better story, so it was the one we ran with.

Sitting on the couch with the two of them, I remembered daydreaming about this very thing the day Desmond went missing. Before the trip to Nepal, before the final showdown, before all of it, all I wanted was a lazy day of reading or napping with Desmond and Christina.

Here it was. My wish.

As I sank into the couch, I was careful not to wake Christina, who was still sleeping with her head rested against Desmond. I was getting ready to pick up *The Illustrated Man* off the coffee table next to me, when I cast a glance over at my partner in crime. There was Desmond looking back at me: ears flopped back, paws tucked under his chin, and eyes brimming with unabashed love, and I realized something.

We both got our wishes.

ACKNOWLEDGEMENTS

Here it goes:

None of this would have been possible without you, Mom and Dad. Every page of this book is a testament to the love of reading you instilled in me, Mom, and the self-deprecating humor I've inherited from you, old man. Just as important, thanks for suggesting the shelter…guess that was the right move, huh? Also, Emily, Aubrey, and Brad, you're pretty rad too. Thanks for reading early drafts, loving dogs, and just generally being some pretty awesome siblings. And, while I'm listing family who helped me, thanks to both sets of grandparents who were willing to listen to my ramblings about history, Bradbury, and reading in general. GG, thanks for everything. Since you guys are *basically* family too, I'm going to include you in this section as well – Tyler Demay and Nic Rider, thanks for everything.

To the history department at Lycoming college: I'm forever thankful for your gentle and supportive handling of a young…unpolished…writer and historian. Drs. Silkey, Chandler, and Pearl, you helped me understand why stories matter, whether they're historical or fiction, and any limited ability I have as a storyteller is thanks to you. Also, even though you're not from the Lycoming Department, I'm going to lump you in this section, Dr. Jeffrey Ludwig (you're a historian, after all.) Thanks for the japes, and teaching me fancy words.

Writing is brutal: rejection letters that lead to self-doubt, more lows than highs, and the constant, slow march towards hopeful improvement, which is an absolute grind. Luckily, I found wrestling early in my life, so these were not completely unfamiliar with me. Coach Roger Crebs, thanks for imprinting values that transcend athletic competition. Lycoming is lucky to have you.

Of course, this acknowledgments page would not exist without Vulpine Press, who I am forever thankful rolled the dice on a first-time writer. And, speaking of Vulpine Press: Commissioning Editor of Horror, Jess Jordan, helped shape this book into publishing form, and her insight was crucial throughout the process. Jess, the time and thoughtfulness you put into each edit will forever be appreciated. I've learned so much working with you, and I can't thank you enough for all your hard work in getting this book ready for print. I care deeply about this book, and I'm thankful it found such a great home.

Last but not least, Natalie and Bruce: Natalie for the talks, and Bruce for the walks. Having you two in my corner is all a guy could want; from reading the early drafts, telling me I could get it published, to supporting me in everything I do. I don't deserve you, Natalie, but I'm sure thankful for ya.

Of course, there's at least a million of you I missed, and for that I'm sorry. I'm trying to keep this short, which is hard to do when I'm blessed to know so many amazing people. But, before you go, one last thought…

How pissed is Bruce going to be that this book isn't about him?!

Zachary Finn is a lover of all things history and horror. He currently resides in central NY with his dog, Bruce, and his girlfriend, Natalie. When he's not working at a museum, reading, or writing, you can find him getting lost in the woods, wandering old cemeteries, or trying to improve his jab.

You can see what mischief he's getting into on:

Twitter: @finzach135

Instagram: @finzach135 or @badboybruce45

CPSIA information can be obtained
at www.ICGtesting.com
Printed in the USA
BVHW070722090621
609009BV00003B/186